Thai Die

Thai Die

Monica Ferris

BERKLEY PRIME CRIME, NEW YORK

THE BERKLEY PUBLISHING GROUP
Published by the Penguin Group
Penguin Group (USA) Inc.
375 Hudson Street, New York, New York 10014, USA
Penguin Group (Canada), 90 Eglinton Avenue East, Suite 700, Toronto, Ontario M4P 2Y3, Canada
(a division of Pearson Penguin Canada Inc.)
Penguin Books Ltd., 80 Strand, London WC2R 0RL, England
Penguin Group Ireland, 25 St. Stephen's Green, Dublin 2, Ireland (a division of Penguin Books Ltd.)
Penguin Group (Australia), 250 Camberwell Road, Camberwell, Victoria 3124, Australia
(a division of Pearson Australia Group Pty. Ltd.)
Penguin Books India Pvt. Ltd., 11 Community Centre, Panchsheel Park, New Delhi—110 017, India
Penguin Group (NZ), 67 Apollo Drive, Rosedale, North Shore 0632, New Zealand
(a division of Pearson New Zealand Ltd.)
Penguin Books (South Africa) (Pty.) Ltd., 24 Sturdee Avenue, Rosebank, Johannesburg 2196,
South Africa

Penguin Books Ltd., Registered Offices: 80 Strand, London WC2R 0RL, England

This book is an original publication of The Berkley Publishing Group.

First edition: December 2008

Library of Congress Cataloging-in-Publication Data

Ferris, Monica.
Thai die / Monica Ferris.—1st ed.
    p. cm.
ISBN 978-0-425-22346-8
1. Devonshire, Betsy (Fictitious character)—Fiction. 2. Women detectives—Minnesota—Fiction. 3. Needleworkers—Fiction. 4. Antique dealers—Fiction. 5. Art thefts—Fiction. 6. Thailand—Fiction. I. Title.

PS3566.U47T43 2008
813'.54—dc22   2008031631

PRINTED IN THE UNITED STATES OF AMERICA

10 9 8 7 6 5 4 3 2 1

Acknowledgments

Many people helped with the writing of this novel. My writers group, Crème de la Crime, as usual kept me on task. Ellen Kuhfeld, curator, editor, and idea person, was a marvelous adviser. Ron Zommick, my Thailand contact, was very helpful. Denise Williams worked long and hard to make her Phoenix design so beautifully reflect the original one. Minnesota locales the March Hare and the Amboy Diner are real places; Lisa and Heidi are real people—even the giant angora rabbit is real.

So is Bangkok, Thailand, with its gentle people, fabled golden temples, and magnificent woven silks.

One

⁓•⁓

I T was early February in Minnesota, and so far it had been a very mild winter—which meant that anything heavier than an automobile was forbidden to drive on the lakes' icy surfaces. Even snowmobiles had a distressing tendency to fall through on occasion. There hadn't been many snowfalls after the first heavy one in early December, so cross-country skiing was curtailed. Gardeners worried that without deep snow cover, any severe cold snap might damage their spring bulbs. There wasn't even the simple pleasure of looking out at the snow-covered beauty of a more typical winter.

Dreary Minnesota was a big contrast with Bangkok, where Doris Valentine had spent the last four weeks. She had sent almost daily e-mails to her friends, describing cloudless days of at least eighty degrees, sun-ripened pineapples for sale on every street corner, and live elephants with their hides painted in ornate patterns standing under banyan trees in the park.

"Here she comes!" called Bershada from near the front door of Crewel World. "She's got a *suitcase* with her," she added, hurrying back to her seat at the library table.

"Wonderful!" said Betsy, who owned the needlework shop. "I bet it's just bulging with souvenirs!"

"Ah, a really big show and tell!" said Shelly.

"Souvenirs from *Thailand*," sighed Alice, who had never been able to travel much. Her favorite song all her life began, "Far away places with strange sounding names . . ."

"Move over, I can't see!" said Emily, leaning sideways to peer around the photographer who stood between her and the doorway. Emily was in her eighth month of pregnancy and tended to stay where she sat until she absolutely had to get up.

It was the first Wednesday in February, and the Monday Bunch was in special session, though they were not there to stitch. Fellow member Doris was coming home, and they all wanted to hear about her fabulous trip.

"What a great tan she got!" said the photographer, a very young man from the *Excelsior Times*, the paper of record for a town so small that a citizen's return from an exotic vacation was news. His camera flashed twice as Doris opened the door, and she drew back in surprise. But then she smiled and came in, with a big suitcase in one hand and a shopping bag in the other. It was marked RAINBOW FOODS, and probably held fresh milk and bread, necessary immediate purchases on arriving home from an extended trip.

There were six people waiting for her: the owner of the shop, Betsy; young, pregnant Emily; schoolteacher Shelly; tall and elderly Alice; retired librarian Bershadaa; and the ambitious young man who was both photographer and reporter.

Phil Galvin wasn't there. A retired railroad engineer and a member of the Monday Bunch, he thought no one knew he was also Doris's boyfriend. But the gossip around the table before Doris arrived was about how he had met her at the airport yesterday afternoon and had taken her out to dinner last night.

Doris, a medium-sized woman of fifty-three, came in smiling. She indeed had a light tan and, instead of her usual complex blond wig and heavy makeup, she wore her own hair cut stylishly short, permed into gentle curls, and dyed a cheerful carrot color. She looked about twenty pounds slimmer than she had before her trip. Her face was almost naked, just touched up a little around the eyes, cheeks, and lips. She looked wonderful; the compliments from her friends at the table were heartfelt, which brought her to another halt, blushing with pleasure. The photographer's flash went off, startling her again. Then she frowned—the photographer was not a member of the Bunch.

"It's all right, Doris," said Betsy. "Someone"—she looked around the table, but nobody confessed or even looked guilty—"someone told the *Excelsior Times* that you were coming home from a month in Thailand, and now it's going to be in the paper. I really hope you don't mind."

"Well . . ." hedged Doris in her husky voice.

"You can object to it later," said Bershada. "Girl, get your beautiful self on over here and open that suitcase! We're dying to see what you brought home!"

Doris smiled. "Yes, of course," she said, as she put the shopping bag on the floor and the suitcase on its side on the table in front of the one empty chair. She began to unzip it.

"First," said the reporter, putting his camera down and pulling a notebook from his jeans pocket, "tell us what you liked the most."

Confronted by a need to speak for the record, Doris hesitated, pulling a zipper around the side of her black canvas suitcase, which still had the airline tag on its handle. "Oh, I guess I liked everything. The people are wonderful, they're beautiful, and *so* friendly and helpful." The Monday Bunch looked interested, so she continued in a more confident voice. "But they're so thin and little I felt like a giant. And I just couldn't help loving Bangkok, it's so . . . Oh, I can't sum it up. It's the most contradictory city! It's huge, with really modern skyscrapers and a brand-new subway system and excellent hospitals. But the air is polluted, and there are beggars on the street with diseases and disabilities we can fix here. It has dozens of Buddhist temples all covered with gold, and monks in saffron robes, just like in National Geographic." She smiled. "But I didn't see a single Siamese cat."

"No Siamese cats . . . ?" queried Emily, confused.

"Well, the country used to be named Siam—and that's where the breed came from." She sat down and finished unzipping the suitcase. "But what I fell most in love with was . . . silk." And she opened the lid, causing gasps all around at the rich colors presented to the group's eyes.

Doris began by lifting out two lengths of silk. These were not the filmy kind of silks, but substantial, opaque, saturated with color: deep, dark blue and rich red, with generous trimmings of bright gold. Geometrical patterns were woven into sections of the fabrics: a slab of unevenly spaced narrow vertical columns terminating in neat arrangements of diamonds and triangles; thin horizontal lines marked at small intervals with tiny alternating circles and squares; geometrical flowers surrounded by big diamonds filled with starlike shapes and surrounded by figures that could be caterpillars from Oz. The lines were woven on the indigo in gold and red; and on the red, in gold and purple. The pieces were big, about six feet long and two feet wide, and not cut off a bolt but woven as individual pieces. Each long end was marked with thin fringe, braided on the indigo and tied into patterns on the red.

The reporter put his notebook aside and flashed his camera again and again. Betsy waved impatiently at him.

"Handwoven," said Doris proudly. "You can tell by the uneven edges, where she turned the shuttle to go back."

"She?" said Bershada.

"These are done by women. Thai girls used to announce they were ready to marry by weaving where men could see how skilled they were at it."

The pieces were handed around, and everyone murmured words of pleasure about the soft fabric and subtle textures of the patterns.

Then Doris brought out a much larger piece that looked like a brocade. There was a lot of gold in its patterns, which gleamed and shone under the shop's ceiling lights. The base color was again that deep indigo, and the patterns this time went diagonally, except for a broad row of highly stylized— "Chickens?" asked Alice, with a laugh.

"Yes," said Doris. "Well, I'm not sure they're chickens. But they're a symbol of . . . something. I can't remember. But they've been doing it for a long time, centuries."

The other patterns on the brocade were mostly diamonds, though one repeating row looked a bit like the fingers of a closed hand, and another resembled pictographs or hieroglyphics. The fabric was heavy, the designs definitely raised—and deliciously smooth under the women's fingers. The photographer took a picture of Betsy running her fingers across it.

"What are you going to do with these?" the reporter asked Doris, his notebook at the ready.

"I don't know," confessed Doris, embarrassed. "Over there they lay these cloths diagonally across their beds as decoration, but I'd just die if my cat, Waldo, sank his claws into this. I guess I'll hang it on my living-room wall and maybe use the others as table runners. I never thought about using them—I saw them and just couldn't resist buying them, they are so gorgeous."

"And inexpensive, too, I suppose," said Emily.

"Well . . . not terribly cheap, not these hand woven pieces. Now *these* were inexpensive." Doris lifted two big rectangles of thin fabric, about forty by sixty inches. "These are saris, imported from India. I bought them on Coral Island off the town of Pattaya. Open-front stores, white sand, blue and green water . . ." She smiled, remembering. "Women were using these as swimsuit wraps. This little old man came down the beach with a huge armload of fabric—he even had a couple of shirts, but they weren't my size. We were bargaining to set the price when this other man, much younger, who'd been by earlier, came storming back and threw his stuff down at my feet and yelled, 'I more handsome than him! Why you buy him, not me?' He pretended he couldn't understand why I wanted an imitation silk scarf but not a purse made out of fake manta ray hide. He was so indignant that I started to laugh, and then he laughed, too, and gathered up his stuff and went on down the beach."

Doris picked up one of the scarves. It was sea green, printed with soft white lines crossed into wavy diamond shapes and even softer red splotches. She lofted it to show its lightness, then handed it around the table. "You *have* to bargain in Thailand. I was actually scolded by our guide when I bought some nuts from a street vendor and paid the asking price. But I didn't bargain very hard for these—they were so beautiful and the price was low. I think I paid about three dollars apiece."

The other scarf had a broad border in marine blues. Its center was yellow and printed with soft black outlines of tropical fish, printed in melted purples and blurred greens and tangerine.

The women held each scarf up in turn, admiring its patterns and colors. Betsy blew on the blue fabric draped across her hand, and it floated away from her in gentle waves. All of a sudden she could imagine herself standing on white sand, looking out over the Gulf of Thailand, its water the colors of this scarf, while an onshore breeze toyed with the fabric around her legs and shoulders.

Then Doris brought out a small bronze statue of a man with four arms and the head of an elephant. The photographer came close to the figure, his camera flashing and flashing. The members of the Monday Bunch turned their heads aside to avoid being dazzled.

The elephant-headed man had a fat belly and bare feet and a

very amiable expression. He wore a skirt with a diamond pattern engraved on it, fastened with a big button. One of his tusks was broken off—but it was part of the design, not an accident, because he was holding the piece in one hand. "This is Ganesha, the god of beginnings," Doris said. "Thailand is a Buddhist country, but the Buddha is not a god, so they can mix other religions in. And they do. I don't know why I like Ganesha. I think it's because he looks so friendly. People call on him to bless the building of a house or the start of a business. He's also the god of writers—he broke off his tusk to use as a pen, in order to write down a story he was hearing so he wouldn't forget it."

"Hey," said the reporter, "I wish I had a statue of him myself!" He was scribbling as fast as his fingers could go. "How do you spell his name?"

Doris spelled out "Ganesha" while the statue made its way around the table. "He's heavy!" exclaimed Emily, nearly dropping the figure when Bershada handed it over. She turned it upside down to see if it was solid bronze. "What's this inside him?" she asked.

"Concrete," Doris replied. "They fill a lot of their brass and bronze pieces with concrete." She smiled. "I think it's so the post office makes extra money when they're sent home. Or maybe it's just to make them feel solid."

She went into the suitcase again and came up with what looked like a folded fan, bent into a gentle S shape. But she unfolded it into a circle and it turned into a hat with a ruffled brim: a bright red, bell-shaped sun hat patterned with golden elephants, held open with a dab of Velcro. "I bought this from a tiny old woman who came into a little restaurant with a bag of them in different colors. No English at all, she had to hold up fingers to tell me how many baht it cost. I liked that restaurant—the food was delicious—but it didn't have a menu, so you ate whatever the owner felt like cooking that day. It was right across the street from the Temple of the Emerald Buddha. Oh, that temple! I never saw so much gold in my life!" And again, all the women sighed, hearing about the exotica of little old street vendors, menuless restaurants, and a golden temple housing a Buddha statue made of emerald.

"Is it made of one huge emerald, or lots of littler ones?" asked Alice.

"Neither. It's called the Emerald Buddha because it's a deep green color—but it's actually made of jade. It's little, only about eighteen inches tall, but it's very old, and the holiest object in Thailand. Only the king can touch it, and he comes three times a year to change its robes. Right now it's wearing cloth of gold decorated with emeralds and rubies and diamonds. There is a constant stream of people who offer it lotus buds and incense sticks. The temple is big, and very tall. The Buddha sits way up high, on a golden throne. Outside, the eaves are lined with thousands of bells and wind chimes to scare away demons, and everywhere there are golden statues of odd-looking creatures to protect it. Women with legs like birds—their knees go the wrong way and they have claw feet—and huge, bug-eyed giants from China. Everything's coated with gold, except what's covered with tiny pieces of glass in all different colors, very strange, but beautiful. The temple is part of a big complex that also includes the old royal palace. In the palace you can see the boat-shaped throne on a set of pedestals. King Rama the Fifth sat on it to welcome European visitors. Remember *The King and I*? That king. They made it high because Europeans wouldn't fall on their faces in his presence like the Thai had to do, and that way it seemed as if they did. The current king doesn't live there anymore, but in a new palace."

Alice had the hat in her hands during Doris's recitation. She surreptitiously held it to her nose, inhaling gently the remaining molecules of air brought home from a place so exotic as to have golden monsters guarding a little jade statue that only the king could dress.

The reporter asked, "Why did you go to Thailand?"

"Because I wanted some surgery that my medical insurance wouldn't cover, and it was cheaper to go to Thailand than to pay for it here, even including air fare. And their hospitals are the equal of any I've seen here."

"How did you learn about going to Thailand for surgery?"

"A friend told me, and then I did some research on the Internet."

"Did your friend go there for an operation, too?" he asked.

"No, she just went there on vacation with two other women. She loved it so much that she wanted to see it again."

"That was Carmen, wasn't it?" asked Shelly.

Doris nodded. "She was supposed to come with me, but her husband got an assignment in Santa Fe for six weeks, starting a week before we were supposed to leave, and her son goes to college in Albuquerque, so she decided to go with him."

Doris went back into the suitcase and brought out a white paper bag sealed shut with gold tape. She pulled the strips of tape away, opened the bag, and pulled out a big fistful of skeins of floss in shimmering gold. The skeins were about the size and shape of a skein of DMC cotton, but the single band around each was white paper with printing in an exotic, curvy alphabet on it, except for two words: THAI SILK. She tumbled them with shy carelessness onto the table. "These are for you. Each of you may have one."

"Oh, they do needlework in Thailand, too!" exclaimed Emily, reaching for one. The photographer took her picture as she laid the silk across her palm and studied the writing on the band.

"Well, only sort of," said Doris. "Over there it's more of an occupation than a hobby. And these are . . . kind of special."

"How so?" asked Betsy, running a finger along one end of the skein. It wasn't smooth like the silk floss she sold. This had a faintly rough grain.

"Well, I got these from a silk factory just outside of Bangkok. It's an interesting story. I wanted to see silk made, and I didn't realize that most Thai silk comes from the north. I found out about this factory, but there wasn't a tour, so I had to go there by myself."

"Brave of you," said Alice.

"Thank you, I thought so, too. Anyway, this factory, it was called Bright Works, was a small place, and it was kind of rickety and noisy. *Hot*, too. The spinning and weaving machines put out heat and there's no air-conditioning. They make fabric to sell to tailors who can make a suit or a skirt or a shirt to your measure in five days."

"Oh, I've heard of them!" said Betsy. "Did you get one?"

"Yes, I did, and it's beautiful, but it's a summer dress, so I can't wear it for a few months. Anyway, a man there spoke enough

English to translate for me. I talked with the man in charge of making solid-color fabrics, and he showed me the whole process, from spinning raw silk off the cocoons, to dying it, to weaving it. And when I asked for a sample of spun, dyed silk, I had to show him the piece of counted cross-stitch I carry in my purse to explain what it was for. He told me I had to talk to his supervisor—who turned out to be an American! He came to Bangkok on leave from the Marine Corps, back during the war in Vietnam, and decided to live there after he got out. He looked like an ex-marine, too, big and tough and kind of battered, but charming—you know?"

Betsy, who had spent a few years in the navy long ago, smiled and nodded. She knew.

"Do you remember his name?" asked the reporter, pen poised.

"Yes, David Corvis."

"Can you spell that? Corvis, I mean. With a *C* or a *K*?"

Doris thought. "I can't remember—I think I've got jet lag. I can find out, if you like. Anyway, he told me to come back the next day, and when I did, he had these all made up for me. Isn't that just the nicest thing? I cried, I literally broke down and cried, and told him I'd send him something from America, anything he wanted."

"Oh Doris!" exclaimed Betsy. "What if he'd said he wanted a car?"

"He couldn't use an American car," replied Doris, "because they drive English-style, so our steering wheels are on the wrong side for them."

"Well, what did he want?" asked Shelly.

"Would you believe a Minnesota quarter!" said Doris,

laughing. "He collects state quarters, and he has about thirty of them, but not a Minnesota one. I'm going to the bank tomorrow to get a nice new one for him."

"How will you send it if you don't know how to spell his name?" asked Emily.

"I've got it written down somewhere. But it wouldn't matter, I'm sure he's the only David at the factory, and I have its address." She looked around the table. "But there's more. I want you to let me know how good or bad Thai silk is for stitching. I haven't tried it myself. They don't make floss, so it may snag or pull apart or just not look as good. But if it is good, he will let me buy silk floss from him to sell over here." She leaned back and began to smile. "I may go into the silk import business!" She raised both hands. "In a small way, of course. Kreinik has nothing to fear!"

The women laughed as each selected a skein. There were more than a dozen of them, and Doris said the rest should be saved for members of the Bunch who weren't present, and anyone else Betsy chose to try out the silk.

"Thank you very much!" said Betsy. She picked up a second skein, saying, "I want Bitsy Busby to try this. If it doesn't disintegrate under her lickety-split stitching, then we'll know something good about it."

The show was over. Doris began to fold up her silk pieces. Bershada, sitting on her left, said, "Wait, there's something else." She pointed to a cardboard box in a corner of the suitcase.

"Oh, that," said Doris. "That isn't mine."

"Whose is it?" asked Betsy. "And what is it doing in your suitcase?"

"David asked me to bring it home to Minnesota and deliver it to an antiques store, which will sell it to a customer already waiting for it. David has a little business on the side, exporting Thai art."

"Hold on, Doris, isn't that illegal?" asked Bershada. "Bringing something home for somebody else?"

"No, he didn't sneak it into my luggage. Besides, I declared it. *And* he didn't pay me to carry it."

"*What* is it?" asked Betsy, a shade impatiently.

"Yes, let us see!" said Alice.

The reporter, who had been about to put his camera into its bag, instead turned on the flash again.

Doris hesitated. "It's a Buddha, and it's stone, not bronze. I don't know if I should open the box, and not just because it's not mine. What would I do if one of you dropped it?"

"We'll be careful!" promised Alice, and the others heartily agreed.

Doris picked up the box and picked away the strips of transparent tape holding it shut. "I think you'll be surprised when you see it. It's not really old, but carved in an ancient style."

The object inside was wound into Bubble Wrap, and under that a length of grimy old cloth, a faded green printed with a complex pattern. Doris laid the statue on the table and carefully removed its wrapping. As she lifted the last fold of fabric away, the camera flashed from behind her left shoulder, apparently catching her in the corner of her eye. She blinked a few times to clear away the spots before she set the figure upright on its low pedestal, turning it to face the group. The camera flashed again.

"That's a Buddha?" asked Emily. The statue, a pale cream color, was of a slim man in a shin-length robe.

"I don't know why he used this old thing," Doris said, leaning sideways to drop the rag into the wastebasket under the table. "The Bubble Wrap was good enough." She turned the Buddha around so it faced them, then put a steadying finger on its head. "So, what do you think?"

It was nothing like the jolly fat man sitting on a pillow, which is the more familiar depiction of the Buddha. This statue was of a slender man with downcast eyes and just a hint of a smile. He wore his robes fastidiously arranged, covering just one shoulder, reaching halfway down his calves. Both hands were upraised with long, slender fingers. His left hand had the little finger and thumb touching, the right had his forefinger and thumb touching. His hair was done in tiny, tight curls, lifted slightly at the crown.

"Ooooh, he's gorgeous!" said Emily, reaching for the figure—she was tired of being the last one to be handed something going around the table. "Wow, it's heavy!"

"Oh, please be careful!" cried Doris, reaching to steady it. "Remember, it's not mine! I don't know what I'd do if one of those hands broke off!"

"Yes, of course, you're right," apologized Emily, holding it more carefully, using both hands. She put it down on the table and turned it around and around, her head tipped to one side.

"It looks dirty," Bershada said, leaning sideways to peer at it through the magnifying glasses she wore well down her nose.

"I think that's called patina," said Betsy in a dry voice.

"Whatever. If it were mine, I'd give it a good scrubbing. I bet that stone is a nice color under the dirt—excuse me, *patina*." She reached for it, hefted it—Doris could not quite suppress another gasp—and then put it down and scooted it along the table.

Betsy tried lifting it with both hands. "It is pretty solid," she said. The grubbiness, she noticed, was lighter on the high surfaces and darker inside the folds of the robe. Whoever carved this copy was careful to get the imitation patina right. She leaned it back to get a look at it and was struck by the expression on its face. "I like this," she said. "He looks very serene."

"Didn't Buddha invent serenity?" asked Bershada.

"*The* Buddha," corrected Alice before Doris could. "He had some other name. Buddha is like a title. He was born in India five hundred years before Christ and invented a religion that is all about rejecting concern over things of the world. 'Wakeful serenity,' they call it."

"How much is that little statue worth?" asked the reporter.

"About two hundred dollars if you buy it in Bangkok, because it's hand carved. It would cost about eight hundred here, wholesale."

"And whatever you can get at retail," said Bershada.

"That doesn't seem like very much," mused Betsy. "I mean, it does, until you think of all the trouble he took to get it here."

Doris shrugged. "It wasn't that much trouble. Besides, he said it was for a repeat customer. He told me he wants to keep on the man's good side."

Betsy nodded. She understood the value of the repeat customer. Still, she had to ask, "Weren't you just a little suspicious about this request? I mean, being handed something in a foreign country to bring to the United States?"

"Well, of course, at first!" said Doris, indignant at being thought a willing cat's paw. "But I went to his office—his other office, where he has his export business. It's on Silom Road—an important part of the city—though it seemed to be just one room, and half of it was taken up with boxes. He said the statue was to go to Fitzwilliam's Antiques in St. Paul, which is an actual antiques shop—I looked it up on the Internet. I've already talked to Mr. Fitzwilliam on the phone. He asked me to hold it until Friday—he doesn't want someone else to see it and want it—but he sounded happy and said his customer would be very pleased to hear the piece is here. So see? Nothing secret about it."

"And you didn't get questioned about it at customs?" asked Alice.

Doris grinned. "Let me tell you about that," she said. "I bought another hat besides that fan one. It's the kind peasant farmers use in the fields. It's beautiful, but it also looks like a lampshade." She bent sideways to reach into the grocery bag, which didn't hold milk and bread after all, but a big stiff hat made of thin blades of rattan. It had a flat top and sides that bent ever more sharply outward into a broad rim about eighteen inches across. She turned it over to show her friends the underside. The rattan strips were supported on the inside with open work of much finer rattan, cleverly woven in small circles. But the interesting part was a beautiful cylinder about six inches across and six deep, woven of even finer rattan into open spirals. It was fastened to the crown of the hat with knots of thread and reached down almost level with the brim. "See," said Doris, turning the hat over and putting it on, "this is the thing that touches your head, not the hat, so there's always air moving over the top of your head. You get shade *and* a breeze at the same time."

The women nodded, smiling, and their smiles kept getting wider and wider until they turned to giggles.

"I know, I know," said Doris with a sigh, taking the hat off. "It looks ridiculous on me. I saw these tiny Asian faces peering out from under these hats and thought they looked adorable. So I bought a hat from a street vendor at a temple called Wat Pho. Our guide almost hurt himself trying not to laugh at me—and the sweet ladies behind the counter at my hotel didn't even try." She handed the hat to Emily. "Go ahead, you try it on."

Emily looked at the design on the inside, then obeyed and they all laughed at her, too. And Alice, and Betsy. Even Bershada, who could wear just about any hat, drew laughter.

"See? It looks ridiculous on anyone but East Asians. Still, I liked it, so I brought it home. I had to carry it in my hand; it won't fit in a suitcase. Then going through customs I wore it, since I had my hands full of luggage. The customs officer said, 'What do you have to declare?' I handed him my list in fear and trepidation—I was two hundred dollars over my limit and just knew I was going to spend the next hour opening suitcases and paying a lot of duty. But he looked at my jet-lagged face under that silly hat and said, 'Go on through.' So I don't care if it looks ridiculous on me, it's a wonderful hat, a lucky hat, and I say God bless it!"

Two

꘎·꘎

DORIS slept late on Friday morning, hitting the snooze button on her alarm clock over and over until she woke enough to remember her appointment in St. Paul. Jet lag was still with her, she supposed. She blundered her way around her small kitchen, burning the eggs, putting too many grounds in the little coffeemaker, settling for warm bread from the toaster when she realized how late it was getting.

It had snowed lightly the night before, so morning traffic moved slowly. She was more than fifteen minutes late arriving at Exchange Street near the Xcel Energy Convention Center where Fitzwilliam's Antiques Shoppe was located. The street, high above a curve in the Mississippi River, was lined with small, old stores in weathered brick. She had to park near the far end of the block, since all the other places were taken. She got out of her aged black car, coming around to the passenger side to get the box with the statue in it. The weather seemed especially cold after four weeks in Thailand, and the biting wind went right through her coat as she tucked the box under one arm while she pulled her knit hat down over her forehead with a mittened hand.

The antiques store looked faded and shabby on the outside—its wooden framework was worn to the point where mere paint couldn't fix it—but then Doris noticed that the gilt on the wooden letters across the façade was fresh and bright.

The display windows looked like the work of a bipolar window dresser. In one were some old standard lamps whose torn shades were draped with sun-faded scarves. But in the other was a pair of very beautiful bowlegged arm chairs upholstered in green and silver damask. A cardboard sign in the glass of the door, black with Day-Glo red letters, announced that the store was open.

An old-fashioned bell hanging on a curved metal spring announced her entrance. There was a smell of aged wood and vegetable soup. A man, tall and thin, with white hair and a close-cropped silver beard, appeared out of the back room. He wore a blue chambray shirt and tan slacks held up with red suspenders.

"May I help you?" he asked in a tentative voice, as if he thought she might be here by mistake.

"I'm Doris Valentine, and I was asked to deliver this box to you," she replied, holding it up.

"Ah," he said, looking more lively. He smiled and his blue eyes shone. "You're here at last."

"I'm sorry to be late," she said.

"That's quite all right, quite all right." He might have been

Katharine Hepburn's brother by his accent. "Will you follow me?" He walked stiffly to a glass counter near the back, and Doris noticed when he turned on a goose-necked lamp that his finger joints were swollen. He reached under the counter and came up with a length of old pink velvet which he spread on the glass. "May I see what you have for me?"

Doris handed over the box. He hesitated briefly when he saw that the tape had been broken and replaced, then picked at the new tape, pulled it off, and opened the box. He paused again when he saw the cream-colored hand towel, then carefully scooped the wrapped object out.

"Did it come wrapped in this?"

"No. It was wrapped in a piece of dirty cloth, which I threw away."

"Hmmm," he said, frowning as he held it in one hand while gently lifting the folds of the towel. But he nodded when he saw the Buddha, and stood it up on the counter. "Who did you show this to?" he asked, but as he spoke he was looking at it, not her. His voice was quiet, but hard, as if he were angry and trying not to show it.

"Just to some friends."

"Who are they? Where did this happen?"

Surprised, Doris said, "It was at Crewel World—"

"What did you say? Cruel?"

"Crewel World. It's a needlework shop in Excelsior. Crewel is a kind of needlework, wool yarn on fabric."

"I know that," he said impatiently.

"There's a group of us who meet in the shop to stitch and talk. I think there were five or six of us, on this past Wednesday.

I was showing them the souvenirs I bought when I was in Thailand, and they saw the box in my suitcase and wanted to see what was in it." He was looking at her with scary intensity. "Was . . . was that wrong?"

The intense look slowly faded. "No, I suppose not. But if you'd dropped it . . ."

"Yes, I know. But I told them to be very careful with it. And you can see, it's all right."

The man took a pair of strong magnifying glasses out of his shirt pocket and put them on. He picked up the statue and, holding it under the light, looked it over very carefully. "Yes, it looks fine," he said at last, and took his glasses off. Doris let loose a breath she hadn't realized she was holding. "Still, I wish you hadn't opened the box," he said.

"I'm sorry, I apologize. I saw the statue in Bangkok when Mr. Corvis showed it to me, and he said it was the Buddha. But it was so different from any statue of the Buddha I'd ever seen, and so beautiful, I couldn't resist showing it to my friends."

"You threw the old wrapping away?"

"Yes, it seemed . . . disrespectful, you know? It wasn't just raggedy, it was dirty. This statue seems holy—I mean, just look at that face—and when I saw that rag, well, I just couldn't put it back around the Buddha."

"I see. Would you like the towel back?"

Doris was a little embarrassed to say, "Yes, please." But the embroidery on one end was one of her better efforts, a row of pink and yellow roses. It would look nice in her bathroom, so she took it when he held it out. "It's brand new, never used."

"I understand," he said. "Well, the old rag kept it safe across

the ocean, anyway. And now its long journey is almost over."
He touched it gently on top of its head.

Doris pushed her little towel into a pocket. "I'm glad it arrived safely."

"So am I. I'll walk you to the door." He came out from behind the counter and stayed at her elbow as they crossed the gray wooden floor, touching her lightly on the back as if to hurry her on her way.

"Good-bye," she said as she walked out, but he had the door shut before she finished the phrase and was turning the sign in the window to white-on-black CLOSED.

Doris hustled up the street, an icy wind flapping her coat at the back of her legs as if it, too, wanted her to hurry.

I wonder what the rush is, she thought breathlessly, as she dug in her purse for her keys. *Maybe he wants me gone before the buyer comes in because he's going to renege on the deal. The way he looked at the statue, as if he were hungry and it were a Quarter Pounder, I'll bet he wants to keep it for himself or sell it for a higher price to somebody else. I'll bet he plans to tell the buyer I delivered the wrong statue—but that plan may be wrecked now because I saw it, and other people saw it, too.*

She found her keys, unlocked her car door and climbed in, shivering, stamping her feet on the floor in front of the brake pedal. *What if the statue isn't a copy but the real thing, and he doesn't want any strangers looking at it, because they may guess? Or maybe there's something wrong with this whole deal, and bringing it into the United States is illegal because . . . because there are* drugs *hidden inside it!* Her eyes widened. *Or gemstones!* Thailand was famous for its sapphire and ruby mines.

She froze, holding the key in the ignition, and her fingers trembled as she frightened herself with more and more scary notions. But hold on, if there were something tricky about this deal, maybe it was a good thing she had shown the Buddha to the Monday Bunch. When there was trickery afoot, eyewitnesses could be wonderful.

She started her car and checked to see if the street was clear. Up the block, she saw a woman get out of an enormous, dark green Hummer parked right in front of Fitzwilliam's. It was so high the driver had to reach down with a booted toe to touch the pavement—and she was a tall woman. She wore a long black-leather coat and a mink hat pulled down over her eyes. She lifted the collar of the coat to cover her face as she came around the front of the vehicle. She hurried to the door of Fitzwilliam's and rapped on it. To Doris's surprise, it opened at once and she went inside.

Oh, of course, thought Doris, *that must be the buyer.* So apparently he wasn't going to get to keep it for himself, if that had been his plan.

As Doris pulled away from the curb, she glanced again at the Hummer. It's as big as a pickup truck, she thought, wondering why someone needed a vehicle designed to carry troops into battle.

Doris wondered how much Mr. Fitzwilliam was going to charge the tall woman for the statue. David Corvis, the exporter in Bangkok, had told her that in America its value was about $800 wholesale. She figured that if her other fears weren't real—and the thing wasn't stuffed with drugs or gems—Mr. Fitzwilliam probably had at least doubled that price. Was $1,600 enough to close the shop to other customers while the transaction was enacted? She didn't know. Maybe it was worth more than that—a lot more than that. Perhaps Mr. Corvis had lied to her, telling her the Buddha was worth far less than it actually was so she would not be tempted to steal it. Doris decided not to be insulted by that; after all, Mr. Corvis hardly knew her. But if the statue really was very old, then its price might be . . . Well, actually, she had no idea.

She took Kellogg Boulevard back up past the Cathedral of St. Paul, then over and back on the freeway. Traffic had thinned, since it was past rush hour, and she was in Excelsior in about half the time it had taken her to get to St. Paul.

Rather than go up to her apartment, she went into Crewel World. Godwin was behind the checkout desk, writing up an order. He looked over as the door sounded its two notes, and his face lightened.

"Oh, my God, Doris! You look *fabulous*!" He dropped the paperwork and came for a closer look, holding out his hands. He took hers and spread them wide, dropped one and turned her around. "Simply fabulous!" he pronounced.

Doris could not help simpering, just a little. "Thank you."

He stepped back to give her a more thorough up-and-down look. "Hair, check. Face, check. Hands, check." Doris had, in fact, undergone some serious massage therapy in addition to three separate manicures to soften and shape her hands and nails. That Godwin should have noticed this improvement at first glance was a tribute to his interest in physical details—and his friendship with her. "Also, you are down what, fifteen, maybe twenty pounds?"

"Seventeen," she said. "I ate and ate over there, but the food is so healthy, the weight just slid off."

"I can see Bangkok in my future," said Godwin, laughing.

Betsy came out from the back. "Oh, hi, you're back! I thought that was your voice. So, tell us all about it. Was the antiques store nice?"

Doris told them about taking the statue over there. She described Mr. Fitzwilliam and how he reacted when he saw she'd opened the box. "He wanted to know where I opened it and who got a look at it. He seemed about as scared as he was angry."

She saw how Betsy was looking at her and quickly added, "But he calmed down when he saw it wasn't damaged." She reached into her coat pocket. "He even gave me back the towel I wrapped it in," she said, offering it to them for inspection.

Godwin said, "Ooooooh, let me see." He took the towel and studied the cross-stitching at one end. "Very nice," he said, nodding.

"What else happened?" asked Betsy, impatient with Godwin's tangent.

"Well, he walked me to the door and turned his sign to 'closed' behind me, but when I got back to my car I saw this woman get out of a big green Hummer and go up to knock on the door. I kind of think she was waiting in the car for me to leave. Mr. Fitzwilliam was waiting, too, because he opened right up and let her in, which I thought was kind of odd."

"So what do you conclude from all this?" Betsy asked.

"Well, it made me wonder if the statue isn't worth a lot more than Mr. Corvis said it was when he gave it to me in Bangkok."

"How much did he say it was worth?" asked Godwin, his attention drawn at last from Doris's stitching.

"Two hundred there, maybe eight hundred here. Wholesale, I think he said."

"I wonder what Fitzwilliam's markup is," said Betsy.

"He might be charging three or four thousand for it," suggested Godwin. "It's not like the buyer can decide that's too much and go to a different store that charges less."

Betsy said, "Yes, and three or four thousand dollars might be a lot of money to an antiques dealer who usually deals in sums a lot smaller than that."

"I'm also thinking it might be a really ancient statue, not the copy he said it was," noted Doris.

"Isn't it illegal to bring something really ancient out of a country?" Godwin asked.

"It is in Thailand," said Doris. "I went to a market there that had old things for sale, and I was warned against buying a bronze statue I liked because of that law."

Betsy said, "So if it's really old, it might not be in this country legally. On the other hand, if this were really an ancient statue, it would be worth a great deal more than three thousand." She made a gesture of agreement at Doris. "So you could be right, it might be worth much more than Mr. Corvis said. And what they're doing is theft, even if Mr. Fitzwilliam—and his customers—are buying it legally. Just like paying U.S. currency for street drugs doesn't make them legal."

Doris asked, "But what about me? Have I broken the law, too?"

"I don't think so," replied Betsy. "It's more like you were bamboozled."

"I'd prefer to think he made a cat's paw of you," said Godwin. "*Bamboozle* is a ridiculous word. It sounds like something you do with a set of drums." He had a thought. "What if he does this a lot? Tell me, was his shop very luxurious?"

"No," said Doris. "Kind of the opposite. Sort of."

"What do you mean 'sort of'?"

"Well, it wasn't one of those places that calls itself an antiques shop but really is a secondhand store. This one had some gorgeous antique furniture and some beautiful old dolls. You know, the kind with porcelain faces and long dresses covered in lace. But it also had some toys that were broken, like a pedal car with only three wheels and an old tricycle without a seat. I don't really know how to rate a store like that."

"Mr. Fitzwilliam sounds like a bad businessman," Godwin said. "Mixing nice things with junk."

"Maybe not," said Doris. "I don't know anything about antiques, so maybe the things I thought were junk were really rare and costly. But anyway, there's no need to make a big deal about it. This was an adventure, it's over, and it's not my problem any more. I did what I was asked to do, Mr. Fitzwilliam thanked me, and the statue is probably already in the hands of the buyer, so that's the end of it."

She turned to go. But Betsy said, "Just a second. Have you seen the latest edition of the *Excelsior Times*?"

"No, why? Oh, has it got a picture of me in it?"

"Well, sort of," said Godwin, picking up a copy and opening it to an inside page. "And three paragraphs' worth of story."

"What do you mean, 'sort of'?" asked Doris, reaching for the paper. The published photograph had been taken from a rear angle that showed off her new curls but did little more than suggest she had cheekbones somewhere around in front. The focus of the photograph was the stone carving of the Buddha, sitting on the table. One of Doris's hands was visible, holding an end of the rag, its raveled end hanging from her fingers.

"Oh, no!" said Doris. "The only photograph they published was of the back of my head!"

Betsy said, "That's because the paper's in black and white. All the pictures the reporter took of the fabric wouldn't be any good without color."

"Besides," Godwin pointed out, "now you have a picture of the statue, the one thing you didn't get to keep."

"That's true," Doris admitted. She quickly read the story, which as usual for a newspaper story had almost as many errors as facts. Her name was given as Lois Valentine, and the article said that she'd spent two weeks in Thailand and that she'd brought the statue home for a friend named David Korvish.

Doris made a sound like *Bssshhh!* and tossed the paper onto the library table.

"No, no!" said Godwin. "You should keep this. Put it in the scrapbook you're going to make about your trip."

Doris went to pick it up, then saw a rumpled green cloth on the table. "Hey, that looks like the rag the statue was wrapped up in."

"It is," said Betsy. "I hope you don't mind that I rescued it."

"Why should I? But what do you want with it? It's just a dirty old rag."

"Yes, but it's an old *silk* rag," said Godwin, going to the table. "And look, that's embroidery on it. Betsy's been thinking maybe she can clean it up somehow."

Doris came closer. "It's embroidered? Well, so it is! And I can see now it was probably beautiful when it was new. But it's all ragged along that edge, plus it looks like someone used it to wash windows."

"Yes, it's in bad shape," said Betsy. "That's one reason I haven't done anything with it yet. I don't want to ruin it completely."

"Do you think it's really old?" asked Doris. "Maybe it's an antique."

"No, I don't think so. I've seen old silk, and old silk shatters—that's what they call it when it splits up and down the warp. And you can see there's no shattering on this."

"Maybe it's not really silk," said Godwin.

"Maybe it's not," agreed Betsy. "But if it is, it's probably less than fifty years old. I'm going to go looking on the Internet for ways to clean it. There's no rush, which is a good thing because we've been really busy lately."

Godwin leaned over the piece and sniffed. "It doesn't have mildew, anyway. The embroidery is wonderful, and I love the pattern, so exotic." The piece was rectangular, much longer than it was wide, and it featured stylized versions of birds and animals embroidered in what might be Celtic style. "I wonder what kind of bird that's supposed to be," he said, touching a leggy creature with a pointed beak and the merest suggestion of a long, curly tail. "It looks like a cross between an ostrich and a

molting peacock. And what do you think, this one's a tiger?"
Along with pink flowers on curling vines, the animals went up
and down the cloth, facing one another in mirror images.

Doris came to look over his shoulder. "But what about that
frayed end?"

Godwin said, "Oh, we can just cut off loose threads and then
a *little bit* of the end and turn a hem. The pattern doesn't run
off into the frayed part, so it'll hardly be noticeable." He ran a
finger over the surface of the embroidery. "Nice feel. It's all
done in chain stitch."

Doris bent for a closer look. "I think it's going to be a lot of
work," she said. "Look right there, for example, the embroidery
threads are broken. How could you fix that? Plus, you couldn't
match the colors exactly. And the stitching is so beautifully done,
every stitch exactly the same—that will be hard to imitate."

"We can do it," Godwin said with his usual show of confi-
dence.

Doris smiled at his assumption of a share in the project.
"Good luck."

She went upstairs to her apartment and put the little towel
into her bathroom. Then she continued with the placement of
her souvenirs. Elephant-headed Ganesha had been easy to place,
he sat on the desk next to her laptop. The hat would make a
nice lampshade; she'd take it to Leipold's tomorrow. She went
through her apartment holding up the silks, changing her mind
every five minutes as she tried to decide on which wall to hang
them, smiling to herself. Her little apartment was going to look
like an upper-class Thai home when she was through.

Three

ᘯ ∘ ᘚ

THE next day was Saturday, and Crewel World was crowded with customers. Almost all of them were knitters, there for the yarn sale. This was just the second time Betsy had tried a one-day-only sale. The turnout was terrific, far more than had turned out for the first sale. The doorway was crowded with at least a dozen customers when Betsy unlocked the door at ten, and more kept arriving. Unfortunately, she hadn't considered that this might happen, and so hadn't enough employees on hand. By eleven, there were thirty-five customers in the shop, and the number never dropped under twenty the whole day. Betsy called her list of part-timers, but none was available on such short notice.

So many customers, each demanding attention, meant there wasn't time to have a friendly discussion with those who needed help—deciding whether to buy wool or a blend, what quantity was needed if the sweater to be knitted was two sizes bigger or what color might go really well with the plum. These discussions were a big reason people went to an independently owned store rather than a chain.

Betsy, Godwin, and Krista worked as hard and fast as they could. Betsy had inherited the shop several years ago, and although she'd started from almost total ignorance, she was now nearly as efficient and swift as if she'd founded the shop herself. Krista was new to retail work, but she had begun knitting at age four and had recently taught her first class in knitting a shawl. She had been a stitcher almost as long as she'd been a knitter and claimed she had learned to read and count by following knitting and counted cross-stitch patterns. Godwin, of course, knew everything about the shop and the use of its products.

But even this accumulation of expertise and experience couldn't keep up with demand, and by two in the afternoon they were all feeling frazzled.

When the phone rang, Betsy, hoping someone else would get it, let it ring six times before grabbing the receiver. "Crewel World, Betsy speaking, how may I help you?" she said all in a rush.

"Miss Devonshire?"

"Yes?"

"I'm calling on behalf of the Minneapolis Art Institute."

Oh God, a fund-raiser! "I'm very sorry, but I can't talk right now. I'm at work, and we're very busy."

"On a Saturday? Oh, of course, you're the one who owns that little shop in Excelsior! Oh, I am sorry! I don't suppose you remember me, I'm Joe Brown, I'm on the board of directors of the institute."

Betsy summoned a vague image of a tall man in a black felt hat. "Oh, yes, I think I do remember meeting you."

"But please don't spend another second chatting with me—I'll call you back some other time. Good-bye."

Well, that was a pleasant surprise, Betsy thought as she replaced the phone on its charger. Normally, getting rid of people out to raise money was like peeling wallpaper with your fingernails. Maybe the rules were different when it was a member of the board calling. Betsy had raised her pledge to the institute considerably in the past two years. Maybe that warranted a higher class of money-grubber.

"Hey, Betsy, how come you have the green Paternayan yarn on sale but not the pink?" asked a customer, and she dismissed Joe Brown to plunge back into the fray.

With all that was going on, Phil Galvin and Doris Valentine went unnoticed for a minute after they entered the shop. Godwin saw the scared look on their faces and wove his way through a mass of shoppers. "What's up, what's the matter?" he asked.

"It's Dorie's apartment!" Phil said in his loud old-man's voice—he was a little deaf.

Heads turned toward him and he said, "We're fine, we're fine!" Shoppers turned back to their search for the perfect bargain.

Doris spoke more quietly, though her voice was trembling. "We just went up to my apartment," she told Godwin, "and someone's been in there. The place is a wreck. I want to phone the police."

Doris lived in an apartment on the second floor of the building, and Betsy was her landlord. "Haven't you got a cell phone?" Godwin asked, a little surprised.

"They don't have a volume control that goes high enough for me," said Phil in a hoarse whisper.

Doris said, "And I can't figure them out. And we couldn't call from up there; the advice I've always heard is not to stay in a place where a burglar's been at work."

Phil said, "We were wondering if we could . . ." He looked around at the seething crowd in the shop and finished, "But I guess not."

Godwin said, "Here, let's step outside, away from all these people."

They did, and Godwin dialed 911 on his cell. "There's been a burglary at Two Hundred South Lake Street in Excelsior, in an upstairs apartment." He explained that he was not the renter, Doris Valentine was, and that she would be waiting at the bottom of the stairs for the police to arrive.

"I'm going back in to tell Betsy," he said upon disconnecting. "Stay with her, Phil."

"Oh, yes, don't worry about that," said Phil, putting an arm around her shoulder. "Come on, Dorie, let's get you in out of the cold."

They're so sweet together, Godwin thought. He went to tell Betsy what had happened. "Are they all right?" was her first question. Reassured, she then asked, "When did this happen?"

Godwin stared at her briefly, then smiled. "I bet it didn't happen in broad daylight. I bet it happened last night. When she wasn't there."

Betsy stared at him for a moment, then smiled back. "That's cute!"

"Let's not ask them, because then they'd have to lie, and it'd be cruel to do that to them."

"Well, the police are going to ask Doris why she wasn't at home," Betsy pointed out.

"Fine. Let her lie to them. But don't you ask her, and I won't, either."

"All right." She looked over Godwin's shoulder. "Yes, Mr. Woodward, what can I do for you?" Gary Woodward was a high-schooler who was both Betsy's computer expert and a superb knitter. He loved exotic yarns but could only buy them on sale.

Godwin smiled at Gary and went to help Mrs. Anderson pick two shades of maroon yarn for a sweater she wanted to knit.

In a very few minutes a squad car, lights flashing, pulled in to the curb in front of a fireplug. A police officer climbed out and went into the center door of the building, where a staircase led up to the second floor. He was tall and broad-shouldered, and for an instant Betsy wondered if he was her good friend Lars Larson. Then she remembered that Lars had been promoted to sergeant and was pretty much working a desk nowadays. He didn't like it, but with a pregnant wife and a toddler already in the household, he couldn't afford to remain just another officer on patrol.

"What's going on?" asked Gary.

"I don't know," Betsy said falsely, as others turned to see what he was talking about. No need to slow the sale while curious customers crowded the front windows to stare. "Do you want all four of those skeins?"

A few minutes later, a dark sedan drove past the big front window of Crewel World and turned into the driveway leading to a small parking lot behind the building. A minute after that, a man crossed in front of the shop. He was slim under his lined raincoat, and his thin mouth was pulled a bit sideways. Betsy recognized Sergeant Mike Malloy, one of Excelsior's two police investigators. He didn't even glance into the shop but went through the door that led upstairs.

Fifteen or twenty minutes later, she saw he was back out front. He paced slowly up and down the sidewalk, his breath smoking in the cold air, obviously waiting for someone. It took a while, but finally he raised one arm to signal a big brown van that pulled up beside some of the cars parked at the curb.

Along the length of the van were two horizontal stripes of blue and gold over a thin red line. Above the stripes the word SHERIFF was printed in gold letters, and below it, in smaller letters, HENNEPIN COUNTY. Inside the van rode an investigative team authorized to assist at crime scenes with technology smaller departments could not afford. Three people climbed out of the front seat—two women and a man—and Mike moved to greet them. They all wore the heavy brown jackets and gray trousers of the sheriff's department. As they spoke familiarly with Malloy, they opened the back of the van and the man went in to retrieve a video camera and several heavy cases. Mike gestured at the center door, and they all followed him into the hallway that led upstairs.

Betsy sat down at the big old desk that served as a checkout counter. So Mike thought that what happened in Doris's apartment was more than a simple burglary. She wanted badly to go up for a look—and it was even possible she had a right to, since she owned the building. On the other hand, Mike would be annoyed. And it wasn't as if the shop could spare her. She sighed and turned around to sell Gerry Schmidt a counted canvas pattern of three ornamental teapots. Gerry was the only customer in several hours who wasn't buying yarn.

But the next customer wasn't a knitter, either. She was Lena Olson, and she was here to pick up a large canvas that Betsy had special-ordered for her. It was by Nikki Lee, and it was a sensitive, hand-painted rendition of Kaguya-hime, Japanese goddess of the moon, rendered in delicate pastels. It was two feet wide by three feet high, and the mere sight of it brought several customers over to exclaim over its size and beauty. Lena was going to work it in silk, a costly fiber which would bring the cost of stitching this project to well over $1,000. Those customers who realized this whispered the information to some of the others, and the crowd around the desk grew large.

Betsy and Lena ignored them and went over the silks Betsy had selected for her—a service she offered to all her customers. Lena made only one change, from a pure pink to something with a hint of apricot in it, a color that matched her hair.

Then Lena got out her checkbook with only a tiny sigh. Betsy sighed, too, as subtly as she could—a sale isn't made until payment is rendered—then smiled with deep sincerity as she put the check in the drawer. But she could not resist trying to add to her profit. "I hope you will bring it back when you've worked it, so my finisher can do a really special job for you."

"I will—but it's going to take me a while." She held up a paper bag bulging with silks and watched anxiously as Betsy rolled the canvas up and taped three of strips of paper around it to hold it closed.

"This is going to be a fantastic heirloom piece," said Betsy, covering the roll with a layer of thin green florist's plastic and taping that in place. "Now if you get stuck for a stitch or anything, I want you to bring it in to Godwin. I had to hold him back when he saw it so the drool wouldn't get all over it. If you had backed out of buying it, I think he was prepared to sell his car to get it for himself."

Lena laughed. "I've been wanting this for a long time—no way was I going to back out! I can't wait to get started. But thank Godwin for the offer to help, I'll probably take him up on it."

Lena left amid a murmur of congratulations only slightly tinged by envy. Then the watchers rejoined the rest of the shoppers.

In about half an hour, Mike came down, followed by Phil and Doris. Phil was looking angry, Doris distraught. "I'm taking her home with me," Phil announced, and marched off with her.

"Good idea," said Betsy, and watched them go. *Poor Doris*, she thought, wondering if the burglar had taken all her lovely souvenirs. *And poor Phil, too.*

"I want to talk to you," Mike said.

"All right. But I don't think I can tell you anything much. Do you want to talk in Doris's apartment?"

"No, the sheriff's department is still working the scene. Let's just go into the back hall."

"All right. I can get you a cup of coffee as we go through."

"Thanks." She and Mike threaded their way through the maze of customers and display racks to the back of the shop. This was where counted cross-stitch patterns and supplies were displayed, and there were far fewer people there. Through another door they went into a small back room where Betsy kept stock that needed frequent replenishing and where a coffee urn and tea kettle stayed warm. They paused briefly while she filled a cup with coffee, black, for Mike, then went through yet another door into a back hall.

There, she turned and found him looking at her with chilly blue eyes. In the past several years, he had gone from active dislike of Betsy's sleuthing efforts to wary admiration. But no admiration was visible now; Mike was seeing her as a possible witness, maybe even a hostile one.

He asked, "When did you see Ms. Valentine last?"

"Yesterday, Friday. She came in to tell me she'd delivered a stone statue of the Buddha to an antiques shop in St. Paul."

"Did she say she had any trouble with the owner of the store?"

"No. She said he examined the statue very carefully, because she had opened the box it came in and showed it to us and he was afraid that it might have been damaged. But he saw it was fine, and then he thanked her for bringing it all that way from Thailand to America."

"Anything else?"

Betsy thought. "Well, she said the person who was going to buy the statue might have been waiting for it, because when she got back to her own car a woman got out of a Hummer parked in front of the shop and went in. She thought the woman might have been waiting for her to leave." She raised a questioning eyebrow at Malloy. "What's this about, Mike?"

"How long has Ms. Valentine lived in that apartment?"

"Nearly six years."

"Any trouble with her?"

"None. She's very quiet, pays her rent on time, doesn't give loud parties, doesn't break things. Plus she's nice, a little shy but sweet."

"Does she normally go off without telling anyone where she's going?"

"No, at least not for more than an overnight trip somewhere. She has a cat—oh!"

"What?"

"Is the cat all right? She was looking so upset when she came down just now . . ."

"He's fine. He was hiding in the back of her bedroom closet. Not a mark on him."

"That's good." Betsy smiled. "I suppose I shouldn't have worried—she named him Waldo because he can be very hard to find."

"The deputies are very good seekers." Was his thin mouth tweaking because he was amused? Or was he trying not to show annoyance? He finished making a note, then asked, "Who was closest to her, family or friend? Besides Mr. Galvin, that is."

Betsy had to think about that. "Well, I guess her best friend is Carmen Diamond. I don't know Carmen very well. Shelly does—they're both schoolteachers, and they both have dogs.

Carmen's not a stitcher, so I think I've maybe talked to her twice."

"Do you have her address or phone number?"

"No, but Shelly does."

Mike made a note. "Who else?"

Betsy named Shelly, Emily, Bershada, and Alice, of the Monday Bunch, and gave Mike their phone numbers.

"Is there anything that strikes you as odd about her? Could she be a secret drunk? Does she light bonfires in the park and dance naked around them?"

Betsy smiled. "I really don't think so."

"Yet she ups and goes to Thailand all by herself."

"Oh, that. She and Carmen Diamond were supposed to go together, and when Carmen had to back out, we were kind of surprised that she decided to go alone. But she said she'd always wanted to spend some money foolishly, have an adventure, go someplace exotic. And she needed some kind of surgery, something elective, and she'd heard the hospitals in Thailand were far less expensive than here but just as good. Her surgery went well, and she had a marvelous time. She sent us an e-mail almost every day she was over there, telling us what she'd seen and done, and we loved hearing about her adventures. And she came home with some wonderful souvenirs."

"What kind of elective surgery?"

"She didn't tell me."

Mike just looked at her, and Betsy said, "I don't know what it was, Mike—but she came home looking awfully good. Very *rested*." She smiled at him, eyebrows raised.

Mike smiled back. Once upon a time, when a movie star had

a face-lift, the euphemism often used to describe the improvement was, "she looks very rested." He flipped back a couple of pages in his notebook to read something. "Now, tell me about this statue she brought home from Bangkok."

"She brought two. One was a bronze of an elephant-headed god named Ganesha." She stopped to look inquiringly at him.

"Yes," he said nodding, "it was on the floor in her living room."

"Ah. The other was that statue of the Buddha."

"What does the Buddha statue look like?"

"Didn't she tell you?"

"Yes, but you tell me, too."

"Well, it's about this high." Betsy held out her left hand, her right hand hovering about seven inches above it. "Some kind of light-colored stone, fairly heavy. It wasn't the fat, bald, Chinese kind, but slim, and standing up, not sitting. If Doris hadn't told us it was a statue of the Buddha we never would have guessed it."

"We?"

"The Monday Bunch, the people who come in on Monday afternoons to stitch. She brought in her suitcase full of souvenirs on Wednesday, and we had a special meeting to see them. We saw the box the Buddha was in, and made her open it."

Mike nodded. "Go on."

She described the statue. "Doris said it is an ancient form of the Buddha, but that the statue is a modern copy."

"Is it possible the statue is really old?"

"I don't know. She said it wasn't—that is, the person who asked her to bring it here told her that. I saw no reason to disbelieve it. Mike, what's the problem here?"

"Didn't you hear about Mr. Fitzwilliam on the news?"

"No, I must've missed it. What about him?"

"Fitzwilliam was found in his St. Paul antiques store around noon on Friday, dead. Murdered. And his store was trashed about as thoroughly as Ms. Valentine's apartment."

"No! Oh my goodness, that's dreadful! That's . . . that's horrible! Oh, and you think this burglary is related to . . . But how can that be? She took the statue over there! Why would they come to her apartment? What are they looking for?"

Instead of replying, Mike asked, "Did you know that Ms. Valentine bought a gun?"

"No, she didn't. Phil bought it for her. I didn't know anything about it until Phil mentioned it a couple of weeks ago. But that can't be significant, since she didn't buy it for herself. Is it missing?"

"No," he said. "It was up there, in her bedroom."

"Was Mr. Fitzwilliam shot?"

"Yes."

"With *Doris's* gun?"

"Probably not. Though we're waiting for the complete autopsy results, he was shot with a small-caliber gun, probably a twenty-two or twenty-five, and the Valentine gun is a thirty-eight."

"So her gun wasn't taken?"

"No, it was found on the floor of her bedroom. Ms. Valentine said she kept it inside a pillowcase."

"So what *is* missing from up there?"

"Ms. Valentine says a piece of handwoven silk brocade, a

ruby necklace and earrings, and a silver ring, all bought in Thailand. And her laptop."

Betsy said, "That sounds pretty much like a burglary to me."

"Well, the stone statue of the Buddha she says she took to St. Paul wasn't found in the Fitzwilliam store. And it isn't in her apartment, either."

"You think she didn't take it over there? And that it was taken from her apartment?"

"What do you think?" He narrowed his eyes, reluctant to admit he really wanted her opinion.

"Of course she took it over there. The way she talked about going over there, the story she told of his reaction, it was all too complicated to be anything but the truth."

"So where is this Buddha statue?"

"In the hands of the person who bought it from him, I'd say. Probably the woman who got out of the Hummer. Paid for it and left, I'd guess. What do you think?"

"I think his murder and the search of his store, and then the search of Ms. Valentine's apartment are no coincidence, and this statue is what they have in common. It could be that Ms. Valentine found out the statue was valuable after all and decided to keep it for herself. In order to do that, she had to murder Mr. Fitzwilliam."

"Apart from the extreme ridiculousness of thinking such a thing of Doris Valentine, you have to assume she shot him with a different gun than the one she owned," said Betsy.

"If she's an intelligent person, sure." Mike was turning pink around the ears.

"But why murder him? Why not just fail to deliver it?"

"Because Mr. Fitzwilliam would want to know why it wasn't delivered, and when he can't get hold of Ms. Valentine, he will contact the Bangkok dealer, who will give him her address."

"Oh. But he wouldn't have had to contact the Bangkok dealer, since Doris said she talked to Mr. Fitzwilliam on the phone. He knew her name and probably that she was coming to his store from Excelsior. But all right, then, how about Mr. Fitzwilliam decided not to hand it over to the customer? And the customer murdered him to get it."

"Fine—except in that case, why come over here and ransack Ms. Valentine's apartment?"

"It was just a burglar in Doris's apartment. Coincidences happen, you know."

"No, this place was tossed by someone looking for something. He left a huge mess, spilling and dumping all kinds of things. He even took the covers off the exhaust fans in the kitchen and bathroom."

Betsy looked up at the ceiling as she pictured the ruins. What a horrible thing to walk into! But a *search*. She quashed her empathy in an effort to think clearly. Why would someone go on a search of Doris's apartment? She couldn't think. She shrugged.

Mike said, "Suppose Doris didn't hand over the Buddha because she found out it is really ancient and valuable? Countries have laws about exporting their antiquities."

Betsy nodded.

"And the person who was to buy it thought Mr. Fitzwilliam was the one holding it back and killed him. If Doris is right and the woman who went into his shop was the customer, she searched his shop, and when she didn't find it, she came looking for Doris."

Betsy bit her lower lip as her heart began to thump. Was Doris in danger? "Do you think that's what happened?" she asked.

"I'm still collecting information."

"You know, if this was such a secret deal, why was everyone being so aboveboard about it, her going to the Bangkok man's office and phoning ahead to Fitzwilliam in St. Paul?"

He said, "I thought Fitzwilliam was upset because Ms. Valentine showed it around."

"Well, yes, but he said that was because he was afraid she might have damaged it. Which was a legitimate fear. The hands on the statue were carved very delicately." Betsy raised her own hands and tried to imitate the pose of the fingers as best as she could remember it.

"Well, maybe," said Malloy. Again he consulted his notes. "Tell me about Phil Galvin."

"He's nice, a retired railroad man. I think he must be well into his seventies, though he's pretty spry. He's been a customer of this shop since before I came to own it. A gentleman, kind of old-fashioned. He's been courting Doris for a long while, and being very discreet about it. Well, anyway, he thinks he's being discreet. It's cute watching the two of them not announcing to the world that they're in love or hooked up or going into business together or whatever the current term is. It's nobody's business but theirs, and that's fine with them."

"Any reports of quarrels lately?"

"No. But as I said, they aren't talking about their relation-ship to anyone. You don't think he's involved in this, do you?"

"I'm just asking questions. Are you thinking you're going to get involved?"

Betsy thought of Phil, angry on Doris's behalf—and Doris, distraught at being caught up in a case of murder without knowing how or why. "Of course," she said.

Four

☙ ∘ ❧

THIS time the customers weren't standing for any polite evasions. They wanted to know what Sergeant Malloy had been doing upstairs and then what he talked about with Betsy. "What's going on?" Shelly demanded.

Bershada reported, "I saw Doris in here a while ago, and she was looking like she was about to scream. Or cry, at least." That last brought several more women away from the yarn sale baskets.

"What's wrong? Is something wrong?" customers were asking.

So Betsy felt forced to explain. "Someone broke into Doris Valentine's apartment—fortunately while she wasn't there—and thoroughly trashed it."

That brought on an exclamatory chorus: "Oh, that's awful!" "Oooh, scary!" "Poor thing!"

Alice asked, "Have the police got any clues?"

"I don't know, they didn't say anything to me about collecting useful evidence," Betsy said.

People who knew Doris came close to the desk. Jeanette Morgan said, "No wonder she's upset. I had a friend who was burglarized, and she actually sold her house afterward. She said she couldn't live there anymore."

"Poor Doris!" said Pat Ingle. "But she isn't going to move out, is she?"

"Who's Doris?" asked a customer.

Linda Barta said, "Doris Valentine. She lives upstairs. Nice woman. She's dating Phil Galvin."

Jeanette said, "I saw them together the other night in that new restaurant, Biella's. He seems very taken with her. And about time, I'd say. He's been a widower for—how many years is it? Fifteen?"

"Seventeen, I think," said Edie Wills. "Doris was kind of slow to catch on he was interested . . ."

Pat, Edie, Linda, and Jeanette drifted away, gossiping about senior dating.

But Bershada, a member of the Monday Bunch, remained at the desk. She looked pointedly at Betsy and said, "I don't know if you know this, but the police don't clean up after a crime."

"Yes, of course, I know that," said Betsy.

"Good, because if you think she's upset now, girl, you better believe she's going to go ballistic when she comes home and there's still that mess in her apartment!"

"Well, what am I supposed to do? I can't leave the shop!"

Shelly, standing by with two skeins of Lucci ribbon yarn, said, "But you're her landlady! You should call someone! You can't leave her to clean up a burglar's mess all by her own self!"

Godwin, having heard the conversation in passing, made a U-turn. "Isn't that double jeopardy?" he asked.

Rosemary Kossel, a very advanced knitter who taught classes at Betsy's shop, said, "It doesn't seem fair, does it?"

Bershada said, "There are companies that will clean up crime scenes, but it's bad enough having one stranger go through your stuff, without inviting more of them. Plus, they aren't cheap."

"But what choice do you have?" Rosemary asked.

She, Bershada, and Shelly looked at Betsy then, who said, "What, you want to surprise her?"

"I should think she'd find it a wonderful surprise," Rosemary said.

"I'm not so sure," Betsy said. "It's one thing to be there when someone is helping to clean up your place, because you can tell them to throw that away and keep this, and thank them. But it's another thing entirely when a bunch of gossipy women go through your things when you're not there, *and* without your permission, and think they're doing you a favor!"

"Okay, you have a point there," said Shelly. "So why don't we ask her?"

This time they all looked pointedly at Betsy, who acknowledged the responsibility with a small nod. "All right," she said, "I'll ask her if we can help, okay?" She looked at each in turn. "That's *we*, as in all of us. Except Godwin, who is taking a late flight to Florida."

"I could put it off," Godwin offered, obviously hoping Betsy would turn him down.

"No, you can't," Betsy said firmly. "You and Dax bought those cheap tickets and you can't change them."

"That's right," Godwin said, relieved.

Betsy looked at the others. "I expect you back here when Crewel World closes at eight."

Bershada and Shelly nodded, but Rosemary's fair complexion turned bright pink. "Oh, wait, I was thinking we'd do it tomorrow! I can't tonight! I'm so sorry. My daughter is taking me out to dinner and a movie tonight."

Bershada said, "But you can't expect Doris to try to sleep in her apartment when it's all torn up."

"I'm really sorry," reiterated Rosemary. "But my daughter and I have been trying to have a private conversation for two weeks. I think she's got something important she wants to talk about."

"Oh. That's different," said Bershada. "We understand. So go ahead, don't worry about it." She turned to Shelly. "What time?"

"Wait, hold on," said Betsy. "What if the police are still investigating in there? Or they have it sealed up for some reason and we can't get in?"

"I'll be right back," said Godwin, pleased to be able to do something in aid of the cause. He was gone only a few minutes. "They're winding up now," he said. "They'll be gone in about ten or fifteen minutes."

"How about we go up now—no, in an hour?" suggested Shelly. "I want to take these things home." She held up a plastic bag of yarn and needles.

"Fine with me," said Bershada.

"But I'm not free until eight—" Betsy began, trying not to

sigh. Her feet were already aching and she had a headache from hours in the shop.

"I'll come," said Alice, who had been standing quietly in the background.

"Thank you!" said Rosemary. Still pink, she went away.

"Yes, thank you, Alice," said Betsy, her tone quieter but just as heartfelt.

Betsy phoned Phil and said some members of the Monday Bunch had volunteered to help clean up Doris's apartment.

"Well, isn't that nice of you!" he said. "I think that's really great! I'll tell Dorie—and I'll be there to help, too. Hold on." There was a conversation on his end, unintelligible because he had put a hand over the receiver. "All right," he said. "Betsy, we'll both be there in an hour. Thank you!"

They were all prompt. Betsy went up with Doris, Phil, Alice, Shelly, and Bershada to have a quick look for herself. The yellow plastic crime-scene tape had been pulled down, but left in a heap on the floor. Doris unlocked her door and started to open it, but when it bumped against something she drew back fearfully. Betsy reached in and pushed the obstacle out of the way—it was the door to the coat closet. It had been left open, and everything in it had been pulled off the hangers or the upper shelf. A box of Christmas ornaments had been upended and many of the glass balls were broken. Two winter coats, and a host of sweaters and jackets were on the floor under a crisscross of hangers.

The entryway led into a small living room with a triple window on the right. They all stood there for a few moments, shocked at what they saw. Lamps were thrown on the floor and broken. Papers were scattered across the carpet, and chairs were overturned. Cushions from the couch had been dumped on the carpet and the couch upended over them. The thin fabric that covered its underside had been ripped away.

"Oh my Lord!" said Bershada. She put an arm around Doris's shoulder. "I thought you said it was a burglar! Honey, this was a *vandal*!"

As Betsy led the way through the living room, everyone walked carefully, but still their feet crunched now and again on something frangible. The kitchen was another disaster. The refrigerator had been opened, and much of its contents had been pulled onto the floor. Every cabinet door and counter drawer had been opened and emptied. Sugar and flour canisters were spilled onto the floor.

Traces of black powder were on every surface, left by the sheriff's department investigators.

Betsy said, "I had no idea it was going to be this bad."

Alice said, "If I wasn't standing here looking at this with my own eyes, I wouldn't believe it."

Shelly said, "Some teenagers once broke into a school where I was teaching and spent hours trashing it. But it didn't look as bad as this."

"I hope this guy left lots and lots of fingerprints," said Shelly in a low, angry voice. "I hope his fingerprints are on record somewhere."

"I hope so, too, baby," said Bershada. She turned to Betsy. "You get back downstairs. We'll get started."

Betsy, shaken, went back to work.

Hours later—only a few, but it seemed like many—the sale ended and the shop closed. Cleaning up, taking down signs, removing colored stickers denoting sale prices from products, counting the money, running the credit card machine and cash register, emptying the coffee urn and tea kettle, washing up, carrying out the trash, and writing up a deposit slip all took additional time after the door was locked. Krista said she'd take the money over to the night deposit at the bank, and Betsy gratefully handed the bag of checks and cash to her.

Then, upstairs again, Betsy looked over at Doris Valentine's apartment door. It was partly open and there were two plastic garbage bags standing in the hall outside it. Betsy could hear the sound of cheerful voices coming from inside.

But Betsy needed to eat something. It had gotten too busy in the shop for her even to grab a snack at noon. She needed to sit down for at least a little while, too; not just her feet but her right leg, the one she'd broken last year, ached from being stood on for so many hours. Right beside her own front door was Sophie, mewing piteously for her supper.

Not that Sophie was as desperately hungry as Betsy was. She had spent the entire long day cadging treats from customers, some of whom knew to bring along a little something for her. In vain, Betsy had pointed at the needlepoint sign hanging on the chair with the powder blue cushion that the cat had claimed as her own: NO THANK YOU, I'M ON A DIET. People saw the sign, laughed, and slipped Sophie a fragment of cookie or bagel.

Betsy unlocked her door, and the cat led the way into the galley kitchen. Betsy followed, to feed her a single small scoop of Science Diet dry cat food, the variety designed for old, fat, lazy cats, though the package didn't put it that bluntly. Betsy bought Science Diet because the package advertised it as a "complete" food, meaning it had all the nutrients to keep a cat healthy— something quite untrue of the goodies Betsy's customers loved to slip Sophie.

While her pet was crunching her swift way through her pittance of cat food, Betsy was building a salad of iceberg and romaine lettuce, sweet red peppers, cucumber slices, one of those little cans of tuna, and lots of croutons. She ate with Sophie's swift efficiency, drinking a glass of iced tea with her meal and then heading over to Doris's apartment.

Order was becoming apparent. Phil and Doris were working in the living room. The chairs were upright and in place, the broken lamps gone. Phil was tacking the loose underside fabric of the couch back in place with a broad thumb. Doris was sorting bills, postcards, letters, and other papers from the floor beside a small wooden desk. She didn't seem to be looking at what she was picking up, but merely stacking them a few at a time and putting them into random drawers. Her face was almost expressionless.

In a few days, thought Betsy, *she'll have to go through all of that again*.

Shelly and Bershada could be heard in the bedroom and bathroom.

Alice was sweeping up the last quarter of the kitchen floor, a pile of flour growing under her broom.

"That must have been spilled toward the end," remarked Betsy.

"Why do you say that?" asked Alice, turning to smile a greeting at her.

"He wouldn't have wanted to leave footprints."

"A careful vandal," said Alice, started to sweep again. "I never heard of such a thing."

"Can I help you in here?"

"It'll need to be mopped pretty soon."

"Call me," said Betsy, going back to the living room.

"Phil? Phil!" That sounded like Bershada, calling from the bedroom.

Phil called back, "I'll be right there!" He looked around, saw Betsy, and said, "Here, give me a hand."

Doris saw what they were about to do and came to help. They tipped the couch up onto its feet and pushed it back against the wall.

"Phil!" called Bershada again.

"I'm coming!" Phil called back. He touched Doris on the arm, and walked away.

Doris went back to the hard wooden chair in front of her desk, hung her head, and looked about to weep. Betsy hurried to put a hand on her shoulder. "Doris, it'll be all right. Trust me, it will be all right."

"I know, I know. But to think of a stranger's hands pulling all my things out and dropping them like they were nothing important, leaving his dirty fingerprints all over everything . . ." She sobbed once. "It's like he's still here, smirking at me from every corner. It's like I'll look in a mirror and see him looking back at me from over my shoulder with a slimy smile." She shuddered. "It makes me want to just walk away, leave every-thing behind, start over somehow."

"No, don't do that," Betsy said.

Doris smiled sourly. "You don't want to lose another tenant, huh?"

Betsy smiled back at this sign of courage. "That's right. You're paying the taxes on this place, you know." She squeezed Doris's shoulder. "Besides, I'd miss you. And Godwin would miss you—him especially. You'd break his heart if you moved away."

"Maybe. I love him—and you, and the Monday Bunch. I'd have to stay in Excelsior. And there's not many places in this town I can afford to rent."

She was right. Excelsior looked like a sweet little country town—and it was—but its residents paid big bucks to live in a safe, clean, attractive, Mayberry-like place this close to the Twin Cities. Betsy had some lucrative investments that made the shop almost a hobby and enabled her to charge less-than-average rent for two apartments and stay in the third herself.

"Once everything gets put away, I think you'll feel better," Betsy said.

"You're probably right." But Doris didn't sound as if she be-lieved it. She bent to gather up the last of the papers and shove them into another drawer.

"Where's Waldo?" asked Betsy.

"Hiding in the linen closet. He hates company."

Betsy went off to see why Bershada had been calling Phil. It turned out she needed help getting the queen-sized mattress back on the bed. It was thick but inclined to sag. Betsy arrived in time to help guide the thing into place. Bershada wadded up the sheets and pillowcases and found a hamper in the closet to stuff them into. On the floor in front of the linen closet in the bathroom, Betsy found a fitted sheet and a top sheet that didn't match, but were in the middle of a heap and therefore clean. She also found a single pillowcase of yet another color. Phil went back to the living room while Betsy and Bershada made the bed.

"She's really upset," said Bershada, pulling on a corner.

"I know." Betsy floated the top sheet out. "I wish there was some way to comfort her."

"I know she's in a lot of pain, but maybe what comforts me when I'm sad will help to comfort her just a little, too," said Bershada. Betsy looked at her inquiringly, and Bershada leaned forward to murmur, "Chocolate!"

Betsy smiled. "I wonder if she has any cocoa in the kitchen."

"Don't just stand there, honey, go and see."

Of course Doris had cocoa, though it was an inexpensive brand that needed just hot water. In a cabinet Betsy found six mismatched mugs, one a thick diner-style claiming to come from the Chatterbox Café in Lake Wobegon. Betsy knew it was Doris's favorite, so she set it aside for her. There was another stamped SOUVENIR OF THAILAND and others printed with many-hued roses. Betsy started the kettle and put into each mug a little more dry cocoa than the carton called for. As soon as the kettle boiled, she filled them, added a splash of condensed milk, stirred, set them on a tray, and called Phil and the women into the living room for a break.

Doris came to sit on the couch beside Phil. Betsy sat on his other side, Alice took the shabby old upholstered chair, Shelly took the desk chair, Bershada sat on the floor. "It's yoga," she said, when Doris remarked on how easily she got down and how erect she sat. "You still goin' to that water aerobics three days a week?" she asked.

"Oh, yes," Betsy replied. "It's horribly early in the morning, but that way it doesn't put a hole in my day. I like the stretches best—they keep my spine flexible."

Phil said, "I worked damn hard all my life, and I said that when I retired the most strenuous thing I'd ever do again was casting a line into a lake or river. Turns out I like weeding a garden, too."

"And walking," said Doris. "We do a lot of walking."

Phil said, "In the winter we walk around Ridgedale Mall; in the summer we walk up to Gray's Bay and back." He smiled at her. "She carries me part of the way."

"And he carries me the other part," Doris said, but she looked down at her hands as she said it, as if repeating a joke so old it had lost its humor.

"Have you taken an inventory?" Alice asked Doris in her brusque way.

Doris widened her eyes in surprise, but then she took a breath and said, "Yes, the police were very nice about that. They made me take my time to be sure I didn't miss anything. The burglar took my wonderful new ruby necklace and ring that I bought in Thailand, and a silver and garnet ring that Phil bought for me, and that silk brocade panel and"—she had to stop for another breath—"my laptop." She looked over at the desk. "What I don't understand is why they had to tear the place apart! How *could* they be so cruel?" She burst into tears.

"There, there!" said Phil, turning to put his arms around her. He gave Alice an angry look.

"I'm sorry," said Alice. "I didn't mean to upset you, Doris."

"They why the hell did you bring it up?" demanded Phil.

Alice gestured around the room broadly enough to take in the whole apartment. "I didn't think I needed to bring it up. After all, what are we here for, if not to clean up the mess the burglar left?"

"You're right, Alice, you're right," Doris said, pulling away from Phil to wipe her face with both hands. "I'm just upset, that's all."

"Of course you are," said Alice. "Anyone would be. Betsy, what do you think? Is this the sort of crime you could solve?"

Betsy smiled wryly. "No," she said, shaking her head. "This is just the kind of thing the police are good at, but not me. You know, fingerprints, fibers, tiny pieces of lint or cryptic footprints. No, not cryptic. What's the word? Footprints it takes ultraviolet rays to expose."

"I really, really liked that silk brocade," mourned Doris.

"More than the ruby necklace?" asked Shelly, surprised.

"Rubies and sapphires are mined in Thailand, and they sell for low prices over there. The stones I bought were small and probably not very high quality—it was just the idea of owning rubies. But the silk, oh the silk! That was special. I've never seen anything like that anywhere."

"It *was* beautiful," agreed Bershada. "I'm so sorry it's gone."

There was a little silence.

Shelly said, "Well, if we're going to get this done, we'd better get back to it."

Betsy, who had taken off her shoes, groaned and began to feel around for them with her toes.

Bershada said, "Now, people, wait just a minute. Look at Betsy, she's been on her feet all day. I think we should send her home and finish up without her."

"No, no—" Betsy started to object.

"Yes, yes, yes," said Shelly.

"But I don't want to go home," Betsy said.

"So don't," said Bershada. "You just sit there. When we want more cocoa, we'll ask you to make it. That's your job for the rest of the night—making cocoa."

"I agree," said Phil, but tentatively. He looked at Doris.

"Fine with me," she said. "What's left to do?"

"The bathroom," said Shelly.

"The kitchen floor needs a scrubbing," said Alice.

Bershada said, "And, Doris, we made a big pile of your undies on the bed."

"I'll be right in," said Doris.

"Let me help you, sweetie," said Phil.

"No, you don't," said Bershada, laughing. "You go scrub the kitchen floor."

In another minute, they were back at it. Betsy at first felt useless to be consigned to the couch while everyone else got busy. But in a few minutes her head fell back and her eyes closed. She wasn't asleep, just relaxed. She wished someone would come and rub her feet; she loved having her feet rubbed. A shame Morrie was no longer her boyfriend—he gave the best foot rubs.

Thoughts and ideas drifted through her drowsy mind. Doris

was a very nice woman, and she sure didn't deserve to have a vandalizing burglar pay a visit. Stealing the silk brocade was an odd thing to do. Who would the burglar sell it to? The teen vandals Shelly had talked about were a group, and they spent hours in the school. Could it have been a group of teens who did this?

But this apartment didn't seem a likely teen target. Or even a burglar's. Doris wasn't a rich woman, or one of those crazy old people who lives alone in a raggedy house and has a reputation as a miser. Yet the burglar had done everything but take up the floorboards. Mike Malloy was right—this was more like a search than anything.

But for what?

Maybe the search was for that lovely statue of the Buddha. No, it couldn't be. Doris had delivered the statue. There was no need to search her apartment for it, when it was not here.

Maybe something else, then: a diamond-studded cat collar or a Rolls Royce concealed in the bathtub—

"Betsy?"

She came to with a start. "Huh?"

It was Shelly, standing in the kitchen doorway. "Have you heard from Susan Greening Davis yet?"

"What? Oh, hum, yes." Betsy squeezed her eyes shut and then opened them again, trying to get her brain to wake up. "Yes, she's coming late this summer. She's going to teach a counted cross-stitch class. Oh, and I've written to Lisa Lindberg asking her to come and do a spinning demonstration."

"What's this? Lisa Lindberg is coming?" said Bershada, coming out of the bathroom.

"It's not firm yet," said Betsy. "You told me she's great at spinning and dyeing, so I decided to ask her. She says she'll see."

"Are you thinking this Lisa will teach a spinning class?" asked Doris. "And then you'll be carrying spinning supplies? I've always wanted to learn how to spin. I even bought a drop spindle, but I can't get it to work."

"Girl, you will love Miss Lisa!" said Bershada. "She spins angora yarn right off the rabbit!"

"What?" said Phil, over Shelly's shoulder. "How does she do that?"

"I don't know, exactly. She starts her spinning wheel, and hooks the rabbit up to it somehow, and the result is angora yarn."

"Well, that I've got to see!" declared Phil.

"Me, too," said Doris, seeing Phil and hastily hiding a small garment behind her back. But the expression on her face as she listened to Bershada was pleased and interested.

"Well, why wait?" said Bershada. "How about we make a day trip and go see Lisa? Amboy isn't that far, just south of Mankato. Lisa also owns a cute little restaurant, makes fabulous pies. And she sells hand-spun, hand-knitted hats and mittens in a store she also owns."

"Busy lady—oops!" said Shelly, suddenly realizing her sponge was dripping. She cupped a hand under it.

"She's a working fool," declared Bershada with a laugh. "But that yarn shop is something to see. She dyes some of her yarn, but the rest she leaves the natural color of the animal she took it from: goat, bunny, or sheep. And her yarn is beautiful stuff."

"Does she sell it? Her yarn?" asked Phil. He had become an avid knitter.

"Sometimes," said Bershada. "Not in great quantities, though," she added to Betsy, who was always looking for new sources of yarn, especially varieties that were hand spun.

Phil said, "Well how about we go tomorrow? Betsy, you're closed tomorrow, aren't you?"

"Well, yes, I am, but I've got my account books, laundry, grocery shopping, and housecleaning to do, so leave me out."

"Shelly?"

"I'm in."

"Alice?"

"I'd be pleased to go, thank you."

"Bershada?"

"Tell me what time, and I'll be there. And how about we take my car? It's old, but it's big and runs smooth." She drew that last word out, and ran her hand in a long, even line in the air, out as far as she could reach.

"Dorie?" asked Phil, and they all turned to look encouragingly at her.

"Yes, all right."

"Well, then, let's get this finished!" said Shelly. "We'll need a couple of hours sleep before we set off, I guess. Is seven thirty too early?"

"Hold 'er, Newt, she's headin' fer the barn!" declared Phil. "I say ten is plenty early to leave."

Alice agreed. "Some of us want to go to church."

"Ten is fine," declared Bershada. "That will get us there in time for lunch."

" 'Hold 'er, Newt'?" said Shelly.

"It's an old saying," said Doris. "Picture a farmer in the days when they used draft horses, and Old Nelly was trying to avoid her day's work pulling the plow. I learned all about it from Phil, who is much, much older than he looks."

"You're only as old as you feel!" said Phil, and in great good spirits, he went back into the kitchen to finish scrubbing the floor.

Five

꩜ ∘ ꩜

"WHERE on earth did you get this thing?" asked Shelly from the backseat of Bershada's big old Lincoln Town Car. The car, a blue so deep it was almost black, was rust-free. Usually, it takes only a few winters for road salt to make a Minnesota car start bubbling around the edges, and this model was thirty years old. There are a lot of Saturns in Minnesota, because they have plastic bodies.

"It comes from Arizona," said Bershada. "I have a friend who subscribes online to several Arizona newspapers. He keeps track of estate sales and reads used-car ads, and when he sees one of these old tanks for sale, he goes and buys it. There's always a market for them up here. I love 'em. This is my third one. My first was twenty years old. The older I get, the further back I reach for my cars." She laughed.

"Okay, I understand where," said Phil, who was also sitting in the backseat. "My question is, Why? Why buy something like this? It must get terrible mileage."

"Well, it doesn't get the best mileage, that's true," admitted Bershada. "But suppose I had one of those modern mini-cars? How would you decide who has to sit in back? Best two falls out of three?"

Phil chuckled. "I'll admit, it is roomy back here."

As they settled back in their seats, Bershada turned off Highway 7 onto 169 South. This would take them all the way to Amboy.

The sky was a mottled gray, but it wasn't windy, and the temperature daringly approached twenty degrees. A scant couple of miles later, the car started across a long bridge over a marsh. Some construction anomaly gave cars crossing it an amusing ride: *kuh-thump* as the tires went over a joint, then a gentle *whump* as they drove over a slight depression. Sixty-two miles an hour was the optimum speed, and with a little effort—the car's big engine thought seventy a nice cruising speed—Bershada held the speedometer right there. No one in the car spoke as they went *kuh-thump, whump; kuh-thump, whump; kuh-thump, whump;* but all were nodding in time to it. Anyone who drove Highway 169 frequently was familiar with this particular rhythm, which worked in either direction, and the few cars in sight were all bobbing across the bridge, *kuh-thump, whump,* as if in some happy ritual dance.

Highway 169 was a freeway until it crossed the deep, broad valley of the Minnesota River, where it turned into a two-lane highway. Bershada tried to go no more than seven miles over the speed limit. The highway was clear of snow, and traffic had thinned to almost nothing, which didn't help with her efforts not to drive too fast. Once across the river, the land was low hills running parallel to the highway. A dense line of leafless trees marked the Minnesota River not far away, and the highway curved now and again to stay near it. They skirted the small towns of Jordan and Belle Plaine, whose apple stands and garden centers looked forlorn in the winter landscape.

Half an hour later, the highway ahead dropped out of sight, and a sign announced the approach of the town of Le Sueur. And there, on top of one of the hills, higher then the naked gray trees, was a huge figure of a green man in a brief costume of leaves, waving a greeting.

"Well, looky there!" said Phil, waving back. "I haven't seen him in a long while."

"Who?" asked Doris, looking vainly in that direction as the car drove by the gigantic billboard and started down into a deep valley.

"Come on," said Shelly, "haven't you bought Le Sueur peas? He's the Jolly Green Giant, and this is his valley."

At the bottom, they crossed a long bridge over the Minnesota River. Not long afterward, then approached St. Peter, a pretty, little, old brick city on the banks of that same river.

South of St. Peter, the skies cleared somewhat, and shafts of sunlight turned the highway here and there a blinding white. The Minnesota River had gone west, on its way to caress New Ulm.

The land beside Highway 169 rose to become very flat; the only irregularities in the scene were old, shallow drifts of snow making curved gray snakes across the barren fields.

"Looks like Kansas out there," noted Bershada.

"Looks like North Dakota to me," said Shelly.

"Looks lonesome," said Alice.

"I think you're all right," said Phil.

Then came another valley as a major city, Mankato, came into view. "Oh my, it's grown a lot since I saw it last," said Doris.

"When did you see it last?" asked Shelly.

"Years ago. I went to college here." Doris blushed faintly. "It was just a technical college—a trade school, really," she said, anxious not to mislead them into thinking she went to the Minnesota State University.

"I did, too," said Phil, determinedly on her side. "We went to the same school, took the same classes. Just not in the same years."

"What did you study?" asked Bershada.

"Steam," said Phil. "We both have boiler's licenses. I was among the last of the steam engine drivers; then years later I went into heating plants. Dorie was one of the very few women after World War Two who worked in a factory maintaining the steam power units." There was pride in his voice.

"Have you two ever watched Lars Larson work on his steam car?" asked Shelly. "He's explained how it works to me a couple of times, but I don't really understand."

"I've seen him driving it around town, but I haven't talked to him about it," said Doris. "I'd love to, though, sometime," she added a little wistfully.

Phil said, "When the weather turns warm, I'll take you over to his place and get him to start the old machine up for you."

"What p.s.i. does he run it at?" she asked.

"Would you believe six hundred?"

"Oh my goodness!"

He nodded. "My old steam locomotive did just fine at two, two-fifty."

"My first factory boiler burned fuel oil and ran at thirty."

The conversation became even more technical at this point, until they saw incomprehension on the faces of the other two and bashfully fell silent.

"Look at this, we're crossing the Minnesota River *again*!" exclaimed Shelly. "Are you sure there's only one river called the Minnesota?"

"Only one," said Bershada, "but, girl, it gets around."

After the excitement of Mankato, the land flattened out again, and there was little to see until Vernon Center, which appeared to consist of a house, a bar, and several shedlike structures gathered tightly along the highway, as if waiting for a bus to take them away to Mankato's bright city lights.

Not long after that, Bershada slowed the car, as it approached a sign along the highway. AMBOY, the sign said, with an arrow pointing left.

"Now, nobody blink, or you might miss it," said Bershada, making the turn.

Actually, there were two blocks of dwellings, nice single-family houses set back a little from a street lined with trees. Some of the houses already had lights turned on inside. Although it was barely noon, the sky had darkened, and clouds were dropping lower as they thickened.

Alice leaned forward and looked up through the windshield. "I think it's going to snow."

"Well, I don't," Phil said. "The weather report last night said cloudy, but no precip."

"The weather forecast this morning predicted light snow," said Bershada. "But my car can go through up to six inches of the stuff, no problem. And here we are," she added, pulling to the curb.

"Where?" asked Shelly. All she could see was a large antiques shop outside the passenger window.

"Across the street."

There, on the corner, stood a picket fence in front of a small lawn divided by a curved walk. It led to a little cream-colored stucco building with a steep, dark roof set with a single small gable. A Model A Ford would have looked right at home parked in front of it. AMBOY COTTAGE CAFÉ, announced a modest sign on the wall beside the door.

"Is everybody hungry?" asked Bershada.

"You bet!"

"Well then, come on!" She climbed out and everyone hustled after her as she crossed the street.

The interior was about thirty feet wide but only twelve feet long, with perhaps a dozen very small, mismatched tables under a high, peaked ceiling paneled in light-colored pine boards. The walls were covered with quilt squares, quaint tchotchkes, small farm implements, and old photographs of the town. Incredibly good smells were coming from the kitchen, which was separated from the front by a pair of small flapper doors, like those in a western saloon. Near the doors was an old-fashioned cast-iron stove. Doris could feel the heat coming from it; she went over to hold out her hands to it. Not that she was cold, it was just a comfort to see a stove like the one she remembered from her grandparents' farmhouse, one that was really used, not a relic.

A very attractive woman—probably somewhere in her late thirties, tall, with honey brown hair and blue eyes—came out of the kitchen. "Are you all together?" she asked.

"Yes," said Bershada, pulling off her dark red wool coat.

The place was nearly full, but the woman gestured toward an empty table under a side window. "I'll bring you some menus," she said. "Would any of you like coffee?"

"I would," said Phil, shrugging himself out of his old army-style parka.

"Me, too," said Doris, and there was a polite chorus of agreement that coffee would be nice.

The woman went into the back room. "That's Lisa, the owner," Bershada said.

"She looks nice," said Shelly.

"Let's ask her about her other shop," said Alice, who was eager to see it.

When Lisa came back with a tray of steaming mugs and menus tucked under one arm, Bershada said to her, "When the lunch rush is over, will you show us your other shop? I've been bragging about your spinning and dyeing."

"Well, if you can wait until two . . ."

"Yes, we can," said Alice firmly.

Doris, still standing, began a struggle to get out of her long wool overcoat, which had a gray houndstooth pattern printed on a cream ground. Phil was behind her in an instant, taking the coat off her shoulders, hanging it on the back of her chair.

She held her knit hat and mittens, felted to make them thick and warm, in one hand.

Lisa gestured at the hat and mittens. "Did you knit those yourself?"

"Yes," said Doris, shyly holding them out.

"They're well made." Lisa said, examining them professionally before she handed them back. "I'll return in a minute to take your order."

Doris sat, picked up her coffee cup and took a sip. The coffee was a Scandinavian brew, strong but not bitter. She took another, deeper, sip and nodded. "This coffee is delicious," she said.

"Let me see that mitten," ordered Bershada, after taking a drink of her coffee.

Doris handed it over. "It's not that good," she said.

"Come on, honey, how can you say that? This is really nice! I like the suede palms."

Doris had sewn a thin piece of suede in the palm of her mittens so they wouldn't slip on her steering wheel. "Thank you."

"I say, I say, I say," said Phil in almost a Cockney's accent, "look at all this, then!" He lifted his open menu to indicate the object of his happy surprise.

Everyone was duly amazed at the variety of foods on the menu. Here were roast chicken and vegetable wraps, spinach quiche, and salads garnished with pine nuts and homemade sourdough croutons.

"And, oh boy, look at the pies!" said Phil. "Makes it worth while to go traipsing through all this highfalutin stuff to get pie for dessert!"

Doris gave him a look and he grinned at her. "Gotta keep up the male side at this party," he said.

"I think I'll have the salad," said Bershada, "so I'll feel less guilty about the pie."

Everyone else ordered the salad, too—except Phil, who had a bowl of chili with whole-grain bread. And he asked for his slice of pie to come with a scoop of vanilla ice cream.

The food was delicious, and everyone cleaned his or her plate—or bowl. Then they went for a little walk, stopping to look into the store windows two doors up, where Ms. Lindberg had her yarns and handmade hats and mittens on display.

"Is that a spinning wheel I see?" asked Alice, shading her eyes to peer into the dimness.

"I think so," Bershada replied.

Phil went to the door and tried it, but it wouldn't open.

"Let's go back," said Shelly, shivering and looking up at the sky.

"What, you're cold?" asked Bershada, surprised. "It's not that cold out here."

"I know, but I'm chilled to the bone. Can't you feel it? I hate this damp cold." She shivered again.

Phil looked at her with his eyebrows lifted and a grin starting, until he realized she said "damp," not "damn."

"It's like England," Shelly went on after making a face at Phil. "I spent two weeks over there many years ago, and I don't think I got warmed up until I was back home for a month."

The others laughed, but they also agreed this was a cruel sort of cold and turned back to the restaurant.

They found it almost empty and Lisa waiting for them.

"You don't have anyone working in your store," said Bershada, faintly accusing.

"No, I don't have a lot of customers—and most of them know to come in here and find me." She pulled on a light jacket—her shop was just a few doors down from her restaurant.

"Well, I want to see you do some spinning," said Alice, childlike in her determined interest.

"Come on then," said Lisa, and led them out under the lowering sky.

B ETSY looked over at the huge, white Baroque-style church on top of a tall, sudden hill to her right. The snow had begun as she started out for St. Paul and was now coming down heavily, blurring the outlines of the cathedral, its dome nearly invisible high above. She consulted her Google map—she was not very familiar with St. Paul, though she recognized the cathedral and could see ahead the immense block that was the Xcel Energy Convention Center.

She hadn't meant to leave Excelsior today. What she had said to the Monday Bunch was true—she *did* have a lot to do. Plus, she really was tired from the sale yesterday. It would have been nice to stay at home, cleaning and doing laundry, catching up on her bookkeeping and stitchery, taking little naps. But she'd started thinking about Doris and the burglary of her apartment, and the fact that Mr. Fitzwilliam had been found dead in the disorder of his own antiques store, and so here she was. She had no expectations, but she'd told Mike Malloy that she was going to get involved in the burglary case and she couldn't think how else to start.

She turned right onto Exchange Street, found a parking place, and got out to walk back up the street.

There were lights on in Fitzwilliam's Antiques, and she could see people moving around inside. The place was pretty much as Doris had described it, except the beautiful upholstered chairs were no longer in one window. The other window was empty, too. Must be good sales lately, Betsy thought, opening the door to enter.

"Hey, who left the door unlocked!" shouted a man's voice.

Betsy stopped just inside the store, waiting for developments, unbuttoning her coat.

From somewhere in the far back she heard a woman's voice reply. "I did! I'm taking stuff out, and it's making me crazy having to put it down to unlock the door, then remember to lock it again when I come back in. Nobody's out in this storm anyhow!"

"I am!" Betsy announced.

There was a startled silence, and then the woman shouted, "Eddie, take care of that!"

A man came out from behind a high shelf that was half full of old dolls, children's books, and toys. He was tall and thin with dark hair and brown eyes. His old twill trousers, very dusty, were held up with blue suspenders. His eyes were red-rimmed and sad.

"I'm sorry, we're closed," he said. "For good, I'm afraid."

"Oh, I suppose I should have realized . . ." said Betsy. "May I offer my condolences?"

"Thank you. Did you know my father?"

"No. In fact I never met him." It was stiflingly warm in the shop, so Betsy pulled her heavy coat open. "I'm here because a friend of mine is involved in this case."

"Who's your friend?"

"Her name is Doris Valentine. She brought something from Thailand to Mr. Fitzwilliam."

"Is that so?" he asked in the tone of someone with his suspicions confirmed. "How do you connect to her?"

"I told you, she's a friend."

He looked Betsy up and down. She was casually dressed in jeans and a green sweater—one of her earlier efforts. And it had cat hair on it.

"You're not a cop."

"No. Or even a private eye." Betsy smiled. "I'm Doris's landlady. But I also do investigations."

"Okay." He was still frowning, but at least he put down the big cardboard box he'd been holding.

"If you like, you can call Sergeant Mike Malloy of the Excelsior Police Department. He can tell you I sometimes do a good job of investigating."

Again he looked her up and down, but this time he nodded and seemed to relax a bit.

Betsy said, "You see, she had her apartment practically destroyed by a burglar looking for something. This happened soon after she brought a statue of the Buddha to Mr. Fitzwilliam, and just after Mr. Fitzwilliam was killed and his shop was torn apart in a search. I think this burglar was looking for the same thing in both places."

"What thing?"

"The statue, probably. Because it seems to have disappeared. Unless you've found it?"

"No," he said.

"Well, Doris is the one who was asked to bring it to Mr. Fitzwilliam from Bangkok. May I ask your name?"

"I'm Edward Fitzwilliam."

She looked around the shop. "May I ask you a few questions?"

"What's your name?" he asked instead, but not in a suspicious tone.

Betsy told him, then asked, "Was this shop on its way up or down? I mean, I'm not an expert on antiques, but it looks to me as if some of the things in here are of very high quality, while other things are . . . well, not."

The man looked around. "It looks like that to me, too—and I *am* a bit of an expert."

"Was your father a poor judge of quality?"

"No, not at all. It's just that things had been sliding for the last six or seven years, and then, more recently, they started picking up again." He stuffed his hands into his back pockets, shoulders drawn up against unhappy memories. "But the comeback was slow and uneven, so he couldn't just toss out all the drek and fill the space with good things."

"Was he a bad businessman?"

"No, but I think he got lazy." He sighed. "Or maybe just depressed when he realized he wasn't ever going to attract the Summit Avenue crowd to his store."

"So what changed his mind?" she asked.

"I . . . don't know," he confessed, his shoulders now up nearly to his ears. "All he told me was that he made a couple of good deals, and he thought things were going to turn around."

"Was he normally secretive about his deals?"

"No, not usually. See, every so often he'd try to get me to come into the business with him. That pretty much stopped when the store started sliding. But it didn't start in again when he started coming back."

Just then, a short, trim woman with dark hair, luminous skin and sober gray eyes came toward them. Betsy hastily moved out of the way. The woman was carrying a large, raggedy cardboard box full of table lamps. "I'm sorry," she said to Betsy, "but we're not selling anything today, and we're kind of busy." She stooped and dropped the box by the front door. It clattered sharply—most of the lamps were made of porcelain—but it didn't sound as if anything broke. She gave the man an angry look and went toward the back of the store.

"I think I'd better get back to work," he said.

Betsy said, "Please, could you call me? I'd like to talk with you some more. Maybe I can help you find out who is responsible for your father's murder."

He studied her face for a long few moments, then nodded. "All right. What's your number?"

Betsy dug in her purse for the her card case, then gave him a card, saying, "E-mail or phone, it doesn't matter. Thank you."

And she left.

Six

LISA Lindberg's woolen-goods shop took up most of the ground floor of the two-story building. The original hardwood floor had been refinished and polished. Lisa had removed the plaster from the walls to expose the original brick, and she had half-finished installing an antique embossed-tin ceiling. On one wall hung a large piece of abstract art, made of thick ropes of hand-spun wool, loosely woven and fastened to a tree branch.

Phil went over to a display of skeins of yarn in soft tans, browns, and grays. Shelly went to try on the various hats made of wool, mohair, and angora, also all in the natural colors of the animals' fur coats. She mugged at herself in the mirror as she pulled the tams into various shapes and positions on her thick hair. Doris went for a closer look at the abstract weaving.

But Alice went directly to the spinning wheel. "Is this for show or use?" she asked.

Lisa smiled. "Use. Want me to show you?"

"Yes, please."

Lisa went to the back of her shop, where she disappeared behind a curtain, then almost immediately came back with a wire cage about two feet long and almost as wide. It contained what at first looked like two large white rabbits. But on closer inspection, they all realized it was only one immense rabbit with long fur.

"What is *that*?" exclaimed Doris.

"A rabbit with a pituitary problem, I bet," said Phil.

"It's a perfectly healthy rabbit," said Lisa. "He's a giant angora, which is a breed, like the silky, English, or French breeds. Most angora rabbits run six or seven pounds, but Fernando here weighs fourteen pounds." She put the cage on the floor beside the spinning wheel, pulled a towel off the back of a hard wooden chair behind the desk and moved the chair up to the spinning wheel, where she sat and draped the towel across her lap.

"Where are your clippers?" asked Alice.

"You don't clip their fur, you pull it," Lisa said. She leaned sideways, opened the top of the cage, and lifted the rabbit by the scruff of its neck onto her lap. It sat there calmly, with its ears—with amusing tufts at their tips—erect at first, then laid back. It had red eyes and a long, thick coat, shorter on the face. Lisa gathered a tuft of fur on the back of the creature with her fingers.

"Oh, don't!" cried tenderhearted Shelly.

"He doesn't mind in the least," said Lisa. "Watch." Using her thumb and two fingers, she tugged gently and pulled out a clump of fur. The rabbit did not wince or even stir. Lisa started the wheel turning, keeping it going by working a wide, flat, wooden foot pedal. There was a short twist of string or yarn coming out the side of a simple mechanism above and to one side of the wheel. It consisted mostly of a wooden U shape lying on its side and surrounding a spindle with yarn already started on it. Alice was sure there was more to it, but she couldn't see because the mechanism had started spinning.

Lisa twisted the clump of white fur onto the end of the yarn, moving her fingers to attach it to the end of the string. With her other hand she pulled more fur from the rabbit and gave it to the hand feeding the yarn. Her fingers moved in a smooth, experienced way and very quickly a length of white, fuzzy yarn went into the mechanism.

Doris said, "I always thought the yarn went around the big wheel."

"No, the big wheel is there to operate the flyer assembly," Lisa said. Her hands were busy, so she simply nodded toward the spinning mechanism.

"Well, I'll be switched!" said Phil, coming closer for a good look. "That is a remarkable thing to see!" He was not speaking of the spinning wheel but of the way Lisa was pulling the fur off the quiet rabbit.

"I don't understand why the rabbit puts up with you pulling its fur out," said Shelly.

"It's not attached very firmly," said Lisa. "And, anyway, all that fur is hot, so he likes having it thinned out."

Indeed, the rabbit sat quietly across her lap—hanging over it actually, because of its size—its nose working in the putt-putt-putt way of its kind.

"They grow new fur fast. I can do this to Fernando about every four months."

Lisa spun until everyone was satisfied by the demonstration. Then she put the rabbit back into its cage and accompanied her visitors as they walked around her shop. The big room was sparsely furnished, with a table and display shelves of felted wool hats and mittens, angora berets and helmets, a couple of knit sweaters in earth tones. Alice tried on a couple of hats, with Shelly supervising, and it was Shelly who chose the angora beret in a silvery gray color for her. Alice frowned over the price, but said she'd take it, anyway.

Doris picked up a brown felted hat with tiny white loops standing up all over it.

"Is this woven? I don't see how you got these picots so even all over it," she said.

"Mohair doesn't felt," Lisa explained. "When I knit the hat, I mixed wool and mohair, and when I felted it, the wool shrank but the mohair didn't."

"Well, isn't that amazing? I just love the effect!" It was obvious that Doris wanted the hat, but she put it back down without even asking the price. She told herself it was because she had spent so much in Thailand—and she had overspent her budget. But in truth, her losses in the burglary made her fearful of acquiring anything nice and new.

Though Lisa didn't normally sell yarn, Phil persuaded her to part with a skein of white angora, enough to put a collar and cuffs on a sweater he was going to knit in sky blue wool.

Bershada picked up some small wads of wool in bright hues of orange, red, and purple. "I thought you only used natural dyes," she said, holding them out.

"Oh, those were done by third-graders in a class I taught.

The dye is Kool-Aid. You have to use it in a very concentrated form, of course. I use vinegar to set the dye."

They stopped to look at a strange machine in the back. About the size of an ice chest, it was made mostly of large and small rollers covered with long, shining wire bristles. It was sitting on a metal cabinet that brought it up to near eye level. "It combs the wool," explained Lisa.

"Wow," was all any of them could think of to say for a few moments. The thing looked dangerous. The mere thought of a hand getting mangled by the menacing prickles made all of them keep a respectful distance.

Phil said, "I never knew, never thought to think, that there was a happy medium between hand-combing wool and having it processed in a big factory."

"Well, there's too much carding for me to do it by hand," said Lisa, "but not enough to send it to a factory, so I'm exactly in that place, Mr. Galvin."

Doris said, "This is a very pretty town, Ms. Lindberg. But it's so small. How do you keep the store going?"

"Tourist trade," replied Lisa. "We get more visitors through here all the time. I used to leave the front door unlocked even when I wasn't here, because local people knew to come to the restaurant to pay for anything they wanted. But with so many strangers passing through, I don't dare do that. I can't afford the losses of a theft."

"I understand," said Doris softly. She turned and slipped away toward the front.

The others had more questions, and then Phil noticed she was gone. "Dorie?" he called.

"I'm up here," said Doris in a choked voice. "And . . . and look, it's starting to snow."

"Is it snowing hard?" asked Phil, hustling to the big front window where Doris was standing.

Shelly started to follow him, but Bershada took her by the arm and shook her head. "She's upset," Bershada murmured. "Let him talk to her alone."

Phil came up beside her. "It's not snowing very hard," he said. "Say, are you crying? What's the matter?" When she did not answer, he said, "Now, Dorie, I know it's something." He leaned close to her ear and murmured gently, "You can tell me."

She turned away. "No." Then she changed her mind and turned to face him. "Well . . . all right. When Lisa talked about leaving doors unlocked, it reminded me how I'd left my apartment unlocked. So it's my fault the burglar got in. Just thinking about it makes me sick and sad."

"Well, you poor thing!" Phil said, putting an arm around her shoulder. "Here I've been admiring you for being so brave, but not realizing what a struggle it's been for you. I think all of us appreciate your letting us help you forget for a little while. When we get home, you can cry all you like, and I promise I'll be right there to lend you my shoulder."

"Thank you," Doris said, in a shaky voice. "I'll take you up on that. Now, give me a minute and I'll be all right." She sniffed, found a Kleenex in her purse, blew, and the tears stopped.

The others came over soon after to look out the window. They saw more than mere flurries, but not a heavy snowfall.

"Maybe we'd better start for home," said Shelly.

"Why?" asked Bershada. "I'd like to visit that antiques store.

The weather forecast this morning was for light snow, and that's what's happening out there. I already told you, my old car can plow through anything up to six inches."

"Yes, but we're kind of a long way from Excelsior," noted Alice. "If this keeps up . . ."

Bershada turned to Lisa. "Is the antiques store open?"

"Yes, and it has some wonderful things. The owner must have three hundred old hats in there, for example, and some clothes that date back to the early twentieth century. And he also has a tame squirrel that climbs all over him."

"That sounds interesting," Phil said, looking encouragingly at Doris.

But Shelly said, "I'm sorry, I still think we should start for home."

Alice, looking out the window, backed her up. "Me, too," she said.

Lisa raised her hand to discourage further argument. "Let me check to see if the weather forecast has changed," she said. She pulled out a cell phone, dialed a number, and listened.

"It's snowing hard in Minneapolis," she said, after she broke the connection, "and the prediction is for six inches as far south as Mankato."

"Uh-oh," said Phil.

"All right, let's go," said Bershada.

They gathered up their purchases, put on their coats, hats, and mittens, and thanked Lisa warmly.

"It's all right," she said. "Come again, soon."

"We will, we will," they all promised as they hurried out the door.

"It's still not very cold," noted Bershada as she pulled her keys from her purse and unlocked the car. "I hope this doesn't turn to freezing rain."

There were groans of anxiety as they climbed into the big old car.

They didn't have any serious problem on the road back to Mankato, so even though it was now snowing harder, they decided to push on. But then it turned bad. Bershada had to drive slower and slower as the snow thickened, blowing directly into the car's windshield, making it hard to see more than a dozen yards ahead. The border between the highway and the shoulder became invisible under all the snow.

Then the sky grew darker, and Bershada's headlights reflected off the snow rather than lighting the road.

Soon she was down to less than thirty miles an hour. She had Phil and Doris take turns looking out the back window for a braver driver coming up fast behind them.

Shelly got out her cell phone but she couldn't get a signal. And when Bershada turned on the radio, she learned the roads were worsening all the way up to St. Cloud—well past the Twin Cities. The radio station was giving such alarming news that she shut it off again. She had barely done so when they all felt a *bump* as the heavy car fell off the macadam onto the shoulder. It almost veered into the ditch, but Bershada, fighting the wheel, managed to get it back on the pavement. Still, it gave her such a fright that she slowed the car even more.

The windshield wipers were set on high, but snow had built up around their edges, and the warm air of the defroster could only turn it to slush as the temperature dropped. Snow built up on the side windows, too, and they were so fogged with condensation that the people in the car began to feel claustrophobic.

"I think we should find a motel," said Shelly in a low voice.

"I agree," said Doris from the backseat.

"It's getting dangerous out there," said Alice, rubbing a side window with a gloved fist. A single huge semi going the other way churned the snow into a thick fog. Bershada slowed to a crawl until they were out of its range.

Phil said, "I'll sleep in the lobby if they're full up."

"I just hope we don't have to sleep in the car," Bershada murmured under her breath, but her passengers were in such a heightened state that they heard her. They were all frightened, and frightened people become superstitious, so no one dared call attention to the remark for fear of having it come true.

"How far are we out of St. Peter?" asked Phil.

"Maybe we should turn back," suggested Alice.

"No, I think we're closer to St. Peter than Mankato now," Bershada replied. "Anyway, if this storm is moving south, it's as bad behind us now as ahead. Problem is, I'm down to twenty miles an hour. Plus, manhandling this old car is wearing out my shoulders."

"I'll drive!" came a chorus of voices.

"No, really, I'm fine. And it shouldn't be much longer."

"We *are* stopping in St. Peter," said Phil. "Right?"

"I think we'd better," Bershada said.

"Is there a nice motel in St. Peter?" Shelly asked, already imagining a warm, snug room safe from the storm.

But Doris was looking out the window. There was nothing to see out there. They might as well be on the moon—no, it didn't snow on the moon. Did it ever snow on Mars?

She kept her desolate thoughts to herself while praying that they'd arrive in St. Peter safely.

Shelly was praying, too, that they didn't slide off the road again. That semi was the first vehicle they'd seen in a long while—and it was going in the opposite direction. If they went into a ditch, they wouldn't be found until morning.

The last time Bershada had had her car serviced, she'd had been advised to get new tires, but tires were expensive, especially the big ones this car took. She'd hoped to make her old tires last until spring. Now she hoped they had enough tread to keep them on the road.

Despite the car's weight, it shuddered a little as a blast of wintry air pushed at it from the side. Phil frowned, then quickly turned to Doris with a smile to say, "Cozy back here, ain't it? This old baby's got a good heater."

And Doris drew yet more courage from somewhere and smiled back. "Oh, yes, I'm nice and warm." She leaned a little sideways and added softly, "Especially with you beside me." She looked past him at Alice, who obligingly was not looking at them. Phil lifted an elbow to subtly touch Doris on her arm, and she smiled again.

Alice asked in her blunt way, "Is there a Motel 6 in St. Peter? I can't afford a nicer place."

"We'll take whatever we can get," replied Shelly, equally blunt. "We'll pool our money if we have to, and of course we'll double up." She looked over her shoulder. "Except poor Phil, of course."

"Awwww, now . . ." said Phil, but then he chuckled wickedly. "I bet not one of you has something I've never seen before."

"That doesn't mean I'm going to give you a glimpse of mine!" said Shelly.

"What if all the motels are full?" asked Alice. "A lot of people will have been caught out by this and will have needed to stop for the night instead of getting on home."

A worried silence fell.

"Finally!" said Bershada as the lights of St. Peter came up gradually from behind curtains of blowing snow. Her relief was enormous.

They passed two motels with *No Vacancy* signs lit, then stopped at a third, despite its sign also indicating a full house. The desk clerk called all the other places in town, but they were all fully booked. As Alice had predicted, so many people were caught out in the storm that every room for rent was occupied.

"The hotel is letting people stay in the lobby," offered the clerk.

"Oh dear," said Doris unhappily.

"I bet I know a place that won't be full," said Bershada.

"Where?" everyone asked—even the desk clerk.

"It's a bed-and-breakfast."

"Why won't it be full?" Phil asked. "Too expensive for the average stranded traveler?"

"No, it's because it's a secret bed-and-breakfast."

"Don't play with us!" said Alice. "There's no such thing!"

"Yes, there is. It's called the March Hare. It's not really a secret, but the owner is still renovating it, so he doesn't advertise."

"Oh, wow," said the desk clerk, who was very young. "I forgot about that place!"

"Can you phone them for us?" asked Phil.

But Bershada said, "No, don't bother, it's just a few blocks from here. If all the rooms are taken, I'd sooner spend the night in their parlor than in a hotel lobby."

They hustled back outside and climbed into the car again—except Phil, who took the brush-scraper out of the back seat and cleared off the side and back windows. He got back in, a little breathless from his hurry.

"Shall we stop on the way for a bite of supper?" he asked.

"Look around," said Bershada. "Everything's closed."

"There's a gas station up ahead," said Phil.

"I'd rather go to bed hungry than eat gas station food," declared Shelly.

Bershada pulled out onto the street. "Me, too," she said. "That gas station, is it a Freedom station?"

Shelly rubbed at the side window with a mittened hand. "Yes."

"Then this place is in the next block." Bershada pulled close to the curb. "It's a Victorian, made of brick, set back from the street. Keep an eye out, everyone."

"Does it have a big sign?" asked Shelly, peering outward.

"I told you, it's a secret place. No sign."

"There it is, I think," said Shelly, her face barely an inch from the window. "Right on the corner."

"Yes, it's on a corner." Bershada glanced off to the side briefly. "This is probably it." She turned the corner and stopped. A tall, untidy hedge lined the other side of the sidewalk. "Great,

I remember that hedge—it was covered with lilac blooms when I stayed here two years ago."

"Heck of a good memory you've got," said Phil. "Come on, let's go knock on the door."

"Use the side door," Bershada instructed. "It's never locked until nine; the manager has a buzzer that sounds when anyone comes in."

The house reared up in the snowy darkness, the outline made irregular by bow windows. The group went up to a screened side porch lit dimly from inside the house. Bershada pressed down the old-fashioned latch on the heavy antique door, whose top half was fitted with thick glass. It opened and they crowded into a tiny hall with a steep staircase right in front of them and rooms to their left and right. The left-hand room had a low-watt bulb shining far back in it. After a moment, they realized in the dimness that they were looking at a big modern kitchen with professional-sized appliances.

From somewhere beyond the back of the kitchen came an attractive young woman with light brown hair pulled back. She was wearing a cream Aran sweater and blue jeans. "Oh, you're here after all!" She looked them over. "But I thought it was a party of eight women."

"No, we're a party of four women and a man," said Bershada in an amused voice, "and I'm sure we weren't expected."

Seven

ᘓ ᐧ ᘔ

BETSY was tired. Tomorrow was Monday; she had to get up early for her water aerobics, and she had a class that evening, so she'd be in the shop late. She ought to get to bed early, but her apartment was getting grubby from neglect. The kitchen floor in particular needed a good scrubbing. Plus she needed to work on an amusing counted cross-stitch pattern that was turning out to be difficult. It was Brett Longley's design of a realistic Dalmatian puppy looking at the floor in front of him where half his spots had spattered off. The name of the piece? "Achoo!" The difficulty lay in the subtle shading on the white fur.

But the Internet was alluring, and she just couldn't quit until she added her opinion to a thread on Jacqui Carey's patterns. That done, she was about to log off when she heard the juicy click that meant an incoming e-mail. She nearly ignored it, but curiosity—and a lack of desire to do housework—won and she went to the screen that held her e-mail. It was from Dorie101. She started to open it, then drew her fingers back. Hadn't Doris's laptop been stolen? What if this was from the thief?

Well, what if it was? Maybe he wanted someone to pay a ransom to get it back. She'd heard sometimes that thieves did that. So she should read it just to see.

And, of course, if it had an attachment, she wouldn't open that.

Hold on, maybe it contained a virus or a worm, and she shouldn't read it at all. She let her fingers rest on the keys while she tried to make up her mind.

But Betsy had a curiosity bump the size of Mount Shasta, and she just had to take a look.

Hi Betsy! We're in St. Peter. The snow got so bad we couldn't continue. All the hotels are full so we were lucky to find this bed-and-breakfast right on the main street, called the March Hare. It hasn't even got a sign in front, because the owner is still renovating the building, though it looks all renovated to me. They rent rooms to groups coming to seminars and things at Gustavus Adolphus College, so I guess they have some kind of deal with the school. The group they were expecting couldn't come because of the storm, and we were stranded, so the manager said okay. She's nice; her name is Heidi. The place is a really old mansion, from the 1870s, and the furniture is real antiques. I have the least expensive room, a servant's bedroom in the back corner of the house. I could see the lilac hedge from here, if it weren't snowing so hard. As it is, I can't see anything.

Hard to believe that in three months the hedge will be covered in blooms. My room is very small, but cozy, and it has a beautiful quilt made of scraps of velvet. We are hoping the snow quits tonight so we can get back on the road tomorrow. Got to go, the manager needs her computer back.

Love, Doris

Ah, thought Betsy, Doris signed on as a guest and used her own account, that's why it came from Dorie101. She was glad Doris thought to e-mail her. She'd been worrying a bit ever since she'd heard the weather report on tonight's news. The snowstorm that was supposed to roar through fast had stalled and there were blizzard conditions all over Hennepin and Nicollet counties.

Secure in the knowledge that her friends were not stuck in a ditch somewhere, she signed off and went out to dust her furniture and mop her kitchen floor.

D ORIS came half-awake when she heard stealthy footsteps outside her room. Then she heard the door to her room open very quietly, and that alarmed her into complete wakefulness. Could it be Phil? Of all the nerve! Then a voice—a woman's voice—said softly, "Doris?"

Doris reached across the bed for the lamp and snapped it on. A woman, tall and slim, dressed in a long, dark coat, stood in the open doorway with a gun in her hand. Doris found she could not look anywhere but at the gun.

"Where's the silk?" demanded the woman.

"What? What silk?"

"Don't pretend, all right? The Thai silk, where is it?" Doris looked up and saw a young woman's face clenched in anger.

Drawing a shaky breath, she managed to say, "At home."

The woman's voice went high with hysteria. "No, it *isn't*! I looked and I looked and it isn't there!" The gun was pointing at Doris's face, although the hand that held it was trembling.

"Honest, I don't have any silk with me!"

"Liar!"

"No, really—" started Doris, but she could see the woman's trigger finger tightening. Without thought, she flung a pillow backhanded as she plunged off the far side of the bed.

The gun went off and wood splinters flew. A terrified Doris, deafened by the noise, rolled to her feet and ran toward the woman—there was no other way out of the room. She slammed straight-armed into her and pushed her out into the hall. The woman grabbed at her, pushing back.

"Help!" Doris screamed. The woman swung the gun and hit Doris on the side of the head. Then Doris grabbed her gun arm and tried to push it up. "Help!" she screamed again.

As the woman moved her arm sharply to shake Doris off, Doris clung with both hands and shoved a bare foot behind the woman's boot to trip her. But the boot was cold and wet, and her foot slipped. Both women were making wordless sounds of effort.

The woman was taller than Doris, and stronger. She smelled of perfume and leather. It was dark in the hall, and Doris could barely see. The woman suddenly moved sideways, stepping on Doris's toes. *"Owwwwwww!"* howled Doris. But she did not let go of the arm.

When the woman moved sharply again, Doris realized that

someone else had grabbed her. "Drop it!" ordered a man's voice—Phil. Thank God, Phil.

The woman choked out, "Let me go!" and kicked backward as she twisted in Phil's grip.

"What's going on?" someone called. Bershada.

"Oh my God, what are you *doing*?" exclaimed someone else. Shelly.

The gun went off again, and there was a sound like pottery shattering.

"Get out! Get away!" Phil shouted. He was pulling the woman by the shoulders, trying to turn her away from Doris, who was still trying to hold on to the woman's arm. The gun went off a third time, and Doris screamed as the flash blinded her. Her cheek burned and she choked as she inhaled burnt powder.

She couldn't clear her lungs, her arms were losing their strength, she was blinded, choking. The woman, as if sensing victory, growled, "I'll *kill* you!" Doris, with all that was left in her, pushed hard.

The woman's arm swung up and she disappeared.

Astonished, Doris fell against Phil and the two of them staggered into the wall near the top of the stairs.

At the same time, there was a big thump, then a tumbling sound, a single groan, and finally, silence, except for Phil and Doris's panting.

As they looked down into darkness, a light suddenly came on. At the foot of the stairs lay a figure, ominously still.

"Is she dead?" rasped Doris.

"I dunno," Phil gasped. "Are you all right?"

Doris coughed and drew a small, painful breath. "I . . . think so." She coughed again. "You?"

"Yes. Oh, hon!" He stroked her hair and her face. "Who *was* that?" His voice was a harsh whisper as he struggled to catch his breath.

"I don't know. Oh, Phil, I was so *frightened*!"

He put his arms around her and the two clung together while they gulped air and waited for their breathing to become less desperate.

"What did she want?" he asked after a few moments.

"I don't know. She told me—listen!" A voice came from downstairs. They looked down, fearful that the woman who'd attacked them was getting back to her feet. But she lay where she had fallen.

The voice was loud, but trembling with fright. "Yes, shooting! . . . I don't know! At least three shots . . . Please hurry!" It was Heidi, speaking to someone on the phone. "And someone's fallen down the stairs! . . . No, all right, I'm not going to go anywhere near him . . . What? I'm sure someone's hurt, all that shooting . . . Yes, March Hare on Minnesota Street . . . No, it's all quiet now—maybe they're all dead up there . . . What? Oh, yes, I'll turn on the lights. But, oh God, hurry, hurry!"

The police were coming, that was good—but Doris suddenly broke away from Phil. She had gone to bed in her underwear, and the idea that the police would walk in and see her, not slim, not young, and indecently exposed, shifted her focus with a shock.

Phil was also nearly nude, standing there in his boxer shorts, the hair on his skinny chest standing up in a silver mist. His broad smile was no comfort.

"I'm going to go put something on!" she whispered, and hurried to her room. She pulled on the slacks and sweater she'd taken off—how long ago? What time was it, anyhow? She picked up the delicate little watch she'd bought herself last Christmas and held it close to the low-watt bedside lamp to read its tiny face. Ten after three. She didn't feel the least bit tired; amazing how being shot at gave one that wide-awake feeling. Fearing the police were already at the door, she finished dressing by slipping her cold and clammy boots onto her bare feet and hurried out into the hall.

Phil had turned the light on. He was standing near the top of the stairs, fully dressed, with that scared grin still on his face. She went to join him, and they looked down at the woman lying ominously quiet at the foot of the stairs.

Eight

෨·ൡ

WHEN the racket started, Bershada pushed Alice in the shoulder. "Wake up, something's happening!"

Alice grumbled, "What?" then sat up, alarmed. "What's all that noise?"

"Someone's fighting. And I think that was a gun going off."

"Where's it coming from?" asked Alice, climbing naked out of bed, grabbing at a blanket. Her voice was frightened.

"It's down at the other end." Bershada went to the door, felt for the light switch, and flipped it on.

Then the door opened, bumping against her. She gave a shriek, which Alice echoed.

"It's okay, it's okay, it's just me," said Shelly. "Let me in, for God's sake! Was that a gun?" She was thickly wrapped in a duvet.

"Yes," said Bershada, who pulled the top sheet from her bed

to wrap herself in it. Then she picked up a big pottery pitcher that was sitting in a painted bowl on the nightstand near the window.

"Come on, let's go," she said.

"*What?*" said Alice. "Are you *crazy?*"

"I'm going."

"Well, I'm not. For one thing, none of us is dressed!"

"Fine. My cell phone's in my purse. Call nine-one-one." She opened the door went out, with Shelly right behind her.

There was only a very dim light in the front part of the hall. Once they'd made it down the two steps, it was very dark. They felt their way along, toward the sounds of struggle.

A small lamp was glowing feebly through Doris's open bedroom door. By its light they could see three figures tangled in a rapidly shifting mass.

"What's going on?" demanded Bershada.

"Oh my God, what are you *doing?*" exclaimed Shelly.

Bershada tried to discern who was where in the fight, and raised the pitcher over her head, prepared to strike.

A shot rang out and the pitcher blew into fragments as a bullet went through it and struck the wall beside her.

"Get out! Get away!" shouted Phil.

The two women hastily retreated back down the hall.

"Oh my God in heaven!" gasped Bershada, brushing fragments out of her hair. "Someone's gonna get killed, someone's gonna *die!*"

The gun went off again, and the two women fled back to Bershada's room, where Alice was talking frantically on the cell phone. "Yes, shooting! Hurry, they're shooting all over the place!"

But even as she said it, a heavy silence fell.

P HIL looked around Dorie to focus on the body at the foot of the stairs. It lay with one booted foot on the bottom step, one arm flung outward, the other shoved under the body, elbow sticking up. An uncomfortable, even painful, pose, but there was not the slightest effort being made to straighten out.

On the other hand, the figure's long coat was shoved upward. Phil couldn't see the face, which for all he knew contained open, frightened eyes.

Who the devil was she? A lunatic who had picked this place for a random attack? Maybe. It had been dark in the hallway, Phil hadn't gotten any kind of look at her. Dorie probably hadn't seen much, either. Now that the lights were on, maybe Dorie or even Phil might recognize her.

He started down the stairs, moving slowly, with one hand on the banister—the stairs were impressively steep. He reached back with his other hand, in an invitation for Dorie to join him. After a few steps he felt her hand slip into his. He could feel her cold fingers trembling, poor kid—not that his own nerves weren't quivering, his heart pounding. This had been a heckuvan experience.

He was pretty sure he knew all, or most, of Dorie's dark secrets—as she knew his—but this? First the burglary, now attempted murder. What in the *hell* was going on?

Downstairs, out of sight, he could hear Heidi's voice, talking more softly this time, so softly he couldn't understand the words she spoke.

About halfway down the stairs, another thought occurred to him: This couldn't be a deliberate attack. Who knew they were going to stay at the bed-and-breakfast? Not even *they* knew they'd be here. But then Phil thought of the fury in the woman's voice when she said she'd kill Dorie. That had sounded personal. She'd seemed to be angry at Dorie, not some stranger. Maybe she'd known they were here because she followed them from Amboy. But why? And how, in that blizzard?

He nearly fell going down the next step because he wasn't paying attention. "Whoops," he said softly as Dorie took a sharp breath. "All right, it's all right, hon," he said.

To his ears, faintly, came the scream of a siren. *Thank God.* As he took the last few steps, he could hear what Heidi was saying. She was on the phone again; this time, apparently, to the owner of the house.

"Yes, that's right," she was saying. "I called the police, they're coming right now, I can hear sirens, but they're moving so *slow*—what? What? Yes, it's snowing like crazy here, too . . . Oh, no, I don't think you should try to drive down, I think all the roads are closed . . . Okay, Mr. Toohey, I'll call you again as soon as I find out what this is all about."

UPSTAIRS, Shelly, hearing the sound of a siren, went to look out the front window.

"I think I see flashing lights," she said.

Alice said, "I think we should stay here until the police actually arrive."

But Bershada said, "Honey, I can't stand just waiting. It's gone quiet out there, and the police are closing in. I think one of us should go see what's going on. I'll go, if y'all want to wait here."

Shelly said, "Now wait, now wait, the shooting may have stopped because someone is reloading. Maybe right this minute he's sneaking up the hallway looking for someone else to kill."

That brought an anxious pause. They all held their breath and listened hard for the sound of footsteps. When no one heard any, they breathed again.

Alice muttered, "Still, I'm staying in this room until a policeman comes knocking to tell me it's safe to come out, and I don't want to be alone, so you both better wait here with me."

PHIL stooped beside the still figure on the floor. He reached out to touch her hand very gently. It was still warm, tanned but flaccid. A gold ring, set with a deep blue square-cut stone, gleamed on one finger. By the look of it, it was real gold and a real sapphire.

"Is she . . . dead?" asked Heidi.

Phil remembered a trick a nurse told him. He reached out and took the top of the woman's ear between his thumb and forefinger and pinched really hard, using his thumbnail. There was no response.

"I'm pretty sure she is," he said.

"What *happened* up there?" asked Heidi.

"We're not sure," said Dorie. "I was asleep and she came into my room with a gun—"

"Where's the gun?" interrupted Phil.

"There, by her hand," said Dorie. It was a black revolver that looked much smaller now than it had when pointed at her. Phil rose, caught the toe of his boot behind it and shoved it into the kitchen. Heidi hastily moved out of the way as it turned once on the vinyl and thumped gently against a counter.

"What did she want? Money?" asked Heidi.

"No," Dorie replied. Her voice was puzzled. "She wanted silk. She asked me where the silk was. I think she must've been insane." Phil stooped over the body and she said, "No, Phil, we should leave her alone, the police won't like it if we move her."

"I'm not going to move her, but I want you to take a good look at her face." He pressed the shoulder of the coat down to expose her face. It belonged to a beautiful woman in her middle thirties, with shining, dark brown hair. If it hadn't been mussed up, her hair would have fallen into that style that made curves like parentheses to just under the ears. Her eyes were closed, and above them her eyebrows were so perfect they looked combed.

"I don't know her," said Dorie. "I've never seen her in my life."

The woman's skin looked flawless. She was wearing makeup, but it's the kind you don't notice on a woman until you realize her skin looks too nice to be real. He could see a golden earring with a dark blue stone that matched the one on her finger. Her hands were thin and beautiful even though the fingernails were short and painted with clear polish. The brown coat was real leather, thicker under Phil's hand than it looked—well, for heaven's sake, look there by her leg, it was lined in mink! He straightened. "Who gets all dressed up like this to go shoot someone?" he wondered aloud.

Dorie took it as a real question, directed at her. "I don't know. Why would a stranger come and ask me a stupid question, and try to shoot me, unless she was crazy?" She leaned over to look at the body from a different angle. "Oh, Phil, look at the way her head is."

Phil moved to get a better look. "Yes, I see." The dead woman's head was bent at an angle no intact spine could assume. It confirmed his belief that she was thoroughly dead. He stood up, his fingers rubbing against themselves as if to dust something off. He grasped Dorie's hand again and took a big step over the body, bringing Dorie with him into the dining room. The siren was getting louder, but slowly—the streets must be really bad out there.

"I killed her, didn't I?" Doris said in a scared voice. "The police are going to arrest me."

"No, they won't. This is clean self-defense. She came here with a gun, and we got into a fight to keep her from killing you. And she fell."

"I pushed her."

"Well, dammit, so did I." Phil didn't think that was true, but Dorie needed reassurance.

"Did you? Well, that's good. And thank you."

"The question about the silk—was it the silk you brought home from Thailand that she wanted?"

"She said she looked and looked and didn't find the silk. But the burglar took my biggest piece of silk. So if that was her in my apartment looking for silk, she found it. That's why this doesn't make any sense."

"Maybe she's not the one who burgled your apartment."

"No, she said she looked . . . Maybe she came after the first burglar left? But why are they after that silk? There were half a dozen panels of it hanging on Ming's wall in the market." Dorie thought for a few moments then frowned. "She knew my name, Phil. She called me by my name and said, 'Where's the silk, the Thai silk?' And she was really, really mad at me, she said she was going to kill me." Dorie shivered.

"God, I wish I knew what this was all about," Phil muttered, as he put his arms around her.

The siren's wail came closer. "I wish it were over, I just wish it were over and we were safe at home," she whispered.

Nine

⁓ ⊙ ⁓

THE siren had been growing louder and louder, and now red and blue lights flashed into the windows as a vehicle, bigger than an ordinary squad car, pulled partway into the driveway at the back of the house. More sirens could be heard screaming from farther away. Seconds later, Phil caught a glimpse of a figure at the side door, holding a gun. "Don't shoot, don't shoot!" he called.

Heidi screamed out from the kitchen, "Be careful! The body's right inside the door!"

The door opened just enough for two uniformed policemen to sidle in. They seemed huge in their dark blue jackets, and they shed snow and melting snow all over everything. They both held guns pointed at the ceiling.

"Who's in the house?" the bigger of the two asked.

Heidi gestured at Phil and Doris near the doorway. "Me, and Mr. Galvin and Ms. Valentine are all the ones down here," she said, "and upstairs there are three women—Bershada Reynolds, Shelly Donohue, and Alice Skoglund. They had the two front bedrooms."

"Is anyone else hurt?"

"Down here? No, just that woman on the floor. I think she's dead."

The other cop had holstered his gun and gone to one knee beside the dead woman.

"Kelly," he said, "go clear the upstairs."

"Right," said Kelly. Gun in hand, he went up the stairs faster and more quietly than Phil would have thought possible.

"Who is she?" asked the kneeling policeman, who was pressing two fingers into the woman's neck.

Heidi said, "I don't know. I never saw her before. I heard the door alarm go off a little while ago, but when I came out, there wasn't anyone here. If that was when she came in, I guess she went right upstairs. It was just a couple of minutes later that I heard some kind of a fight, and a gun went off three or four times. I was calling nine-one-one when she fell down the stairs."

"Where's the gun?"

Phil said, "I saw it near her hand when we came down, and I kicked it away."

Heidi stepped back a little and pointed to the floor near a counter.

"Was that the gun that was fired?" asked the cop.

Heidi said, "I think so."

"Yes, it was," said Dorie. "At me."

The policeman looked at Dorie so sharply that she took a

step back. "Who are you?" he asked, even though Heidi had already told him.

"My name is Doris Valentine," she said, with a tremor in her voice.

"I'm Phil Galvin," announced Phil. "We're together." He took Dorie's hand. "All of us, Bershada, Shelly, and Alice, and me and Dorie, were coming up from Amboy when the snow got so bad we had to stop here in St. Peter."

"Are you from Amboy?"

"Nossir, we're from Excelsior, and we were headed back there."

The policeman nodded. "The both of you just stand there a minute, okay?"

"Yessir." Phil gave Dorie's hand a reassuring squeeze.

The policeman went over to the gun, bent low, and said, "It smells like it's been fired." He turned to Heidi. "Is this your gun?"

"No, sir."

"Do you have a gun?"

"No, sir!"

Then he looked at Doris and Phil. "Not our gun, either!" said Phil, and Dorie shook her head emphatically.

The officer pushed a button on a microphone clipped to the shoulder of his jacket and said, "Base, this is Officer Max here. We're in. Kelly's clearing the upstairs. I've got one down, a DOA, at the foot of the stairs right inside the back door. Three people here with me—one's the manager, two are guests. The rest of the downstairs not cleared."

They must have been waiting on the front porch for Officer

Max to say something. Phil heard a rattle and then a thumping as someone tried the front door.

"Locked," apologized Heidi. She crossed the kitchen, came through another door into the dining room, and disappeared into the parlor. Phil heard the door open. He leaned backward, looking through the dining room, and caught a glimpse of two people in brown as they entered the front door. Sheriff's deputies. One peeped into the dining room, and Phil straightened hastily. The deputy waved briefly at the cop, then went back out of sight. The other came into the dining room. Her brown jacket was soaked, and her trousers were wet to the knees. "Whatcha got, Max?"

"The DOA's a female, unidentified as yet, and there are supposed to be three more females upstairs. Kelly's gone up to have a look. Is Hansen watching the front?"

She nodded, pulling off a pair of heavy leather mittens. Phil noticed that they looked like shooters' gloves: There was an overlapping split in the palm so fingers could come out without removing the mittens.

"Whad'ja do, Amhurst, walk over?" asked Max.

"That's a big roger, Max," she replied, matter-of-factly. "We heard shots were fired, so we came the fastest way. All our SUVs are out on the highway working accidents and bringing in strandeds. Is your DOA shot?"

"Not that I can see, but I haven't moved her. Three shots fired, according to the witnesses, but none of my three here are wounded."

"She fell," said Dorie. And when the law turned its regard on her, her tone became defensive. "Well, she did! She had the gun, but we fought—"

"Who fought?" asked Max.

"The three of us," said Phil. His gesture took in the dead woman, Doris, and himself. "She was like a crazy person. We don't know why she attacked us."

O FFICER Jack Kelly quickly searched the back bedrooms and bathroom, reporting them cleared via his radio to Max downstairs. He found quite a lot of pottery fragments on the floor of the back hall, including a broken handle. Then he went around a corner, up two steps and down the carpeted hall to the front bedrooms. He went all the way to the front of the hall and waved at the sheriff's deputy at the bottom of the stairwell. The twist of wooden stairs made an interesting and dizzying shadow play as he moved around the top of it.

The door to one bedroom was open. He did that sly, rolling-around-corners entry that had been drilled into him at the academy—he was new to all this, and halfway between excitement and terror. He paused to look around, with his gun at the ready. The light was on, but the room was empty. The bed looked very disordered, a blanket half on the floor. The bathroom had a set of women's underwear hanging on the shower curtain bar.

He went across the hall, listened briefly at the door, then rapped sharply on it. "Police! Open up!" he barked in his deepest register.

There was a louder murmur of voices from the other side.

"I said, open up! This is the police!"

"All right," said a woman's voice near the door. "But please, there's just three of us, all women, and we're scared."

"I am not going to hurt you," Kelly said in a milder tone.

The door opened and behind it were, as advertised, three scared females: a slim attractive black woman, a tall elderly white woman, and a medium-sized young white woman with lots of disheveled brown hair. The black woman and old woman were dressed, but the woman with all the hair was wrapped in a duvet, which she held as if she might be nude under it. *Well, well, kinky*, he thought. All three pairs of eyes were wide with alarm.

"What's going on out there?" quavered the woman in the duvet.

"We're still figuring that out," he replied. "Is anyone else in here with you all?"

"No, just us," said the elderly woman, surprising him with her deep voice.

But he took a quick look around anyway, in the closet and the bathroom—where more women's undergarments hung drying—ignoring their slightly insulted faces. He'd been warned never to take civilians' words at face value no matter how innocent their appearance.

"Now," he said, "what's going on here?"

Ten

❧ · ❧

ANOTHER siren announced the arrival of emergency medical crews. Two women and a man made up their party, and again the mysterious intruder was checked for signs of life. And, as before, none were found. They stepped away and stood in the kitchen awkwardly, professionals with no call for their profession. The investigators had their work to do, though the woman was not officially dead until the coroner, who had not yet arrived, said so.

"Have you called Dr. Sholes, Max?" asked the man.

"No, I decided to wait until a thaw clears the streets." Max said this so deadpan that it took a moment for the emergency tech to laugh.

One woman tech said, "He'd wade through drifts taller than this to come here. Nothing he likes better than to be at the scene of a nice, juicy murder."

Which was true, so it was a sorrow to him that St. Peter was such a quiet, friendly town, despite its being host to both the large Gustavus Adolphus College and the Minnesota Security Hospital, where the dangerously insane were held and treated.

"Now, hold on, this may not be a murder," warned Max. "The story I'm hearing is that this woman came here with a gun to attack an innocent guest of the inn, and they engaged in a struggle. The result was that this woman fell down these stairs."

"So we assume the dead woman is the attacker, not the innocent guest?" asked the other female tech.

"Yes. The guest, also a woman, yelled for help and another guest came out of his room. If their story checks out, this was simple self-defense."

"Poor Dr. Sholes," said the female tech. "Not so juicy. Still, I'm betting he'll enjoy hearing the story. But meanwhile we're in for a long wait, because if he turns up in the next hour, it'll be a miracle. The roads are about as bad as they can be."

A loud, rough, grating noise, like a giant bicycle bell with croup sounded from the front of the house. "What the hell's that?" demanded Max.

"Front doorbell," said Heidi, rising. "Shall I answer it?"

"Did you lock the front door when you came in?" Max asked Amhurst.

"Nope," said the female deputy.

The noise sounded again. "Good manners, maybe," said one of the med techs.

"I'll get it," said Amhurst. She hurried out and in a few moments a man's voice called, "Wow, it's terrible out there! Tell me, where is it? What have you got for me?" By the sounds he was stamping snow off his boots and slapping it off his coat in the little foyer.

"We're here by the back stairs, Doc," called Max. "We've got a DOA female."

"Don't you want a professional opinion about that?" asked Doc.

"All right, if it'll make you happy, come and look." He said in a lower voice, "Though a man who can't check for his own self whether a door is locked or not—well, I just don't know."

"Here, let me help," the deputy was heard to say. More stamping and brushing noises could be heard. "Hold still, let me get your back. You look like a snowman."

A short, stocky man in Wellington boots and a camel hair overcoat came into the dining room. He was smacking a purple knit hat into one gloved palm. The deputy was behind him, dodging flying snow and reaching fruitlessly for the hat. A snow-clogged purple scarf was already in her hand.

"All right, all right," he said abruptly, realizing what she wanted though she had said nothing. He handed her the hat, pulled off the gloves—thick brown leather lined with fleece—and handed them to her as well. Then came his heavy wool overcoat. He sat on a dining-room chair and pulled off his Wellington boots, which dripped ice, snow, and water on the beautiful antique Persian rug under the table.

"Thank you," said the deputy faintly, as she staggered off with her burden.

Dr. Sholes's silver hair had been squashed flat against his head by the hat, and his cheeks were red from cold. His face was broad, his mouth wide and friendly, his big nose shapely and even redder than his cheeks, his eyes small and very blue. His voice was a gruff baritone but not harsh in tone. "Well, well, well," he murmured, already focused on the body, intensely interested. He walked to it slowly, eyes taking in detail, then stooped with a little grunt—he was rotund—to check the carotid with two fingers and lift an eyelid. "DOA, all right." He looked up the stairs. "Steep sucker. She take a tumble down this?"

"That's what I'm hearing," said Max. "Though she may have been pushed." He spoke into his microphone. "Kelly, you done with those three females yet?"

"Yeah. I let one go back to her own room and put on some clothes. All they know is there was a fight and shots were fired. They locked themselves in this bedroom waiting for rescue. Want me to bring 'em down?"

"No, you stay up there with them. Detectives are on their way."

"Copy."

Officer Max looked at Phil and Doris and said, "Investigators are coming. They're going to have a whole lot of questions for the both of you, so how about we put one of you in one front room and the other can stay in the kitchen."

"I'll start a pot of coffee," said Heidi.

"No, you come here into the dining room and have a seat. We'll want to talk to each of you separately."

"Yes, sir." Max stepped out of the way, but Heidi repeated her trick of going to the back of the kitchen and into the dining room through another doorway.

"The kitchen used to be two rooms," she explained.

"Fine." He called in that this was an official homicide and

asked if a team could be sent over to process the scene. Then he raised his voice to call, "Hansen!"

"Yo!"

"Come here and take Ms. Valentine into the front room."

"May I have the library instead?" asked Doris. "It has a fireplace, and I seem to have kind of a chill." Phil had noticed she was shivering and wished he'd thought to make that request first.

"Sure."

Now that he knew about the other doorway, Max took Phil through it into the kitchen and sat him at a little table under a window.

"I know how to make coffee," volunteered Phil.

"No, you just sit tight, okay?"

"All right."

D ETECTIVE Mark Shindler struggled through growing drifts and wind blowing a gale full of snow into his face, up his sleeves, or down his neck, depending on which direction he was walking. It wasn't all that many blocks from the police department, but it seemed miles in that storm.

He was joined a few blocks from the station by two investigators from the sheriff's department. St. Peter was the Nicollet County seat, so their department was headquartered here. Having companions to share the misery did, as advertised, halve it.

The house, when they reached it, was ablaze with lights, glowing even through the twisting veils of snow whirling in front of it and around its corners.

The trio paused on the big front porch to consult—briefly,

both because the routine was familiar and because the thermometer was sinking like an anchor.

"There are supposed to be five guests at the inn plus the manager," said Shindler. "Mandy, you take the manager, she's the one who called this in. Heidi's her name."

"Yeah, I know," said Mandy. "She's my cousin."

"Whoops, then Paco, you take Heidi. Her last name's Mogenson. Mandy, there are three naked women on the top floor." He shook his head. "Don't ask, that's all I was told about it. There are four big bedrooms up there. Separate them before you talk to them. I'll tackle the woman who was allegedly attacked by the victim. Whoever finishes first can tackle the man who helped her. Ready? Let's go." He opened the big old front door and stepped gratefully into warmth and light.

A N HOUR later, Deputy Paco went out to look at the cars parked on the street. He found a huge flat-backed vehicle with squared-off headlights and a severely rectangular windshield: a Hummer. There seemed to be slightly less snow on it than on the other parked cars. The grill was cold when he put a bare hand near it, but when he gently brushed at the snow in the middle of the hood he found a thin layer of ice. The same on the windshield. So it had been parked here warm, after the snow started. The first layer of snow had melted, then turned to ice.

He bent and brushed away the snow and road crud on the license plate, using his flashlight to read the three letters and three numbers. He wrote them down in his notebook and went back inside.

He told Detective Shindler what he'd discovered, was duly praised for his enterprise, and was asked to call the plates in.

In a few minutes he was told that the plates were registered to a Hummer belonging to one Wendy Applegate of St. Paul.

Shindler tried the name out on everyone in the house, but he drew another blank from everyone but the Valentine woman, the would-be victim. She thought she might have heard the name before. Then again, she was so rattled she thought she might have heard her boyfriend Phil's name before. *Stranger and stranger*, he thought.

Eleven

ᏕᎧ . ᏕᎧ

"**B**UT they had to let us go for lack of evidence that we'd committed a crime," said Doris to a thunderstruck Betsy. "Then they said that they would keep in touch, and they'd appreciate it if Phil and I wouldn't take any trips out of the country."

"Oh, Doris!" said Betsy. "This is so horrible! I can't believe it! This woman actually tried to *kill* you?" They were in her shop on Monday afternoon—the five had ridden home in Bershada's luxury automobile, then taken lengthy naps before coming to talk to Betsy. Shelly was with them; the schools were closed because of the snow.

"I don't think that was her intent, not at first," Doris replied in a low voice. She was sitting on a chair at the library table, a cup of tea sitting untasted in front of her. A white bandage was coming loose from her cheek, and she was wearing the same clothes she'd worn on the trip. "She wanted a piece of Thai silk from me. She said she'd looked for it in my apartment and couldn't find it."

"So the person who burglarized your apartment was this woman."

Doris nodded. "She said in those exact words that she'd looked for the silk and it wasn't there."

"But the Thai silk *is* in her apartment," said Alice, in a tone meaning she'd made this argument before. "I saw it with my own eyes when we cleaned up. Except the piece that was stolen—and it was stolen by this woman."

Doris nodded uncomfortably. "I know, that's what the police in St. Peter are having trouble with, they think I'm lying about why this woman came after me."

The cordless phone on the table began to ring. Betsy had turned off the answering machine, so she had to pick up. "Crewel World, Betsy speaking, how may I help you?" she said.

"Ms. Devonshire, this is Joe Brown."

"Mr. Brown, you have a superb talent for calling at awkward times," said Betsy crisply. "I will consider increasing my pledge, but not at this particular moment."

"I apologize. Look, this is important to the institute. Perhaps you could call me at a more convenient time?"

"Oh, all right," grumbled Betsy, and she wrote down his number. She hung up and said, "Whew! Where were we?"

"Who was that?" asked Bershada, taken aback by Betsy's short tone.

"Fund-raiser."

"Oh," drawled Bershada, and the others nodded comprehendingly.

"*I* think the woman in St. Peter was some kind of nut," said Shelly, defiant on Doris's behalf.

"I think this is a case of mistaken identity," said Phil. "For some reason she's confused Doris with some other person. Maybe one of the people who was supposed to be at the March Hare."

"I'd agree with you, Phil," Betsy said, "but Doris said the woman called her by name."

Alice, still stuck on the detail of the silk, said, "I think she thinks Doris has some other kind of silk."

"What other kind of silk?" asked Phil.

"The kind she didn't find when she searched Doris's apartment."

Phil said, "That doesn't make any sense!"

Betsy said, "Wait, maybe it does! Doris, remember that old silk rag you threw away?"

"Yes, you pulled it out again and showed it to me. You said the embroidery on it was pretty." She sounded indifferent.

"I remember an old rag," said Bershada. "It was wrapped around the statue of the Buddha. You're telling us it's a valuable silk cloth?"

"Well, it might be. I want to research how to clean it. I think it could be as much as a hundred years old."

Alice said, "But you told us silk can't be more than fifty years old, because it shatters."

Betsy nodded. "I thought that was true. But then I did a little research on the Internet and found some pictures of very old silk." She looked around at Doris, Alice, Shelly, Phil, and Bershada. "*Centuries* old. That rag might be just an old rag—or it might be a valuable antique worth more than the stone statue it was wrapped around."

"Thai silk," said Doris softly, coming into focus. " 'Where's the Thai silk?' That's what she asked me."

Bershada said, "Do you seriously think that raggedy old thing is the Thai silk Wendy Applegate came looking for with a *gun?*"

Betsy frowned and shifted her shoulders in an uncomfortable shrug. "I don't know. I didn't think that might be the reason for the burglary or for Mr. Fitzwilliam's murder. I thought it was about the statue. But now Doris says this woman wanted the Thai silk that wasn't in her apartment. Still, my rescued embroidery doesn't *look* like Thai silk; I mean, the embroidery doesn't look *anything* like the patterns in the woven silk that Doris brought home."

"Woven patterns might not look like stitched ones," Shelly pointed out.

Doris said slowly, "When I was buying silk from that woman in Bangkok—Ming was her name—she showed me lots of different kinds of embroidery from Thailand, Laos, and Vietnam, and I didn't see anything like what was on that rag."

Shelly asked Betsy, "So how old do you think it is?"

"I don't know. It might not be very old at all. It may be just what it looked like, a worn-out piece of embroidered silk, not worth anything. But if the rag had been tossed into a chest and left alone in a dry, dark basement, it could be sixty, eighty, even a hundred years old. The really, really old silk fabrics—two-thousand-year-old silk, can you imagine?—were found in tombs in China."

Phil said, "Come on, you think this rag you're talking about could be two thousand years old?"

Betsy said, "Oh, no, I'm sure this isn't that old. The photographs I saw of really old silk were just plain cloth, though they were striped in very bright colors. And there were pictures of half-rotted fragments, hard to tell what they were like when they were new, but they didn't look like Doris's cloth, either. I think this is much newer."

Alice said, "Maybe it's from the early nineteen hundreds, something an English missionary stitched while she was in Thailand."

Betsy said, "Well, for heaven's sake, Alice, I think you've put your finger on it! That could explain why it reminds me of Celtic designs. If that's what it is, it might be worth three or four thousand dollars. Maybe more—have you seen what really old samplers sell for?"

Bershada said, "The rag I saw didn't look anything like a sampler."

"Did it have an alphabet on it?" asked Alice.

"No," said Betsy.

"Well, I've stitched more than a few samplers in my day, and they all had alphabets on them—that's what makes them samplers."

Doris pulled them back on topic, saying, "But you think this is the silk that woman was after?"

"I'm willing to think so."

"Four thousand dollars isn't worth killing someone over," Shelly pointed out.

Alice said, "No amount of money is worth a human life."

Just then, the door sounded its two notes, and in came Gary Woodward, teen knitter. He had a Crewel World bag in one hand and was smiling the way a scholar does when school is unexpectedly out.

"What's up, Gary?" Betsy asked.

Gary's smile vanished into an apologetic look. "Well, it's this skein of yarn I bought on Saturday." Gary took it out of the bag, a bright, furry, shimmery mass in red-orange and maroon, appropriately called Flame. "I bought two. The other one's fine, but this one—" He pried it apart a little and showed Betsy a bite-sized fragment of a chocolate bar melting its way into the delicate filaments of the yarn.

"Oh, gosh," said Betsy. "Well, go get another one—if there is one."

"I hope so, I already started the hat with my first skein."

The people at the table watched him wander off, and when they judged him out of earshot they leaned in and took up the conversation again.

Betsy said, "Maybe Shelly's right, the dead woman was insane, asking for a piece of Thai silk she had already taken from Doris's apartment. But on the other hand, I have a piece of old silk fabric. Doris brought it home from Thailand, and no amount of searching in her apartment would have found it."

Bershada said, "Well, all right, maybe that thing is what she was after. But even a hundred-year-old piece of silk can't be worth much when it's a mess like that one was. I've seen those expensive samplers, and they're in beautiful condition."

"Yes, of course you're right. But I've been researching how to clean and restore it."

"Will that make it valuable?" asked Alice.

"Maybe."

Phil said, "I think the biggest mystery of this whole thing is, how did Wendy know where we were? *We* didn't know we were staying at the March Hare until we got there!"

"I knew almost as soon as you did," said Betsy. "Doris, you sent me an e-mail, remember?"

"Yes, that's right." She looked across the table at Betsy and asked, not quite succeeding in keeping the accusing tone from her voice, "Who did you tell?"

"No one."

"Oh, but you must have!" declared Alice.

"No, not anyone!" said Betsy, her eyes flashing for an instant. "I didn't talk about it on the phone, or send an e-mail, or forward the e-mail Doris sent me. So unless there's a psychic out there somewhere reading my mind, I am not the source that told the dead woman you were staying at the March Hare in St. Peter."

"Well, isn't that dandy," said Phil. "*Someone* must have told her. How else did Wendy Applegate find out? Either she read Dorie's e-mail, or someone told her about it." He looked around at the other women. "Did any of you make a phone call from St. Peter?"

They shook their heads.

"I didn't, either," said Phil.

"Heidi," declared Bershada. "It must've been Heidi."

"Why on earth," asked Phil, "would Heidi call someone and tell her Dorie was staying there?"

"Did any of you talk with Heidi at all?" asked Betsy.

"We all did," said Shelly. "After supper we sat in the library—it's a beautiful room, with a bay window almost as big as the whole wall, and lots of books, and a fireplace. We talked to her about our trip to Amboy, and that set off some talk about stitching. Heidi crochets and she brought out a doily she's been working on. I showed off the mohair tam I bought, and Doris said she'd been to Thailand and had brought home some silk floss."

"Doris, did you mention the silk you bought in Thailand?" asked Betsy.

"No. I didn't even talk about my trip, or the silk I bought, or the stone Buddha and the rag it was wrapped in. In fact, until you mentioned it just now, I think I'd pretty much forgotten about it."

"So if the rag is this old silk the woman was after, how did Heidi know about it?" asked Bershada, interestedly, and Alice nodded. They had enormous respect for Betsy's deductive powers.

"One of you must have told her," said Betsy.

But since none of them had known the old rag was silk, they were able to deny that.

"But someone must have led that woman I killed to the March Hare!" said Doris.

"Stop saying that like you're a murderer!" said Phil sharply. "I told you it was self-defense! And, anyway, it might've been me who gave her that final push!" She bowed her head under the rebuke in his voice, and he reached to touch her shoulder in apology.

" 'Murderer'?" Gary had detoured from the checkout desk to the library table, where they were all sitting. "Who got killed? Ms. Valentine, I don't believe you could really kill someone. Betsy, are you going to get mixed up in another mystery?"

Gary had once played a key role in solving a computer mystery for Betsy.

"It's a mystery but not a murder, Gary," replied Betsy. "It was a terrible accident. A woman fell down some stairs."

"But the police think it was Doris who pushed her down the stairs," said Alice, ever ready with an uncomfortable detail.

"Wendy Applegate," said Shelly, thinking out loud. "I told the police I had never heard of her, but now I have this feeling I've heard that name somewhere."

"Where?" demanded Phil.

She thought for a moment, then raised her hands, palms up. "Sorry, but I just don't know. It could've been some gossip in the teachers' lounge." She frowned, then shook her head, unable to retrieve the information. "I'll Google her."

Doris said, "I know who she is."

"*What?*" exclaimed Shelly. "Did you tell that detective in St. Peter?"

Doris frowned. "I told him I thought her name was familiar. I was upset, I couldn't remember."

"We were all pretty upset," said Phil, shaking his head sadly.

"Well, who is she?" asked Shelly.

Doris said, "She went with Carmen Diamond to Thailand. She and another woman. I think her name was Linda, or maybe Lana."

Shelly exclaimed, "*That's* why I sort of remember! I met Carmen at a teachers' conference last year and we went out for coffee. She told me about her trip to Thailand with two friends." She looked at Doris. "It was kind of fun to learn that we have a friend in common."

Betsy tapped her lips with a forefinger. Was it important that Wendy had been to Thailand? With Doris's friend Carmen?

Alice began, "But why would someone break into Doris's apartment—"

"She didn't break in," interrupted Doris in a pained voice. "I never lock my apartment door. I mean, I never used to."

"I never did, either," said Betsy firmly. "People in Excelsior usually don't, or didn't until this got into the news. Excelsior is the kind of town where you didn't think you had to. Mayberry of the North." That was a title Betsy herself had given Excelsior.

"I heard that you got burglarized," said Gary. "What was it they took?"

"Her best silk panel, and some jewelry, and her laptop," said Phil.

"They took your laptop?" Typically, Gary was far more interested in a computer than silk, or even jewels. "Wow. What kind was it? You canceled your e-mail account, I hope."

Doris said, "It was an old Dell. And no, not yet. In fact, I used it yesterday evening to send an e-mail to Betsy, telling her where we were."

Gary stared at her. "And you're wondering how this woman found out where you were? *You* told her!"

"No, I didn't! I only told Betsy!"

Gary resorted to very basic language. "When you used your account, the person who stole your laptop could read your e-mail."

"Oh, for heaven's sake!" said Betsy. "*I* knew that!"

Gary explained to a still-puzzled Doris, "All they'd have to do is log on—if you stored your password, of course."

"Stored . . . Oh, you mean, so I didn't have to type it in every time I logged on? Yes, I did that. Doesn't everyone? But I used someone else's computer!"

"But you used your own e-mail address, didn't you?"

"Yes," said Doris. "I already told you that."

"Oh, honey," Bershada said, "I've done that before and then seen the e-mail on my own computer. It saves it to your account, and your account is on your computer."

Doris stared at her, wide-eyed. "Oh my God, then this is *all* my fault! I wrote Betsy where we were. I even told her my room was the little one in back, overlooking the lilac hedge. That's how Wendy knew which door to open. Then I fought with her and pushed her—" She stopped before Phil could rebuke her again.

There was a profound silence for a few moments.

"Betsy, I'm sorry," said Alice, sounding penitent.

"So am I," said Doris, wretchedly.

"That's all right, really," said Betsy, as if it were of no importance—but that was because she was thinking. She nodded to herself as she came to a conclusion. "You know what this means, then. This *proves* the person who burglarized your apartment is the dead woman. Because otherwise, how did she read that e-mail off your laptop?"

"Well, okay, that's true," said Doris dully.

"Well, then, don't you see? You're safe."

"Safe?" said Doris, her head coming around.

"You see, Mr. Fitzwilliam's shop was searched, and he was killed. Then your apartment was searched, and the person who did that came after you . . ." She moved her hand, gesturing at her deduction.

"Ah," said Alice, "but now the person who did those things is dead herself."

Doris sighed as if in relief, choked, and burst into strange, awful laughter.

Twelve

෴ ⋅ ෴

B ETSY was up to her eyebrows in bookkeeping when some-one knocked on her door—and it wasn't a gentle knock, but a loud thumping that made her hands jump on the keys, turning 178 into 194784.

Betsy deleted the gibberish while shouting, "All right, I'm coming!"

Greatly annoyed, she hustled to open it.

Doris was standing there in slippers, pink corduroy trousers, and an oversized gray sweatshirt. Her eyes were wide with alarm.

"What's the matter?" asked Betsy, her anger and indignation replaced by concern.

"Lena Olson's dead."

"Oh, no!" Betsy gasped. "What happened?"

"Suicide."

"Oh, I don't believe it! Come in, come in!" Betsy led the way into her living room. "How did it happen? Are they sure?"

Doris went to the couch and sat down. She put her hands over her face and said, in a muffled voice, "The police say so. She was found in her car in the garage of her house."

Betsy said, "How awful! She just bought that beautiful Lee needlepoint canvas. She was so excited about getting it at last. Do they know why? Did she leave a note?"

"No. When I heard about it, I thought it might have something to do with this Thai silk mess."

"What could . . . Oh my God."

"What?" asked Doris.

"Lena Olson—you said the third woman's name was Lana or Linda. Lena Olson was the third woman on that trip to Thailand, she went with Wendy Applegate and Carmen Diamond. Right?"

"Yes, that's right. The police have her name. They must've gone to talk to her. And if she was helping Wendy with whatever she was up to, then she—Lena—might have panicked. I called over there a little while ago, I wanted to talk to her, to see if she knew about Wendy. Her husband answered the phone and he was crying, I could tell."

Doris clenched her fists in her lap. "Do you know who found her? Their son, Burke. He's just fifteen. Can you imagine? He came home from basketball practice and found her in her car. He was all mad because she was supposed to pick him up, and he couldn't find her in the house and he went to see if the car was gone and . . . Oh, it makes me so *angry*! What a cruel thing to do to your own child!"

"Yes," said Betsy softly. "How much does Lena's husband know about this Thai silk business?"

"Nothing, I would guess. What could Lena tell him? If she confessed, she'd be in jail, not down at the morgue."

"She must have felt totally desperate and sad. Which is precisely the opposite of the way she was acting on Saturday."

"What are we going to do?"

"I don't think there's anything we can do. For one thing, we don't know that Lena was involved in the smuggling operation. For that matter, Carmen went to Thailand with Wendy and Lena. If Lena's a part of it, could Carmen be, too?"

"Oh, no! I'm sure she's not!"

"Where does Carmen live?"

"Wayzata. Lena was from Maple Plain." Wayzata was just across Lake Minnetonka from Excelsior, but Maple Plain was a half hour away.

Betsy didn't know any members of the police department in Maple Plain. And she did not think intruding on the Olson family with some scary questions was a good idea right now.

"I'm going to phone Mike Malloy. Maybe he knows something."

But he didn't. "It's out of my jurisdiction," he said. "And none of my business. It ought to be none of yours."

"Now, Mike," Betsy said, "if it's connected to the mess Doris is in, it *is* my business. And it ought to be yours."

He sighed gustily. "All right, yeah, you're right. Oh, and speaking of that, the gun that Ms. Applegate was carrying in St. Peter is the same gun that killed Oscar Fitzwilliam in St. Paul.

So there, at least, is a case that's closed. I tell you what: When I get a copy of the report on Lena Olson, I'll let you know."

"Thank you, Mike."

Betsy told Doris about Wendy's being the murderer of the antiques shop owner.

Doris said, "She'd already murdered someone?" Her eyes were wide with shock. "I touched a murderer?"

"You were very brave," said Betsy. "You did just the right thing."

"I wasn't brave, I just wasn't thinking," said Doris. Still, Betsy's praise calmed her enough to go back to her apartment across the hall.

Betsy returned to her bookkeeping for a while, but by eleven she was in bed and fast asleep. Then, a noise that began gently and quickly grew into barrage, woke her. Sophie the cat leaped onto the floor and ran under the bed.

Betsy got to her feet and slid her feet into her slippers. "All right, all right," she grumbled as the loud banging continued. She fumbled in the dark for her robe. She was still trying to get into it as she came into her living room, pausing to flip on the light switch with a robe-covered hand. "Ow!" she muttered as the light came up like thunder out of China 'cross the bay.

"All right, all right, I'm coming!" she shouted.

Getting her hand through the sleeve with a last savage shove, she yanked the door open.

Doris was standing there, one hand clutching an old pink chenille robe closed at the neck, her other hand raised to knock again. Her eyes were enormous in her pale face, and her short red hair was more tousled than Betsy would have thought possible. There were brown smudges under her eyes and a scared look to her mouth.

"What's the matter, what's happened now?" asked Betsy, alarmed.

"I'm so sorry to wake you, but may I sleep in your guest room? I just can't stay in my apartment—there're strange noises, and I keep having nightmares."

"Yes, of course." She stepped back. "Come in, come in. Sit down."

Doris obeyed, going to sit hunched on the couch, still holding her robe closed. It was several sizes too big; its shoulders came halfway to her elbows. On her feet she wore fleece-lined pink slippers. She was staring sightlessly at the carpet.

Betsy looked at her for a moment and said, "I'll make us some cocoa."

A few minutes later, Doris took a second sip from her steaming mug and this time her teeth did not chatter against the rim.

Betsy sat down in her easy chair, took a drink of her own cocoa, and said, "This is such a terrible time for you. I wish I knew what I could do to help. I'm not surprised that you're all upset. I'd have nightmares, too, if I were you."

"I was such an *idiot* to agree to bring that statue back with me!" Doris's voice was low, but trembling with vicious self blame.

"Now, not necessarily," said Betsy. Then curiosity won out over sympathy. "But why did you agree to do it?"

"I already told you," Doris said, her voice turning sullen.

"I guess I mean, what was it about him that made you decide

to trust what he said? Doris, you're normally very level-headed, you aren't at all the kind who is constantly being taken advantage of. Yet, in this case, there was no alarm going off in your head, right? And you'd think there should have been, considering the mess it led to. So why?"

As Doris stared at her, a frown slowly formed. Distracted from the late-night horrors by the need to think logically, she sat back and considered Betsy's question. "You're right," she said at last. "I'm not usually taken in by strange men trying to talk me into doing something common sense says not to."

Betsy sipped her cocoa and waited.

Doris thought some more. "I think it was because everything else over there was so foreign, so exotic. Don't get me wrong, I loved being in a place that's really exotic. That's the purpose of travel, isn't it? To see things you don't see at home? But Thailand is truly different, in every way. Palm trees, banyan trees, strange flowers. The people don't look like us. They speak a language I couldn't understand—I couldn't even pick up a few phrases, because it's one of those languages where intonation can change the meaning of a word. Even the writing isn't like anything I'd seen before. And their religion is not like Christianity, either—or Judaism or Islam. Their culture shares our attitudes in some ways, but then you suddenly realize they're coming at life from a whole different direction. Again, this wasn't bad; it was exciting and interesting. But suddenly, in the middle of all this was an American, an ex-marine, tall and strong and . . . familiar." She looked at Betsy. "Do you understand?"

"Yes, I do. You meet someone in a foreign place who's from

your own country, and while back home you would barely talk to him, overseas he's a good friend."

"Yes, that's it, exactly. I felt comfortable with him right away."

"Wasn't there some other American you met over there?"

"Yes, Ron Zommick. But he was only there for a few days. The manufacturing end of his company is in Thailand, but its headquarters is in Los Angeles, and he was winding up some business over there before he had to go home."

"You talked about him in your e-mails. How did you know to contact him?"

"You know Lillian Banchek? Of course you do. You introduced me to her online—she lives in New Jersey, I think."

Betsy nodded. Lillian, a funny, opinionated woman with a clever needle, was a regular on RCTN, a stitchers newsgroup.

"Well, Ron is her ex-brother-in-law. She and I were exchanging e-mails about a pattern I was working on, and when I mentioned I was going to Bangkok, she told me to contact him and gave me his e-mail address. So I did, and he told me to call him in Bangkok, so I did." She took a drink of her cocoa. "He was great. He took me to some interesting restaurants and to some really amazing temples. But like I said, he had to get back to L.A., so we didn't get much time together. He was very charming." Doris smiled. "Good looking, too."

Betsy smiled back. "Yes, you sent us a photograph of him. Was he the one who put you onto the other American—what was his name?"

"David Corvis. No, he wasn't the one who told me about David. It was . . ." She rubbed her face with the palms of her hands. "I can't think very clearly."

"Want to turn in?" asked Betsy, trying to keep the hope out of her voice.

"No, not yet. Even thinking about closing my eyes starts the ugliness."

"All right, I understand."

Doris sighed. "But I apologize for keeping you up. If Goddy were only back from Florida, I'd've gone knocking on his door."

Betsy was surprised at that. "Goddy?"

"Oh, yes. He and I are really good friends."

"I know you're friends," said Betsy, "but I didn't know you were that close."

"Well, we are. Have been right from the first day I came into Crewel World. Remember? He sat down with me and showed me how to do the cross-stitch. He was so nice and friendly—" Doris broke off with a sob. "When will he be home?"

"Sunday. That is, his plane gets in late Sunday night so we probably won't see him until Monday. Doris, what else happened on your trip to Amboy?"

Doris set off on a ramble about the trip, the long drive, the nice restaurant, even the immense rabbit. She told Betsy about the blizzard and how scary it was driving through it. "I wish we had stopped in Mankato. I'd have liked to see the old place. I went to school there. So did Phil—we took the same courses, a few years apart, so we weren't classmates. Interesting how we both got into steam. He's going to introduce me to Lars Larson's Stanley in the spring."

Betsy said, "I've ridden in that car."

"Really? What's it like?"

"The car? Well, it looks pretty much like any other antique

car. You know, thin, flat fenders, wheels with wooden spokes, a running board. His is from 1911, I think. But its insides are really different. For example, under the hood is a boiler, and there's an enormous, complicated tangle of pipes running all over the underside of the car. The motor is about the size of a dishpan and it's on the underside, near the back. And there are levers and dials and gauges that let you know you're not dealing with an 'explosion engine.'"

"What's an explosion engine?"

"Internal combustion—the kind of car we all drive nowadays, or will until they get the electric cars figured out."

"Does it go huffing along like a steam locomotive?"

"No, it doesn't make any noise at all. Unless it blows up."

Doris looked alarmed. "You mean it might actually explode?"

"Not the boilers. A Stanley boiler has never blown up. But it has two fuel systems. One is for the pilot light in the firebox, and the other heats the boiler. The pilot light pipes are very thin, and they can get clogged. And if that happens, the pilot light will go out. If the car's been running for a while, the firebox is hot enough to ignite the fuel continuing to spray into it. This isn't an internal compustion engine—the fuel is sprayed into the firebox, not contained in a piston.

"The Stanley brothers designed the firebox to withstand this happening, but it will scare the bejesus out of folks for a mile in every direction. I was out riding with Lars when his Stanley erupted. The car doesn't jiggle like most antique cars, and it doesn't have an engine noise. So I was admiring the spring flowers when all of a sudden there was a strong smell of gasoline.

Lars pulled over and started to say something when the world turned upside down with the most enormous *bang*!"

Doris started, her eyes rounding, but then she giggled.

Betsy continued, "Red flames shot into the air, black smoke came up all around us, and I was standing across the road with not a clue how I got there. I don't know how many people dialed nine-one-one and the fire department came, too. It was all very embarrassing, because we were just fine. So was the car. In a few minutes Lars had cleared the blockage in the pipe of the pilot light with a wire, relit it, rebuilt a head of steam, and we were on our way as if nothing had happened.

"But that's when I really, really understood: a steam-powered automobile might look pretty much like any other old touring car, but it isn't."

Doris giggled again, then fell silent. Betsy yawned, but Doris was not ready to turn in yet. Casting about for a new topic, she said, "Did you know silk was discovered in China?"

Betsy had recently done a lot of research on silk, so she did know that, but she said politely, "Oh, really?"

"Yes. There's a legend that a Chinese princess was having tea in her garden and a silk cocoon fell into her cup. The heat melted the glue that holds it together and as she was fishing it out with her chopsticks she noticed a loose filament. She pulled at it and the cocoon began to unwind. She saw how strong the filament was, even though it was very thin, and after a while she figured out that twisting several strands together might make it into a good sewing thread. She would have had enough from just that one cocoon to experiment—there are about five hundred yards in every cocoon."

Betsy nodded, although she refrained from remarking that it was very doubtful a real Chinese princess ever did any sewing. Embroidery, perhaps, but not sewing. She also knew that wild silk cocoons were not only smaller than the 500-yard domesticated ones, but an ugly brown, not suitable for embroidery. A real Chinese princess would have called for a servant to bring her a fresh cup of tea. It was more likely that the humble servant, who could not afford more than one cup of tea a day, would go fishing for the cocoon with a pair of chopsticks. And it would be someone who didn't mind brown sewing thread who discovered how to spin it from a dead worm's shroud. Because the unwrapping of the silk cocoons involved the death of the budding moth.

Betsy couldn't stifle another yawn.

Doris, heedless, nattered on. "They've domesticated the silkworm now. They breed them for bigger white cocoons, and because they don't have to live in the wild, it doesn't matter that the moths that come out nowadays are blind and can't fly. They have to let some become moths, of course, so they can get more worms. They keep the worms in big barns, thousands and thousands of them packed together, and feed them mulberry leaves. David told me that when you go into one of those barns where the worms are eating, it sounds like a hard rain."

Betsy hadn't read anything about that. She and Doris fell silent as they imagined that sound. A soothing sound, like rain . . . Betsy felt herself slipping into a light doze; she wriggled her shoulders to get back awake.

"China kept the secret of silk to iself for hundreds and hundreds of years," said Doris.

Betsy knew that, too. Even its own people didn't know about it. At first, only the emperor and his family had silk garments. But then the nobility were permitted to wear it, then the gentry. It became a very important export, and traveled a trade route across the heartless Taklimakan desert to India, Egypt, and points west, a route that came to be called the Silk Road. Silk was used as money, and even as paper, in China.

Inevitably, of course, the secret escaped, partly because the border of China shifted through the centuries. First it was discovered in Korea, then in northern Thailand and parts of Vietnam. Then India received what its history says was a "tribute" of silk and silkworms. Silkworms slipped into Byzantium in the sixth century, brought by monks who hid the worms in their hollowed-out staffs. By the thirteenth century Italy had the *Bombyx mori* worms at work for them.

Betsy's head fell sideways, startling her back to wakefulness. She looked over at Doris, and saw that her friend had tumbled over, asleep. She roused her gently, supported her into the guest room, removed her robe, and folded her into bed.

As she crawled into her own bed and greeted Sophie, who came purring for a brief cuddle, Betsy decided she would remodel Doris's apartment. Take down the wall between the kitchen and living room, replace it with a breakfast bar, maybe. Retile the bathroom. It would be like a new place—that should destroy the ugly associations. And as long as she was at it, she'd remodel the other apartment, too. It was while deciding what color to paint the remodeled living rooms that she fell asleep.

Thirteen

꧁ ᴑ ꧂

Betsy barely woke up in time to get to work the next morning. She had no more than opened the store when her phone rang. "Crewel World, Betsy speaking, how may I help you?" she said as she answered it, and was dismayed at the lack of levity in her voice.

"Ms. Devonshire? This is Eddie Fitzwilliam."

It took a moment. "Oh, of Fitzwilliam's Antiques! Good morning!"

"I wanted to tell you that we've finished clearing out the store, and there was no sign of the Buddha." His voice was quiet but a little hoarse, as if he'd had to do an unexpected amount of talking lately. "That is, there was no sign of the standing Buddha the police were looking for. There were several of the laughing fat ones, and a beautiful Buddha hand cast in bronze, but no slim young man with upraised hands."

"Oh, that's too bad."

"Is there anything else you want to ask me?"

"Yes, but it's a hard question."

He sighed. "I doubt it could be harder than what the police have asked."

"Is it possible that your father was involved in something dishonest?"

"What do you mean, dishonest?" He sounded depressed but not surprised at the question; doubtless the police had asked him that, too.

"Well, he was waiting for the delivery of a very beautiful statue of Buddha that was being brought into the country under somewhat peculiar circumstances. You told me his store was improving its sales but in an irregular manner. And now he's been murdered and the statue has disappeared. Have you gone over his books?"

He sighed and said in his roughened voice, "All right, I guess you are a detective. We've just started going over his books, and there are some . . . irregularities. I'd say yes, he was involved in something dishonest, probably involving the sale of stolen art objects. There was money coming in with no explanation. There were objects sold—not for very great amounts—that didn't have inventory numbers, or were obviously added to inventory after the fact." He stopped and then continued in a lower voice, "I believe he was taking additional money under the table for these things."

"That's very interesting."

His voice turned much harsher. "Interesting? Oh, *very* interesting! What I'm giving you is evidence of a man destroying his whole life! No wonder he didn't want me anywhere near him—he didn't want me to see what he'd become, or to get myself involved in his predicament! I'm happy you find that *interesting*!" The connection was broken with a crash.

Betsy had to go sit down for a minute. The pain and anger in Eddie's voice were a shocking wakeup call. He must have been devastated to discover his father had become a criminal, and she was dismayed that she hadn't realized that. Of course he was insulted when an insensitive amateur came strolling by to find the wreck and remark that it was "interesting." Betsy's own father would have been disappointed in her.

Betsy went to make herself a strong cup of black tea. She sat at the library table in her quiet shop and sipped it slowly, letting it finish her waking-up process while increasing her feeling of shame. What a wretched business sleuthing was, turning hurting human lives into an "interesting" puzzle!

She finished the tea and, looking around the shop, decided she couldn't afford to wallow in misery. A bit of shop business might put her back on track. She began a search for Joe Brown's phone number. She remembered scribbling it—somewhere. After a minute, she found it in the margin of a Nordic Needle catalog. She was about to dial it, then backed off and first called a fellow member of the Minnesota Art Institute.

"You don't know who Joe Brown is?" Jenna said, surprised.

"Well, yes, sort of. I know he's a big noise in the financial world. But I want to ask him for a favor, and I'm hoping you can tell me what my chances are."

"Okay, let's see. He's a money manager, big-time, earning big bucks in the upper echelons of an investment company in St. Paul. He's on a hospital board, a museum board, and the local public television board. He's got a Ph.D. in economics from the University of Chicago, so he's a brain to the nth degree. He collects art, some modern but especially ancient—Egyptian, Chinese, Greek—and he really knows his stuff. But you'd never know any of this by talking to him. He's funny, *and* kind, *and* charming. He'll probably be delighted to do you a favor, both because he's nice and because he's after some money from you. I didn't realize it was pledge time already—have you noticed the gap between pledging and asking for more pledges is getting shorter every year? Meanwhile, he's called you twice and you haven't agreed to up your pledge? You are probably the only person in the area who hasn't succumbed to his charm."

Armed with this information, Betsy was less on her guard as she dialed the number for Joe Brown and waited for the phone to be answered. To her surprise, it was a direct number and he answered it in person.

"Mr. Brown—*Doctor* Brown," she addressed him. "This is Betsy Devonshire."

"Well, hello!" he said warmly. "I really didn't expect you to call me back. After all, I am a beggar—on behalf of the institute, but nevertheless a beggar. So please, call me Joe."

She laughed. "All right. Joe. But this isn't about money. I'm afraid I have another reason for calling you."

"Uh-oh," he said, but he sounded more amused than wary. "I hope I can be at your service."

"I have a piece of damaged needlework that I can't figure out how to fix, and I wonder if you could get me an appointment with someone who does textile restoration at the institute."

For some reason he seemed a trifle taken aback at her request. "May I ask what it is?"

"Well, it might be an old Cari Buziak design."

She could hear bemusement in his voice. "Who is Cari Buziak?"

"She's a Canadian who designs cross-stitch patterns in the medieval Celtic style mixed with modern elements."

"Oh, contemporary."

"Well, probably. Or it might be some blend of styles cooked up by a Christian missionary—probably not earlier than twentieth century. But the person who stitched it was extraordinarily talented, and I think it might be very beautiful if it's cleaned up. But I can't seem to find the time it would take to research the repair, and I don't want to ruin it. I thought that since you're on the board of the institute, and since I'm a member in good standing, perhaps you could do me this favor."

"Not to mention the fact that I'm trying to talk you into a hefty increase in your annual pledge and you feel entitled to use that on me."

"Since you brought it up, I don't have to mention it, do I? But I *am* prepared to succumb to your charm."

"You've been talking with Jenna, haven't you?"

She laughed. "Yes. So can you help me with this?"

"Hmmmm," he said, which might be an indication that this was a bigger favor than he thought she'd ask for—or that he wanted her to think so. "You want someone over there to do the research on it?"

"No, I can do the research if someone will narrow the field, point me in the right direction."

"Ah. Do you know what the fabric—"

The door sounded its two notes and Betsy looked up to see Leona Cunningham enter the shop. "I'm sorry, I can't talk more right now, I have a customer. But you can tell whoever you talk to that this won't take more than ten minutes, I swear."

"Let me call you back," said Joe.

Leona was looking for a pattern suitable for an altar cloth—but not the kind found in churches. Leona was Wiccan and kept a small altar in her home. She changed the cloth four times a year in honor of the four seasons. She'd recently come into an inheritance and so had decided over the next year to buy four really nice pieces of even-weave linen for the altar. Currently she was planning a summer cloth, and wanted to embroider an emblem on it for Lammas.

"Lammas?" echoed Betsy. "But that's a Christian word."

Leona nodded. "It means 'loaf mass,' after the first loaf of bread made from the first ripening grains, put on the altar as a summer thanksgiving. But celebrating harvests wasn't invented by the Christians. It's as old as agriculture—older, maybe."

"Yes, of course," said Betsy. She helped Leona search the patterns and they selected one of a sheaf of wheat tied in a red ribbon.

"Are you going to just have the sheaf on it?" asked Betsy.

"No, but I already have patterns for the four elements," Leona replied. Wiccans—rather, some Wiccans, Betsy knew, since it's a very individual religion—think of the four sabats or major holidays, as each relating to one of the four elements: air, earth, fire, water. Lammas was earth, so the altar cloth was a rich brown. Betsy gave Leona one of Doris's gold silk skeins, asking for a report on how useful it was. Leona paid for her purchases, and as she left, Betsy reflected that she was learning more than she wanted to know about Wicca.

At noon Betsy called up to her apartment and persuaded Doris to come down and go next door to buy them each a sandwich. "I'd ask you to fix me one upstairs, but I'm out of bread."

She was just taking her second bite of a roast beef sandwich on rye when the door sounded its two notes. Betsy glanced up—and dropped her sandwich to go give Godwin a big hug. His good wool overcoat was cold from the outdoors and his "man bag" slid off his shoulder and thumped her on the leg.

He laughed as he hugged her back. "So good to be home!" he said.

"How come you're back early?" she asked, because Godwin was not one to leave a warm, sunny place for a cold, snowy one.

"Oh, the weather turned bad. The forecast was for three days of rain, so instead of the Everglades tour I bought a new ticket home."

"Bless Florida's bad weather, because I'm really glad to see you!" She stepped back. "Wow, what a nice tan you have!"

He made a little face. "You think so? I got more sun than I meant to—not good for the skin, you know." He looked over Betsy's shoulder.

"Doris, is that you? What's the matter? Is something wrong?"

"I'm all right," she mumbled, and forced a smile. "I'm so glad to see you."

He looked from her to Betsy, back to her, back to Betsy. "*Not* all right, I think. Who's going to tell me what's going on?"

He took off his coat as they took turns telling him, and his mouth hung open in amazement through most of it. "Strewth!" he exclaimed at intervals. At the end, he came to sit beside Doris and give her a sideways hug. "Oh my dear, dear sweetie, how very brave you are to be sitting here at all! I'd be quivering in a closet, alternately screaming and crying, and eating Valiums like they were M&M's."

Doris leaned her head on his shoulder. "You are the very best, thank you."

Betsy went in the back to give them a little privacy.

"So, you and Dax had a good time?" Doris asked Godwin after Betsy retreated.

"Yeah," said Godwin, but he drew out the word until it sounded more like a question.

Doris looked sideways at him. "Already?" she said.

"What do you mean, already?"

"I know that tone. It's over, isn't it?"

"No, it isn't," Godwin asserted, but falsely and Doris looked slantwise at him, so he shrugged. "Oh, all right, maybe it is."

"Why?"

"Don't ask that kind of question. Because you know how it is. You're sitting across the breakfast table one morning and you realize you can't stand the way he butters his toast. It's not personal—well, it *is* personal, but there's no *reason* for it. Yesterday you loved his eyelashes, today the shape of his earlobes bothers you." He sighed. "I guess I'm just not meant to find someone I can love forever."

"No, I guess you aren't," said Doris, solemnly. So solemnly he began to smile.

"Hush, you," he said.

Hearing a cozy silence, Betsy came back to find the two looking at Godwin's latest version of a white cotton sock—he was always knitting white cotton socks, claiming the dye in commercial socks made his feet break out. Like Betsy, he never went anywhere without a stitching project. His "man bag" was on the table and from it trailed the white yarn. The sock was a pattern of his own invention, a white-on-white argyle, the pattern discerned by subtle variations in the shades of white and the use of stitch changes to outline the diamonds.

He looked up at Betsy and said, "Are you going to let Doris stay with you for a while?"

"She can stay as long as she needs to, as long as she wants to, for that matter. I'm going to redecorate her apartment so thoroughly she won't even recognize it."

"But that will take a while," Doris said. "Meanwhile, I'm in the way. You use that spare bedroom for an office. Anyway, you haven't had a roommate for years—neither have I, for that matter—and while we can get along for a few nights, I'd better find a temporary apartment really soon."

Godwin said, "Maybe after a couple of nights away, you'll be ready to go back to your old place."

"No, I won't. I'll never go back, never."

Another customer came in. Her name was Gwen, and she was an immigrant from Liberia. She had discovered counted cross-stitch in America and was here to select the new floss she needed to work Stephanie Seabrook Hedgepath's beautiful Mabry Mill counted cross-stitch pattern. Its depiction of a water wheel on the side of a gray-weathered mill with rhododendrons in bloom was "so very American," she said. "I will send it to my aunt in Katata."

Betsy took her to the back portion of the shop where the counted cross-stitch materials were displayed.

After a few minutes back there, she heard the door again sound its two-note alarm. This was followed by squeals of joy. Betsy looked out between the stacks of box shelves to see Doris embracing a slim, attractive blonde while Godwin stood by beaming.

"Carmen!" cried Doris.

"Doris!" cooed Carmen. "We're just back from New Mexico, or I would have been here sooner." She was pulling off her gloves, which covered beautiful, slim fingers. Even from the back of the shop, Betsy could see the diamonds glittering on several of her fingers.

"Now, you must tell me yourself about this dreadful mess you got involved in," she heard Carmen say to Doris. "I've been hearing all sorts of stories, and I'm sure half of them aren't true."

A few minutes later, Betsy added up Gwen's purchases, walked her to the door, then turned to the three people seated at the library table. Where there had been joyous greetings, there was now sorrow and worry.

"Betsy, this is Carmen Diamond," said Doris. "She's the one who was supposed to go to Thailand with me."

"I'm very pleased to meet you," said Betsy, coming to the table.

"Diamond, what an appropriate name," she added, noting there were diamonds in the woman's ears as well as on her fingers.

Carmen laughed complacently. "I'm so glad I didn't marry a man named Potts."

Betsy declared, "My next husband is going to be named Mr. Sapphire."

Godwin laughed, then put on a serious face. "I told Carmen you're just like Patricia Wentworth's Maud Silver." He offered his most guileless smile. "Only not *quite* as old."

"Goddy!" said Doris with a smile, but Carmen looked shocked.

"It's all right, you get used to him or you learn to ignore him, one or the other," said Betsy.

"Seriously, Betsy," said Carmen, "what we would like for you to do is find out what all this mess is about."

"I'm already working on it," said Betsy.

"Well, that's wonderful! What have you found out so far?"

Betsy sat down. "It's all sad news, unfortunately."

"You mean you haven't found out anything important?" Godwin said, surprised.

"No, I've found out things, and I think some of them are important, but all it's doing is making the mystery uglier, without showing me any solution."

"Like what?" asked Godwin. "What bad things?"

"For one, the owner of the antiques shop, Fitzwilliam, apparently has been involved in the sale of smuggled antiquities for several years. His son discovered this when he was going over the books, after closing the shop."

"That *is* sad," said Doris. "But not really a surprise, right?"

"I suppose not."

"What else?" asked Carmen.

"Lena Olson has committed suicide."

"Doris was telling me," said Godwin, "and it's awful news. But what does she have to do with this mess?"

"I hadn't finished!" said Doris. "Lena Olson and Wendy Applegate went to Thailand with Carmen here, where they met David Corvis. Lena, Wendy, and David took a trip up to Chiang Mai in the north of Thailand. Then Wendy and Lena started an import business when they got back home, and now both of them are dead.

"I go off to Thailand and meet David Corvis and next thing I know, I'm bringing something back with me hidden in a suitcase. What's more, the day I deliver it to Fitzwilliam's Antiques, who is sitting out in front waiting for me to leave? Wendy Applegate."

Doris turned to Carmen. "I never met Wendy, so I didn't recognize her climbing down from her Hummer outside Fitzwilliam's Antiques. But she was the same woman who attacked Phil and me in St. Peter. That's how I discovered who she was—when the police identified her."

Carmen said, "Was there another person with Wendy in St. Paul? A short woman, with curly red hair?"

"No," said Doris. "Or at least I didn't see anyone with her."

"But hold everything," said Godwin. "Are we saying *our* Lena Olson was involved in a *smuggling ring?* And *committed suicide?* I don't believe it! Why, she was here on Saturday, to pick up that Japanese moon goddess canvas! No one as happy as she was on Saturday commits suicide three days later!"

Carmen said, "I talked to her on Sunday. She told me about that moon-goddess thing that she had started to work on it. She said it was going to take her at least a year to finish. But she was thrilled to pieces about it, she said it was something her great-great-grandchildren would cherish."

"See?" said Godwin. "*Not* suicidal."

Doris said, "I told Betsy that if the police came by to ask questions after Wendy was killed, she might have panicked."

"What do you think?" Betsy asked Carmen. "Oscar Fitzwilliam was murdered, you know. Mike Malloy told me that the gun Wendy was carrying was the gun that killed him. That might make Lena an accessory. Was she the kind of person who might panic if she thought she was going to be arrested for murder as well as smuggling?"

Carmen thought for a moment. "I don't know." She paused again then said, "She was a happy sort of person, all bouncy—like Tigger, you know? Her son actually bought her a Tigger T-shirt for Christmas a few years ago. Which she wore only once, because it was too big and she liked to show off her figure. The way she'd flirt and tell naughty jokes would embarrass poor Burke—he's just fifteen—to death. But she had a serious side; she had a fine arts degree from Northwestern, and she liked artsy things—she was a member of the Walker Museum and the art institute and she always bought season tickets to the Guthrie. She was the hardest worker, worked even harder than Wendy. Well, no, that isn't true. Where Wendy would get quiet and determined, Lena would get loud and cheerful and pushy. Maybe that was because she wasn't very tall; you know, short people need to speak up to get noticed. She loved life, she did everything full bore, whether it was selling a house, traveling to Thailand, cooking a Thanksgiving dinner, even doing those canvas paintings, needlepoint. The harder it was to do, the better she liked it." Carmen's voice faltered; she was near tears. "No, no, you see? I don't believe it! I can't believe she saw any problem as so big she had to run away from it!"

Betsy shared a look with Godwin. "Maybe she didn't."

Godwin nodded. "I bet you're right."

Doris cried, "Oh, please no! Not another murder!"

Carmen stared at Betsy. "Oh. Oh, well, yes, if there are only those two choices." She put an arm around Doris. "Now, darling, it's got to be. I knew Lena, and I know she wouldn't take that way out, no matter how hard things got for her."

But Doris said, "Only think about it. How she died. You don't kill someone by putting her into her own car in her own garage and starting the engine. Not without tying her up—and that would leave marks, wouldn't it? You'd have to sit there with her, pointing a gun at her. And then you'd die, too."

But Godwin was reaching for the cordless phone in the middle of the table, punching numbers into it. He handed it to Betsy. "Tell Mike," he said.

Fourteen

ᏀᎧ · ᎧᏀ

A FTER Betsy finished talking with Mike, who promised to share with her the results of the police report on Lena's death, Carmen said, "If we're right, this is very scary. First the antiques store owner, then Wendy, now Lena."

"No," said Betsy, glancing at Doris. "Wendy was an accident. Until this business with Lena, I had been thinking Wendy murdered Mr. Fitzwilliam. If it turns out that Lena did commit suicide, then I'll still think that." She turned to Doris. "And that would mean you're still safe."

Godwin said, "What about the silk?"

"What about it?" asked Betsy.

Doris said, "I was telling Carmen that the statue I brought back was wrapped in an old piece of embroidered silk. It was filthy and raggedy, so I threw it in the wastebasket, but you pulled it out again. And I explained that you were thinking that was the 'Thai silk' Wendy came after me for."

Betsy said, "Yes, well, you said Wendy was demanding the Thai silk and while that piece is silk, I don't believe it's Thai."

"Ohhhhhhh," groaned Doris.

"But Doris brought it from Thailand!" Godwin said.

"Yes, so maybe it is what Wendy was after. On the other hand, the design isn't at all like the patterns in the silk Doris brought back. Or like any other Asian patterns I've seen. It looks kind of like . . . well, I had been thinking it looked like a riff on Celtic, but now I think it looks sort of Scythian."

"*Scythian?*" said Carmen.

"Last time I went to the dentist, I read an article in an old *National Geographic* magazine about an excavation at a burial mound in Siberia of some ancient people called Scythians. And there was a golden reindeer that kind of makes me think of the embroidery on the silk that was wrapped around the statute that Doris brought home."

"Celtic or Scythian—that's a weird pair of choices," said Carmen.

"No, it's well beyond weird," said Godwin.

"Like I said, the design is not really *like* anything I've ever seen. I think whoever stitched it was familiar with many different styles of needlework. I'm going to try to get an appointment with someone at the art institute who maybe can identify it, and tell me if it's worth my while to try to repair it."

Godwin said, "But if that old rag Doris threw away is what Wendy was after, that must mean it's not just an old rag but something much more important."

"Yes," said Doris slowly. "But if it's important, why was it treated like a rag? And why did it look like a rag? Shouldn't it have at least been washed? I guess I don't understand this at all."

Betsy sighed. "Welcome to the club. Carmen, you knew Wendy, didn't you?"

"Yes, though apparently not as well as I thought."

"What was your impression of her?"

Carmen thought briefly. "She was driven. Everything she did, she put all her effort into it. Marriage, children, career, even vacation—she got more out of that trip to Thailand than Lena and I put together."

Doris made an odd sound in her throat, and Betsy saw her sit back in her chair, as if she were trying to put some distance between herself and Carmen. Then she saw Betsy looking at her. "It feels weird to hear you talk about Wendy," she explained. She rubbed her upper arms with her hands as if to wipe away the tactile memories of that nighttime struggle.

"I'm sorry, but I have to know."

"I know, and it's all right. It just makes me uncomfortable."

"Do you want to take a walk while we have this conversation?"

"No, I guess not."

Then Betsy turned to Carmen. "Was Wendy any kind of expert on silk, or embroidery, or antiques?"

"She thought she was, enough so that she and Lena started this little company, a part-time thing, selling Asian art.

"When they were in Thailand, Lena and Wendy just went berserk at the markets and among the street vendors. They couldn't get enough souvenirs. It was obvious to me they had buyers' hypnosis—you know, 'Aunt Kate would just love this,' when they know perfectly well Aunt Kate wouldn't have it on a bet. They're just finding reasons to buy, buy, buy."

Betsy nodded. "Happens to me all the time at the grocery store."

Carmen laughed. "I'm like that when I get to the shoe department. Anyway these two, Lena and Wendy, ended up shipping two big crates full of stuff home because there was no way they could check it all on the plane. But then, when the crates arrived in the States, they opened them and came to their senses.

"Even if they wanted to keep all that stuff, there wasn't room in their homes. So rather than rent a storage place, they decided to try to sell it. They set up an account on eBay and got such high bids that they started going around to local art galleries and antique stores. It was less trouble, you see. They were getting three, four, even five times what they paid for it back in Thailand."

"Wow," said Betsy.

"So that gave them another idea: Go get some more."

Betsy didn't say what she thought of that idea, just nodded and sipped her tea.

Carmen went on. "Lena went back over there—this is when the housing market was going through the roof, so with her real estate commissions she could afford it—and bought two more crates of stuff. And the second load of artifacts she brought back sold just as well as the first. Well, this was much more fun than real estate or buying clothes for Target. On the profits of that second trip, Wendy went over. At one of the markets, she met a man who knew his way around. He took her to wholesale markets even few Thai ever visit and helped her buy some things from Laos, Vietnam, even China and Japan."

"Was his name David Corvis?"

Carmen stared at Betsy. "You know, I didn't think of that. I don't remember if they told me his name. I know he had an export business, selling Asian artifacts to markets in Europe and America. Anyway, Wendy sold everything she brought home at a big profit, so she and Lena formed a company they called Exotic Asia, Inc. And eight months later they went broke."

"Was it a failure because they didn't know how to run a business, or because they didn't know enough about Asian art?"

"Both, really. I mean, they spent an awful lot of money renting an upscale place and taking out some big ads, which was probably not the smartest thing to do just starting out. Then taxes hit them hard. I remember Lena moaning about the import and sales taxes. And the rent and utilities—I don't think they ever broke even, not one single month the whole time they were in business. But their stuff wasn't all that good, either. Well, at first it was, but when they realized how high their expenses were, they dropped the quality of their goods. Got into imitations, then bad imitations—*plastic*, you know?"

Godwin said, "They shouldn't have dropped their quality. Didn't they know that every small business loses money the first year?"

Carmen stared at him. "They do?"

"Sure," said Godwin nodding. "So eight months wasn't even a fair trial."

"Did they quit their other jobs?" asked Doris.

"They didn't, thank God. Lena cut back to part time, but

Wendy stayed at her job as apparel buyer and worked at this import business part time. Neither of them went back to Thailand anymore, because this exporter over there agreed to buy stuff for them. They thought they knew what they were doing, but they didn't, not really. I think they were in over their heads right from the start. I don't know all the ins and outs of owning a business myself, but I do know that once it started going down for them, it was like being on a playground slide." She made a steep downward move with one hand. "The final straw was some kind of tax trouble. Or maybe it was insurance. Poor things, they tried, they really did. But there's a knack to running a business, I guess, and they didn't have it."

Betsy nodded. "Neither do I," she said.

Carmen looked around. "You don't?"

"I'm operating closer to the edge than it looks." Crewel World was a little more than paying its way but only because Betsy didn't draw a salary. She had other sources of income, which was a good thing, because now and again she also had to draw on it to keep the shop open. She made the shop pay it back, of course, but it was scary when Crewel World slid into the red like that. She felt better about her shop when she learned there were other needlework shops kept open as hobbies by women—usually retired—with more money than sense. Those who made them pay had a work ethic that had to be seen to be believed.

Carmen continued, "So it turned out they were glad they kept their regular jobs. Even though the housing market had—what's the word they use? 'Softened,' that's it. So Lena wasn't earning what she used to. But it turned out Wendy really needed her job, because after a couple of years of fighting with her husband, he decided he wanted a divorce. And he was being a total bastard about it. It was costing her all her savings to keep her end up in the custody battle for their two kids. Lawyers are bloodsuckers, but you have to hire them, and you have to pay them. He could afford it, but she was really struggling."

"What does he do?"

"He's a surgeon—wait a second while I think of his specialty. Orthopedic, that's it. Bones. There must be good money in bones, he's practically gold plated."

"How old are the children?"

"Let's see, Pippa is eleven, Mick is nine. Very, very bright children, they both go to Mounds Park Academy, which is what Wendy called a posh school. I guess that means high tone. High cost, certainly, but one of the best schools in the area."

"What does Lena's husband do?"

"He owns a construction company, building mostly private homes. But that's a softened industry, too. If you can't buy an existing house, you don't want to build one, either. It's not like they're broke, of course—they're just reining in the spending a bit. Tad wanted a new boat and couldn't get one, Lena wanted a new kitchen and couldn't afford to put one in—like that. Not exactly going to the food shelf once a week." She chuckled, sat back in her chair, and took a drink of tea. "You're too easy to talk to. I'm telling an absolute stranger things I don't tell my husband."

Betsy smiled and lifted her cup. "Tell me about your husband."

Before she could stop herself, Carmen said, "His name is

Richard, and he owns a management consultant company called Information in Action."

"WELL, poor things," said Carmen a half hour later. She sighed and began looking around for her coat. "Okay, are you ready, Doris?"

"Ready for what?" asked Betsy.

"Shopping," said Carmen. "Nothing she owns fits her anymore. I'm taking her to buy new clothes."

Godwin spread his arms at Doris. "You go, girl! Nothing like shopping to cheer a person up! You'll have to stop by later and show us all your new pretties."

Doris struggled to find a smile in response as she obediently rose and put on her coat.

After Doris and Carmen left, Godwin said, "How about I come over tonight and take another look at this Scythian/Celtic embroidery?"

"I'd love to have you, except I've got a date."

"Who with? Is it that Minneapolis detective, what's his name, Omernic? I *told* you he was a sweet man, and just right for you!"

"No, it's not Sergeant Omernic. This man is not connected with the police at all. And"—she held up her hand, palm toward Godwin's nose—"no more questions. It's none of your business who he is." Sometimes Betsy felt Godwin was just a little too interested in her love life, and she was determined to draw the line before it became embarrassing.

Fifteen

ႮჂ · ႮჂ

DORIS was standing in front of one of those oval mirrors
with a wooden frame that's fitted into a stand. She could
tip the whole thing forward and back until she found the right
angle to see her whole self in it. She was wearing a new black
dress that had looked good in the dressing room at Marshall's,
but—as sometimes happened—might be too small at home. But
in the flattering soft light of Carmen's guest bedroom, it was
just perfect. She smoothed its matte textured fabric over her
backside with both hands as she turned a little to the left and
then to the right. Yes, it fit very well—she was a bit long-waisted,
so it was sometimes hard to find a dress that suited her figure. It
had a square neckline she liked, too. She picked up a smoky
gray tweed jacket and put it on over the dress. The length was
right, but maybe she should have picked the smoky green one?
She twisted at the waist to study the effect of movement. The

embossed pattern on the jacket's silver buttons twinkled in the soft light as her fingers deftly fastened and unfastened them.

She caught a movement in the window behind her, reflected in the mirror. Before she could turn around, there was a double crash as a bullet slammed through the window glass and into the mirror. Shards blew all over the room and into her face and her hands, which she threw up to defend herself.

She fell like a rag doll onto the carpet and did not move.

B ETSY'S date that night was with an old friend named John Wagner, who was blind and very quietly gay. He had two season tickets to Theater in the Round, and each time a new play would open he would spread the wealth among his friends, asking one who hadn't been been able to go with him in a while. Betsy liked his company at plays. His opinions were interesting, both because he was a sophisticated theater buff and because he "saw" things differently. Betsy and John went out after the play for a late supper and to talk about the theater's terrific performance of *Arsenic and Old Lace*. Betsy had especially liked the part where Dr. Einstein made his way across a darkened stage to open a window so his partner, Jonathan, could bring in a dead body, singing *sotto voce* as he went, "Cream of Wheat is so good to eat, you should have some every day . . ." About half the audience had been old enough to be familiar with the reference and laugh. John wasn't one of them, so his great baritone guffaw came after the play, as they ate their salads. They lingered over cups of hot cocoa, comparing the play with the movie version starring Cary Grant. And their conversation naturally segued into a depressing discussion of how the world had changed from when they were young—not that they were old, of course, especially John!—so Betsy was late getting home. She was too tired to notice the phone message light blinking and went right to bed.

D ORIE sat on the couch in the Diamonds' living room. She was not weeping, but she shivered from time to time, though it was warm in the room. Carmen was sitting in a wing chair, and Richard was perched on its arm, holding his wife's hand.

Phil had his arm across Dorie's shoulders. Carmen had called him from the emergency room. He had broken several traffic laws getting there, then followed them more sedately to the Diamond house when Dorie was released. He thought Dorie was comforted by his presence, though he might simply have been hoping it were true. He'd stopped saying anything to her. He'd said all he could think of, twice already, and her replies had consisted mostly of two-word phrases like "all right" and "thank you."

Carmen was studying Dorie with sympathetic eyes, but she, too, was out of words.

Dorie herself looked like she had survived a grenade attack. There was a shaved place on her scalp with a bandage on it that was even bigger than the one on the other side of her head, put there in St. Peter. Her left hand was thickly covered with a gauze-and-tape mitten. She was resting it tenderly on her other arm. Various small scrapes and scratches were marked with Betadine on her forehead, nose, neck, and left cheek; her right cheek had been protected by another St. Peter–acquired bandage. There were more scrapes on her right hand and forearm and on her shins. Her new dress was torn. Her face was so white that the Betadine looked black by comparison.

The police had been brisk and officious, and not very comforting. They had asked a lot of questions, taken a lot of photographs. They'd found an old plastic milk crate—Carmen had put it out to be carried away by the recycling truck, due the next day—under the guest bedroom window, and footprints in the surrounding snow indicated that the shooter was a woman or a man with smallish feet, wearing badly worn boots. None of the neighbors had seen anything. The window was five feet nine inches off the ground, so even a tall man would need a box to bring his arms up high enough to shoot through it. The police theory was that the man had shot Dorie's image in the mirror by mistake.

They were very interested in Dorie's immediate history of burglary and another attack—the details of which were mostly given by Phil, as Dorie wanted only to sit in a deep, silent corner of the couch, with an occasional tear sliding down her cheek. But they noted that very few people knew she was at the Diamond house, and so the attack was more likely aimed at Carmen. They advised them all to go somewhere else for the night, maybe for several nights.

"Where can we go that would be safer than here?" asked Carmen. "I won't leave the dogs behind, because who knows how long we'd have to be gone, and they're like identifying markers to anyone who knows us." She was the devoted "mama" to a pair of identical white miniature poodles.

"I'll go," volunteered Dorie, the first thing she'd said in an hour.

"No, you won't!" said Richard. "For one thing, we don't know for sure if Carmen was the target. It might be you. So think how we'd feel if we put you out there and something happened. And another thing, unless you're willing to go to jail—God forbid—there's no safer place than here. We've got steel doors with deadbolt locks and even a couple of rooms without any windows." He smiled. "Okay, two are bathrooms and the other's a walk-in closet—but still, no windows, no outside walls. You're our guest and we don't toss guests overboard when things get a little tight. Which reminds me, how about a drink?"

The police refused, of course, and after promising to make extra patrols, they left.

Richard went into the dining room and began to make clinking sounds.

Doris said to Phil, "Did you call Betsy? She should know about this."

Phil said, "Yes, I left a message, but she hasn't called back. I've phoned around to see if anyone knows where she is. Goddy said she went out on a date."

Carmen said, "I phoned and sent her an e-mail. She'll get in touch, hon, just be patient."

Richard came back with a tray of short, stout glasses. "Here we go!" he said, more jovially than he probably felt, setting the tray on the coffee table. He looked around, as if to see if the recent excitement had marred the room. This prompted Phil to look around, too.

The room, a big one in an old, sprawling ranch, was both

comfortable and comforting, its pastel-painted walls lit by standard and table lamps. Even Carmen was wearing a soothing dress, a lightweight wool in soft lavender. The two white dogs lying on a big, flat pillow nearby were possibly the best-behaved miniature poodles on the planet. They sat up to watch Richard put the tray down, but didn't come over to wrap themselves around his legs in an attempt to trip him, or climb up on the table to sniff the drinks, or begin barking for no discernible reason. They merely sat up, like polite little animals acknowledging the arrival of a senior member of the pack. That, too, was soothing.

Carmen smiled fondly at the pair. "Love you, babies," she said to them, and they turned their heads in unison to grin at her.

"What?" asked Dorie, raising her head.

"My puppies are behaving well, so I told them I loved them."

"Oh," said Dorie. "Yes, they are sweet."

"I always try to praise them when they do well. I think they understand when I say nice things to them."

"Yes, they probably do," said Phil, a trifle too enthusiastically. "She really can talk to these two," he said to Dorie. "I've been watching her."

Richard pressed a glass of scotch and soda into Dorie's hand. "Try this and tell me if it's okay." He handed the other drinks around. Carmen shared a smile with her husband as she took hers.

Phil took a small swallow, and his face lit up. "Wow, this is *nice*!" he said.

Dorie took a sip of hers. "Nice," she agreed, but absently.

"Take a bigger drink," urged Phil. "It'll make you feel better, I promise."

"Nothing . . ." began Dorie, but then she obediently took another swallow. "It's good, thank you," she murmured.

"Doris," said Carmen, putting her drink down untasted, "this is ridiculous. That doctor at the emergency room gave me some pills for you. The two you agreed to take are for pain, but the other two still in my purse are to make you sleep. I'm going to insist you take them. You really, really need more help to get through this than any of us, or even a whole bottle of scotch, can give you. What you need is a nice, long sleep to give you some distance from this."

"No, no!" cried Dorie. "What if he comes back, and I'm asleep?"

"Wait right here," said Richard as he turned and strode swiftly from the room. He was back a couple of minutes later, holding under one arm a Remington 870 pump shotgun, twelve-gauge with a barrel you could park a small automobile in, and in the other hand a big, matte black semiautomatic pistol. "Phil, do you know how to use one of these?" he asked, nodding toward the pistol.

"Of course I do," said Phil. "I have a sharpshooter's medal at home somewhere. Back of my sock drawer, I think. It was a while ago, but I cut my army teeth on a semiautomatic."

Richard handed the gun to Phil, then stooped to look Dorie in the face, laying the shotgun on the floor at her feet. She stared at it. "Listen to me," he said, and her eyes went obediently to his. "Phil and I are going to stay up while you sleep. We will lock all the doors and windows in the house, and we will walk through the house every fifteen minutes, looking into every room, out every window, checking every door. And I swear to you that Phil or I will blow away any son of a bitch stupid enough to try sneaking up to hurt you or my darling wife."

Dorie blinked at him, but did not reply.

Darling wife Carmen said, "The dogs will stay up as long as anyone in the house is awake. They're too little to be of much use in an actual fight, of course, but they will bark if they see or smell or hear a stranger. Nobody, nowhere, no how, is going to bother us." She came over to kneel at Dorie's feet, resting one hand on her knee. "I am going to sit up with you in one of those windowless rooms. I've been meaning to learn to knit, and I've got some yarn and a pair of knitting needles and a book of instructions." She smiled. "The frustration alone will keep me awake."

Dorie looked up and around at them, her face a white blank. "Thank you," she said.

WEDNESDAY morning Betsy nearly shut the alarm off when it started playing classical music at five fifteen. She got up extra early on Mondays, Wednesdays, and Fridays, so that she could drive to the Courage Center in Golden Valley for water aerobics. It was the only exercise program she had ever managed to stick to, mostly because it was early enough in the morning that it didn't put a hole in her day. Also, she'd become good friends with everyone else who participated. She was already at the bottom of the stairs when her phone began to ring, so she didn't hear it.

At six thirty Betsy waded gratefully into breast-high warm water and began taking broad side steps, raising and lowering her arms in the water. The Courage Center's Olympic-sized pool had flat platforms that stepped down at wide intervals, rather than the sloping bottom of most pools. There were about nine other women there, most of them her age or older, and two men, all stepping sideways, warming up. Greetings were murmured as they passed one another. Classic rock was playing, not too loud. Instructor Vicki stepped into the pool and called them to order. First head-to-toe stretches, then a slow jog, and pretty soon they were stepping lively, their heart rates at or close to where they needed to be.

Betsy was blithely doing jumping jacks while everyone else had moved on to cross-country ski movements. Vicki's instructions were tangled up in thoughts about the Thai silk case.

Her first thought was about Doris. She recalled the bright and happy woman who had come home from Thailand, and the subdued, frightened, humbled woman who had haunted her apartment the past couple of days. Doris seemed to be suffering posttraumatic stress disorder, and small wonder. What an ugly reward for helping out an American doing business in Thailand!

"Hopscotch!" called Vicki, and Betsy came to herself and began swiftly reaching for her right foot with her left hand, then reversing the gesture.

Had David Corvis known Doris was coming to visit his silk factory? Was she somehow pointed out to him or pushed in his direction? How? And by whom? Or could it be a coincidence that David met an American woman who lived within easy driving distance of Fitzwilliam's Antiques? Maybe he had a whole set of addresses all over the United States and would use whatever tourist he connected with who came near one of them.

Now Vicki was doing one of her strange combinations of arm movements and Betsy had to stop musing and concentrate. Vicki called the chant: "Out, out, wide, wide, up, up, in, in."

It was a few minutes later, while doing the grapevine step across the pool, that Betsy noticed a situation forming. One of her classmates Dave Waterfill had an amusing predilection for gently nudging or splashing April and then claiming loudly that April was picking on him. But April was home recovering from surgery. Betsy saw him look around, as if searching for another victim. He was a handsome man despite his balding head, with a strong build and a captivating Kentucky accent. He came to the pool because he was facing arthroscopic surgery on his knees and wanted to stretch and strengthen his leg muscles in preparation.

Dave's eye settled on Irene, who was stocky without being fat and who had the most beautiful smile Betsy had ever seen. Her mouth was shapely and she had deep dimples. When she smiled, everyone in range felt better. On the other hand, she was black and Dave was a southerner, so when Betsy saw him focus on her, she held her breath. Dave moved subtly out of his path to nudge her on the shoulder as they passed one another. It could have been an accident: They each murmured "Sorry," and kept going.

But Irene evidently saw something in Betsy's face when this happened. She flashed her smile at Betsy and continued grape-vining placidly across the pool. On her way back, Irene deftly avoided another collision and flicked a few drops of water, hard, onto the back of Dave's head. Dave saw Betsy watching and shouted, "You saw that! You saw that! First April, now Irene! Can't get a moment's peace in this place!" Amid the laughter Betsy was reminded that not all southerners were bigots—and that in her own concern for Irene, she was herself guilty of condescending racism.

B ACK home, Betsy had a quick breakfast and gave Sophie her meager breakfast of Science Diet dry cat food. She was engaged in an ongoing battle with Sophie. She wanted Sophie to lose weight, and Sophie felt every ounce gained was more insurance against famine. Betsy would have won long ago, if only her customers would stop sabotaging her efforts by slipping the cat little bites of candy, bread, cheese, or whatever else they brought into the shop—some of it deliberately meant for Sophie.

She brushed crumbs off her trousers. It was going to be an overcast day, so she wore a bright pink pantsuit and matching shoes. She powdered her face lightly, darkened her eyebrows, applied lipstick, and put on her sterling-silver earrings. It was not yet nine; the shop opened at ten, so now she had time for the Internet. She usually read parts of the *Washington Post*, the *St. Paul Pioneer Press*, and James Lileks's blog, Bleat.

But today she noted an unusual number of e-mails waiting for her, almost every one from the Monday Bunch.

The latest one, from Phil, had just an exclamation point in

the subject line. She clicked it open and was confronted with an angry message:

> Don't you ever read your goddamm e-mail or listen to your phone messages??? Someone took another shot at Dorie, and she went to the emergency room last night for stitches in her head and her hand. She'll be all right, but someone came after her with a GUN! AGAIN! We're at Carmen's place, give us a call.
>
> —Phil

Betsy pulled her clenched fists against her chest while she read the message. *She'd told Doris she was safe, but she was wrong.*

The woman who came after Doris in St. Peter was dead. Who was this new person?

She hurried into the living room, looked up and dialed the number of the Diamond house.

"Hello!" said a curt male voice.

"Mr. Diamond?"

"Who is this?"

"Sorry, I'm Betsy Devonshire, Doris's friend."

"All right. But you can't talk to her, she's asleep."

Betsy asked warily, "Is something wrong over there?"

"There better not be. Phil and I are armed and dangerous."

Good Lord! "May I speak with Phil?"

"Hang on. Yo, Phil! Front and center!" Now he sounded like a drill sergeant.

"It's me, Betsy," she said when Phil answered. "And don't

yell at me, I'm just sick that I didn't find out until now! Is Doris all right?"

"Yes. We finally talked her into taking a couple of sleeping pills the doctor gave us, and she's asleep. Richard's touring the house, and Carmen's asleep—she sat up all night watching over Dorie. It was rough getting Dorie to take those pills. She was scared to go to sleep."

"I can imagine. What happened last night?"

"Well, they told me things went to hell around eight. Dorie was in the guest room trying on a new dress, and someone shot at her through the window. The police think they shot at her reflection in a mirror instead of her—I guess the light wasn't good. She's got cuts and bruises all over her."

"Why is she still there? Why didn't they take her into protective custody or something?"

"Because they're not sure the shooter was after her. It might've been Carmen, you know. She was standing with her back to the window, after all."

"So why didn't they take both of them?"

"Because Carmen won't go without Richard and her dogs, and Dorie won't go if Carmen is staying. Damn fool women!"

"Why would someone want to kill Carmen?"

"Nobody seems to know—how could there be a reason? Carmen is an elementary school substitute teacher, and she's not teaching this quarter. The one thing she did that ties her into this mess was go to Thailand with Wendy and Lena two years ago, and now both of them are dead."

"Do the police have any suspects?"

"No. Not a clue. None of us do."

"So if you didn't go away, how did you get through the night?"

"We stayed up all night with guns. You wouldn't believe the fantastic Remington shotgun Richard has or the gun he loaned me, a Colt forty-five semiautomatic, a model 1911. Beautiful weapon. He's got that magazine holder polished so slick the magazine falls completely out when you release it, ready for a reload. And he gave me two magazines to carry. I'm telling you, we're loaded for bear. We locked the doors and made regular tours of the house all night. We told each other war stories until I was almost hoping our shooter would come back so I could pop a cap in him."

"Phil!" said Betsy.

"Well . . . No, dammit, we were *ready*! And if he did come back, we would have put an end to this nonsense."

Betsy sighed very quietly. "All right, maybe you're right."

"So what do you think the next step should be?"

"I don't know." Betsy thrust her fingers into her hair. If this was about the silk—or the statue—and Wendy and Lena were involved in smuggling it, why didn't one of them bring it back? Why leave it to sit for two years and then get an outsider to carry it here? She said, "Hmmm," because she had no idea.

Then she asked, "Are you going to stay there?"

"Yes," Phil responded. "At least until Dorie wakes up. Then I'm taking her away—and I'm not telling you or anyone where we're going."

After trying fruitlessly to talk him out of that, they hung up.

Betsy thought it possible that the shooter was after Carmen, because this time there had been no demand of Doris that she turn over the silk.

But if the shooter were after Carmen, the question still remained: Why?

Sixteen

꘎

T HE shop had barely been open half an hour on Thursday
morning when Betsy had to explain—again—to one of her
part-timers that the customer is always right. Good employees
never, ever argue with a customer over her choice of pattern,
floss, wool, or canvas. Her other part-timer was avidly eaves-
dropping, which aggravated Betsy very much, since she'd had to
give her the same lecture a week ago.

The phone rang, and Betsy, thinking she was starting to rub
the young woman's nose in it, said, "You have a kind heart,
Mary, so I'm sure you'll do much better from now on," and
went to answer it. "Good morning, Crewel World, Betsy speaking, how may I help you?"

"Good morning, I may have good news for you."

"Oh, good morning, Joe! A little good news might be very
welcome right now."

"Were you serious about needing just a few minutes of a textile expert's time?"

"Why, yes, I was."

"Good, because if you can get here by twelve thirty, you can see Dr. Edyth Booker for fifteen minutes. That is a serious time limit, because she has a luncheon engagement and has to leave at twelve forty-five."

"That's wonderful. I may not even need the whole fifteen minutes. Who is Dr. Booker?"

"She's our new curator of textiles, very knowledgeable about anything woven, though her specialty lies in things Asian."

"Wow, the curator herself! Thank you very much!"

"No problem. I hope she's able to help you. I'd spend a few minutes right now begging for more money, but I've got an emergency meeting in Roseville I have to get to. You can rest assured I'll call you later."

Betsy laughed. "All right." She hung up and checked her watch. There was barely time to call another part-timer to replace one or both of the ones now working, but should she? These two tended to rub up against one another until sparks flew. On the other hand, they were experienced in retail sales and even better at the minutiae of needlework.

She decided simply to ask and called them to the desk in front. "I have to go out unexpectedly for a noontime meeting. I'm thinking of calling Goddy in as an emergency supervisor, or maybe sending one of you home and calling Chelsea as a replacement."

"Oh, don't do that!" And, "Of course you can trust us!" they insisted, ashamed she'd even thought to propose such things, as if they were unruly children.

Well, it wasn't as if she was going to leave them alone the rest of the day.

So at twelve Betsy left the shop and headed up Highway 7, exiting on the fringe of downtown Minneapolis. In a few blocks the white, classical front of the art institute came into view. It sat atop a low hill and had a magnificent set of about a hundred white granite steps leading up it. But since that was not handicapped accessible to a ludicrous degree, it was no longer the main entrance. She parked on Third and went through a much more modest entry lined with heavy glass doors.

The entry lobby was light and airy, floored with highly polished tan marble. To the left was the Children's Theater, on the right was another set of big glass doors leading into the museum proper, where the tan marble floors continued.

The private offices of the museum were on the third floor, and carpeted.

Betsy had rolled the Thai embroidery in a white cotton towel and carried it in a purse almost big enough to be an overnight bag. She wished she'd remembered to bring a small knitting or counted cross-stitch project. Experience had taught her that handwork made waiting easier on her nerves and her temper.

But today there was no waiting. The secretary showed her right into a medium-sized office, where Dr. Edyth Booker waited beside her desk. Betsy had never met her, so she paused for a moment in the doorway to take her measure.

Dr. Booker was a woman of late middle age. She had a somewhat stocky build and she wore her blond hair in a short and prickly cut. She was wearing a flowing black ankle-length skirt printed with big spirals of aquamarine and gray, and a severely cut white shirt. She had turquoise jewelry and sported rings on almost every finger. When she smiled at Betsy, her dark blue eyes twinkled.

"So you're the one who won't let me gather my thoughts before I have to go ask the board for an interim increase in my budget."

"Oh, I'm sorry. I thought you were just having lunch!" Betsy said.

"It is over lunch," said Dr. Booker. "I find that a couple of bottles of a good wine with an ample meal loosens pinch-penny minds."

Betsy laughed, but then Dr. Booker looked at her watch, which had a silver and turquoise band, and turned abruptly serious. "So, what is it you want to ask me about?"

"I own a needlework shop in Excelsior, and recently I rescued a beautiful piece of silk embroidery from the trash. The more I look at it, the less I can figure out what it is and how to repair it." She reached into her purse, brought out the towel, and said, "May I show it to you?"

"All right," said Dr. Booker warily, probably afraid this was going to take longer than she'd hoped.

She went behind her desk, a very solid antique piece constructed of pale oak, almost clear of papers and totally devoid of personal items. Betsy put the towel on one side of the desk and unrolled it with a swift movement of her fingers. The silk had been folded in half lengthwise; she unfolded it, then stepped back.

Dr. Booker stared at the piece, her mouth moving as if she

could not quite remember how to whistle. She bent over for a closer look and whispered, "Where did you get this?"

"A friend went to Thailand a few weeks ago, and when she came back she brought a beautiful stone statue of the Buddha. It was wrapped in this piece of fabric. The Buddha was to go to an antiques shop in St. Paul, but my friend thought that delivering it with this dirty rag was disrespectful, and so she threw the fabric in a wastebasket. I fished it out and I've been trying to think how to clean and restore it. But I can't find any information about this style of embroidery on the Internet—it's silk, isn't it?"

"Yes, it's silk." Dr. Booker's tone was neutral. She moved her hand along the surface of the fabric, almost but not quite touching it.

Betsy continued, "And the weave is unusual, kind of like twill, don't you think? The embroidery is very attractive but I can't find any style like it, either. I don't want to do anything to it until I know what I've got here. It's dirty, but is it safe to wash it?" She saw the way Dr. Booker was staring at her, and said, "What?"

"You say you rescued this from a wastebasket?"

"Yes. There's more to the story, but—"

"I don't doubt that," interrupted Dr. Booker. "Will you excuse me for just one minute? Don't go away, I'll be right back."

"Certainly."

Dr. Booker hurried out of the office, closing the door behind her. Betsy waited a minute, then walked to the window. It overlooked a courtyard piled with snow. A sidewalk between the entrance lobby of the museum and the new wing across from it had been cleared with a snow blower. The Target Corporation had donated the wing, and while it wasn't marked with anything so obvious as the Target logo, there was a very large circle deeply cut into the façade over the entrance. The tan of the stone seemed deeper in color than Betsy remembered it, but that was probably because of its contrast with the sparkling new snow that covered the courtyard. Along the walk it was piled higher than the head of the man walking up it. Only the very tops of several small trees and an abstract sculpture could be seen under the drifts.

Betsy sighed and turned toward the door, which remained shut. She took her coat off while she looked around. Beside the window was a small table on which rested a flat-screen Sony Vaio computer, a secretarial chair in front of it. A file cabinet so old it was made of real oak came out from an adjoining wall, making something like an alcove for the computer setup. An equally old oak armchair, recently reupholstered in green leather, stood on the other side of it.

Betsy took a seat and waited some more. She wondered if her part-timers were behaving. The thought made her sigh with impatience for Dr. Booker's return.

She was just reaching for her bag to get her cell phone out when the door opened and Dr. Booker came striding back in. For the first time Betsy noticed how firm and square her jaw was. Dr. Booker went back behind her desk and said, "I want you to tell me how you came by this piece of silk."

"Is there a problem?"

"I'm not sure." Dr. Booker's eyebrows were raised, like a

high school principal waiting for a delinquent to explain himself.

So Betsy told what she knew of Doris's adventures in Bangkok, and of what had happened since her return. Dr. Booker's eyebrows didn't come down once.

"So this friend of yours is apparently mixed up in a *murder*?" Dr. Booker said when Betsy finished.

"Yes, and I'm afraid that if she had been at home when the burglar came into her apartment, she might also have become a victim."

"Have you any idea what this person or these people are after?"

"The only thing they have in common is that statue of the Buddha that Doris brought back from Thailand. I am starting to think it wasn't a copy, as the man in Bangkok told her, but the real thing. I assume it could be extremely valuable?"

"It could be. Someone would have to examine it—not me; I'm not an expert on artifacts that aren't made of fabric."

Betsy gestured at the piece of embroidered silk on Dr. Booker's desk. "Unless . . . It couldn't be the silk, could it?"

"No, no, no, it's not the silk. As you suggested, it's probably a modern design. Could you describe the statue to me again?"

Betsy did, even raising her hands to show the position of the Buddha's hands. Dr. Booker nodded. "Well, I do know that that's a very early pose. All of the positions have meaning, you know—a command to cease fighting, a command to contemplate the beauty of the earth. What you are demonstrating is the oldest-known pose—and no one knows its significance."

Betsy looked at her raised hands, left and right. "Interesting."

"I will pass your story along to our Asian curator, who may contact you with questions of his own. Now, about this embroidery. It is a beautiful thing, and it would be a shame if it were just tossed away or damaged in an attempt to restore it. I'll be glad to do a little research on it for you." Her left hand hovered over the piece, but again she did not quite touch it. "It won't take long—" Her eye was caught by her watch. "Oh, my, I'm going to be late! Let me call you when I've got some answers for you." She came out from behind her desk and walked rapidly to the door. "It should be by next Wednesday at the latest." She opened it and waited for Betsy to go through. "This will be a pretty little problem for me, and thank you for bringing it in. Good-bye."

Betsy found herself on the other side of the closed door, not sure if she should feel insulted at this very mild bum rush. It reminded her of the way Doris was treated in that antiques shop.

When she turned away, she was surprised to see a large and muscular private guard standing by the secretary's desk. He smiled coolly at her and gestured as if giving her permission to leave. Which she did.

Seventeen

ൟ•ൟ

BETSY had meant to go directly back to her shop, but on the elevator going down she buttoned her coat and kept thinking about Dr. Booker's reaction to the silk. Was it possible the curator wasn't merely surprised at the ragged old embroidery but astonished? And where had she gone, leaving Betsy alone in the office for all those minutes? Had it been to summon that burly guard? The guard had given Betsy a look that suggested he thought she had some precious artifact hidden in her purse. Had he been there to stop Betsy if she had tried to leave with the embroidery?

Betsy gave an indignant snort. So what if she had picked it up, not surreptitiously but openly? It was hers, after all. The Bangkok exporter had used it as packing material, essentially throwing it away. Doris had literally thrown it away. So Betsy, who had rescued it from the trash, could claim it as hers, right? She was here merely to get an opinion about restoring it, not to present it as a gift. Yet she could not shake the feeling that she would never see that piece of silk again.

What if it's not just an old rag? Betsy had thought it worth rescuing and restoring; so, it seemed, had Dr. Booker.

Annoyed with herself for not standing up to the curator and demanding the silk back, or at least demanding to know what the heck was going on, Betsy halted with her hands against the big glass doors that led to the entry hall. Maybe she should go back up there. Someone at the information desk gave her Dr. Booker's number and directed her to an internal-use phone. But Dr. Booker had left for a luncheon engagement, said her secretary.

Frustrated, Betsy looked around and saw in the outer lobby that the glass wall opposite the entry was also made up of doors. They opened onto the snow-lined walk that went to the new wing.

She'd been over there before. She had come to the grand reception that marked its official opening because one of the galleries in it housed an amazing display of modern fabric art.

But another feature of the new wing was a library. Art history, art auctions, art education, art museums—lots and lots of information, all in one place, and all on one topic.

She was more than halfway up the walk before it occurred to her to ask what she was going to use as the topic of a search. She slowed and would have turned around, except it was by then a shorter walk to the library than back to the main lobby.

The circular atrium in the wing was beautiful, modern without being stark. The volunteer behind the desk just inside the door said the library was to Betsy's left. Raising a sardonic eyebrow at the large porcelain statue of a snow white dog with a red ring around one eye, Betsy obediently turned left out of the rotunda and entered the library.

It was empty of patrons, and the woman behind a less grand desk than the one at the entrance was pleased to have a conundrum placed before her. "I want to find some information on a piece of embroidered silk," said Betsy. "I think it might be a valuable antique. It came here from Thailand, but it doesn't look Thai. Someone suggested it was embroidered by an English missionary in Thailand. I don't know how old it is. It's covered with very fine embroidery of odd-looking birds and animals among curling vines of tulip or lotus blooms."

The young woman at the desk had dark, spiky hair, a silver knob on one nostril, and a tattoo of Betty Boop on her upper arm that was only partly covered by the gray short-sleeved sweater she was wearing. She led Betsy to a low counter with three computers along it, gave her a brief tutorial on how to use the search engine and some suggestions for places to look, then retreated. Betsy took off her coat, sat on the office chair and first followed Ms. Boop's suggestion that she search for Asian textiles offered at art auctions—it was a revelation to her that there were places online where one could see copies of old catalogs from Christie's, for example, or Sotheby's. These had photographs of items, with art-language descriptions, what the estimated value was, and how much the item actually went for. But there was nothing online that resembled the embroidered silk on Dr. Booker's desk.

She next went on a search for Asian embroidered silk, but it only had more of the things her home computer had shown her, and none of those items resembled her piece.

She sighed and was about to sign off when she got another

idea. If the silk was brought into the United States illegally, under the guise of packing, then it might possibly have been an attempt to avoid duty—but it most likely was stolen. Next, she tried searching for a list of stolen art, and the search engine called up three. Each list was heartbreakingly long. After a discouraging journey down the first several dozen screens, she narrowed the search to stolen Asian fabrics, and a much shorter list came up. Most of them seemed to be carpets, with an admixture of robes and kimonos. She scrolled faster—and almost went past the one she was after. She hastily lifted her finger to stop scrolling, then went back three screens.

And there it was: a color photograph of the green embroidered silk, except it wasn't dirty or frayed. She clicked on it and instead of an enlargement got a detail. It was a close-up of the strange bird Godwin had called a cross between an ostrich and a molting peacock. A brief caption described it as a phoenix.

She clicked to close the detail photo and moved the cursor over to read the text, which began in red letters, STOLEN. Under that she read with growing amazement:

Eastern Han Dynasty (174–145 BC): From Chu Tomb #1 at Mashan Chiang-ling, in the Szechuan Province: A unique green rectangle of Mashan silk 7.5 inches (17 cm) wide and 24 inches (61 cm) long, depicting, in chain-stitch embroidery, stylized birds, tigers, and other animals in facing pairs, with lotus blooms, in coral, blue, black, red, gray, and gold.

Wait: 145 BC? Impossible! That was twenty-two *centuries* ago! She clicked again on the photo. No doubt about it, that was her silk. It was clean and unfrayed, while hers was raggedy and dirty—where had it been?—but that was her silk.

She just sat there for a minute with her hands resting on the keyboard, staring at it. What an astonishing thing, a piece of embroidery over 2,000 years old! What might it say to an archaeologist about the culture that produced it? The noble woman who owned it? The humble stitcher who made it? Her fingers trembled in awe as she remembered how she had handled the thing so casually.

Then her lips tightened and a slow anger warmed her chest. Such arrogance, exchanging this important piece of history for mere money! This was theft on a grand scale, theft not just of some valuable piece of art but of history, of—what was the word? Patrimony, a country's very heritage. "Unique," the announcement said. Suppose it had been delivered to Fitzwilliam in St. Paul? In a year or two the money paid for it would be spent, but the silk's beauty and historical value would have been lost forever. Good thing that thief was too clever for his own good!

It *was* clever to disguise an item by making it look subservient to something else. Using a soft old rag to soften the shock of travel for a stone carving seemed obvious enough. She looked again at the photo of the silk. The Han silk she had handled seemed to have been in just these proportions, not shorter in length, and there was no additional row of figures on this one missing from the one up in Dr. Booker's office. You don't get a couple of inches of loose threads by tearing off a thin slice. Could that mean the fraying was fake? She tried to picture the silk in her mind, but she hadn't paid close enough attention to it. But it wouldn't be hard to fake, just pull threads the size and color of the warp of the fabric through the edge with a needle. How stupid of her not to have noticed that!

Her sitting motionless for so long drew the librarian's attention. She came over to ask, "Is something wrong?"

"No, it's just that I'm stumped," Betsy said. "I found this piece and it's exactly . . . uh, what I'm interested in. How can I find out more about it?"

The librarian leaned closer. "Well, isn't that an odd-looking thing." She read the text. "Early Chinese . . . embroidered silk . . . tomb excavation. I could find you a good history of China, but China's history is so huge, something like this would probably get a one-sentence mention. Maybe a book on silk?"

Betsy said, "I own two books on silk, but they don't have this piece in it—which surprises me, since this is unique as well as very old."

"Hold on a minute." The librarian went to the next computer, sat down, and began a search of her own. Minutes went by. She had a tight little smile on her face, the sign of a huntress hot on the trail. But Betsy began to feel impatient, and not just because she wanted more information. She shouldn't be spending so much time away from her shop. That pair of young part-timers were almost certainly up to mischief by now. It was Betsy's fault; she should have realized she might be away longer than she'd hoped. She looked at her watch. If she had started back as soon as she came away from Dr. Booker's office, she'd be in Excelsior right now, scolding them for whatever they'd done.

But she couldn't leave, not when this might be the key to the whole mystery. She bit her lips and wriggled on the chair—and thought about knitting. Godwin had once told her that if knitting with the hands wasn't possible, knitting in the mind was equally soothing. Last week she'd helped a customer choose the yarn to knit a "lover's knot" afghan from a free pattern offered on the Internet by Lion Brand Yarn. The customer had needed assistance following the pattern for the big clustered-braid panel, but that was too complicated for Betsy to do now just in her head. Instead, she began to construct the smaller OXOX panel, which was only twelve stitches wide. She would imagine knitting a very long, very skinny scarf in, say, mauve or dusty pink.

Twelve stitches was far too narrow, of course. So knit ten, purl eight, knit ten, that was easy. Turn and purl ten, knit eight, purl ten. Easy. Repeat row one. She could feel her fingers twitching as they imitated the knitting movements. So all right then, let's see, purl ten, slip two stitches onto a humpbacked cable needle, drop it back of the work, knit two, then knit the two on the cable needle back onto the regular needle, and purl two—no, ten. Repeat rows one through three. Then purl ten, slip two stitches to the cable needle and put it in front of the work, knit two, then purl the two from cable—no, *knit* the two from the cable needle. Was she doing it right? It didn't matter, no one would ever see this scarf. Purl ten. Then—

"Excuse me?" It was the librarian, who was looking at her strangely. *Probably thinking I was having a petit mal attack*, thought Betsy, blinking herself back into reality.

"I'm sorry," Betsy said, "I was thinking about something."

"That's what I thought," said the librarian politely. "Anyway, here's an article about that stolen silk."

"Oh, you found something? How wonderful! Thank you!"

The librarian went back to her desk and Betsy slid into the chair in front of the second computer. The article was brief but enlightening.

This silk piece, it said, is one of the oldest examples of embroidery in existence. It was woven and embroidered during the Eastern Han Dynasty, which ruled a part of China from 174 to 145 BC. The piece was owned by a noble woman named Xiu and was one of many found with her body in a small tomb deep underground. Xiu, who died at about forty-five years of age, was wrapped in many layers of silk, of a quality more suited to royalty. And she held rolls of silk in each hand.

Could it be, thought Betsy, that it was no humble artisan who did the embroidery but Xiu herself? Or perhaps Xiu owned a company that produced the silk, hiring the artisans who spun, dyed, and embroidered it and so felt entitled on her death to be buried in robes like the ones her business had produced for the royal families.

The tomb was opened in 1982 and the silk, amazingly intact, was among the artifacts recovered. The Zhin-Zhou Regional Museum in Hubei was designated to receive the silk, but this piece vanished on its journey there and was thought lost. But it turned up at an unadvertised auction in Hong Kong in April of last year and was purchased for the equivalent of US $25,000—not nearly its real value, but it had no provenance and so only was alleged to be what it was.

The purchaser was the owner of a private museum in Bangkok, but the silk was stolen again, apparently upon its arrival at the Bangkok airport. Its current whereabouts were unknown, concluded the article.

Not anymore, thought Betsy. It currently rests on the desk of Dr. Edyth Booker, of the Minneapolis Art Institute. Unless she had locked it in a safe, which was extremely likely.

Twenty-five thousand dollars was not nearly its real value, noted the article.

Then what is its real value? wondered Betsy. *A hundred thousand? More?*

No wonder Dr. Booker was so anxious to hold on to it, a rare item like this. Betsy recalled the expression on the curator's face, which she now thought was an effort to conceal her joy and excitement.

Betsy ordered the computer to print a copy of the article—and of the listing from the stolen art Web site. When she went to collect them from the printer, she found that it had printed the entire list of stolen items. She sighed and went to pay for the copies, only to find that the library didn't charge for copies. So she dropped a generous donation in the wing's clear Plexiglas donor box on her way out of the museum.

Eighteen

∽ · ∾

BETSY drove back to her shop in Excelsior in a daze, thinking about the astonishing find. She found herself admiring the noble Xiu. Forbidden by sumptuary laws to wear the magnificent garments she created for royalty during her life, she boldly wrapped herself in layers of them—and even grasped rolls of embroidered silk with her hands—in her tomb.

Betsy also wondered about the women who worked in Xiu's shop, spinning and weaving and dyeing. Were they slaves, bond women, or employees? Were they treated kindly? Paid a living wage? Did they love their work? Their boss? The woman, forever anonymous, who made the thousands of tiny, perfect stitches that formed the complex, beautiful, exotic pattern on that one piece of green silk—did she have the same determined patience that modern stitchers had? Surely she did, and the talent that only worked when linked to hard-earned skill, to produce such a work of art!

How amazing to stand at this remove in time—twenty centuries!—and feel a connection with both the shop owner and her talented worker.

Betsy recalled Dr. Booker moving her hand across the face of the embroidery, not quite touching it—proof that she knew, or at least suspected, what it was. Fabrics of this age and rarity were rarely handled, and then only by antiquarians wearing thin white cotton gloves to protect the cloth from the natural oils on human hands. Betsy remembered the weight and textures of the Han silk in her fingers. Hers were probably the last that would touch the piece unprotected.

And she wondered why, if Dr. Booker recognized the silk for what it was, she didn't tell Betsy.

Betsy parked in front of her shop rather than in back—she needed to do a little shopping after Crewel World closed this evening—and saw a customer standing in the doorway, peering inward. As Betsy approached, she could hear some noise from inside. The customer—Sharon Morton, who spent a lot of money in Crewel World—made a *tsk* sound, then turned and walked away.

Anything that ran a customer off was very bad. Betsy hurried to look in, heard shouting and saw movement. She opened the door, prepared to slam it and run.

But it wasn't a robbery or assault. Her two part-timers were standing on opposite sides of the library table, screaming invectives at one another, faces red, fists clenched, and fingers pointing.

Betsy had to shout twice to get their attention, but when she did, the noise stopped as if it had been hit with a hammer.

"What's going on?" Betsy demanded, pulling off her mittens.

The two started explaining, talking over one another, and in a few seconds then were back to shouting. It seemed to have something to do with a missing candy bar.

"Stop it, stop it!" Betsy yelled, waving her knit hat like a warning flag. They obeyed. "How many times have I warned you about this?" She took a calming breath and went on, much more quietly, "No more warnings. You're both fired."

That started yet another explosion, but this time all Betsy had to do was raise both hands to make them stop. "I said, you're both fired. As I came up the sidewalk, I saw Sharon Morton walk away from the door without coming in. Obviously the racket in here scared her off. I wonder how many other customers you ran off? This is not the first time you two have caused trouble in the shop. I can't have this, I don't have to put up with it."

"But she—" started one.

"No, it was *her*—"

"I don't care who started it or whose fault it was! It took both of you to make the quarrel! This is final—get your coats and go away!"

There were a hot few minutes of silence as the young women gathered their belongings, their faces set hard in anger and flushed pink. They pushed against one another as they tried to go out the door simultaneously. Outside, the cold seemed to vanquish their anger; they looked at each other as if waking from a dream, then went in separate directions, one of them with her mouth pulled down, trying not to cry.

Betsy dragged off her coat, pushed her fingers through her hair, and went to make a cup of tea. She brought it back and sat at the library table. Her knees felt weak, her thumbs numb. Her eyes ached with angry, unshed tears. She wondered which of them would think to start a lawsuit first.

As her heart rate slowed, she thought, not for the first time, that the shop was far more trouble than it was worth. *I do my best*, she thought. *And what do I get? Heartaches! Nuthin' but heartaches!* That was a quote from somewhere—but who had said it? She groped around in her memory until, accompanied by a smile, she came up with answer: Barney Fife. She took a sip of her tea. Nuthin' but heartaches.

But Barney was wrong, in his context—and hers. She might dream of quitting, but she knew she wouldn't. The rewards were simply too great.

She finished her tea and put in a call to Mike Malloy. He was out, she was told, but was expected back in a half hour or so. Betsy said it was urgent but not desperately so and hung up.

Then, because she was too shaken to stitch and couldn't think what else to do, she pulled a writing pad to her and started to compose a help-wanted ad. It would go online and in the local paper. *Wanted: part-time retail worker for needle-work shop.*

A new customer came in and interrupted her. She was interested in making a needlepoint pillow for her family's condo up on Lake Superior. She sighed over a half-dozen seashore-themed painted canvases for twenty minutes, sighed again at the prices, and left without buying anything.

Betsy made herself another cup of tea and sat down to write

the next line for her help-wanted ad: *Wages negotiable, depending on experience—*

Then the phone rang. "Crewel World, Betsy speaking, how may I help you?" Betsy said, in a bad imitation of her cheerful voice.

"Did Dr. Booker prove helpful?"

"Oh, hello, Dr. Brown!" The cheer felt more real now.

"Don't you remember? Please, call me Joe."

"All right. Joe. Well, she was sort of helpful. She said the fabric was silk, all right. Then she asked if she could keep it for a while to do some research on it."

"Did she tell you what time period it was from?"

"No. Did she tell you anything about it at the luncheon?"

"No. Should she have?"

"I think so, if what I found out on my own is correct." She told him of her investigation at the art institute library. He kept making odd little snorts of surprise all through her narrative but fell into a seconds' long silence when she finished.

At last he said, "You mean to tell me that the Karen Boozer embroidery you wanted identified was really a piece of *Mashan silk*?" He sounded indignant, even angry.

But Betsy could tell he wasn't really angry. "I'm so sorry!" she said with humor in her voice. "If you had asked around, people might have told you I can't tell Cari Buziak from Han Dynasty embroidery!"

"Yes, of course," he said, and added, his tone turned reverent, "My God, what an extraordinary story! Do you know how privileged you are to have had that piece of Han Dynasty silk in your hands?"

"I didn't know at the time, of course, but now I do. I don't know why Dr. Booker didn't tell me what she suspected it was. The look on her face when she saw it makes me think she recognized it. But all she would say was that it was 'interesting' and could she keep it for a few days."

"Maybe you're wrong, maybe it isn't what you think."

"Again, I'm not an expert, but there was a close-up photograph on the Web site of a very peculiar-looking bird, and to me it looked exactly like the bird on the silk. Even the colors were the same."

"Oh my, that does sound as if you rescued an important artifact from a landfill."

"Yes. I almost just let it stay in the wastebasket—I would have if it had smelled bad. It would have gone with the paper trash—ended up recycled, maybe, into paper towels."

"But it didn't, it didn't," he said, as if to reassure the both of them.

"I don't understand why Dr. Booker didn't tell me what she thought it was."

"Perhaps she was afraid you would insist on taking it back, with an eye toward selling it."

"Is it terrifically valuable?"

"Oh God!" he groaned, and she recalled he was an Asian art collector. But there was that current of amusement running through his voice again.

"Ah," said Betsy. "But then why didn't she tell you the news over lunch?"

"Oh, for a very good reason," said Joe. "This wasn't a gathering of friends, but a special meeting of the board of directors of the institute. Minutes were taken. She would not say anything on the record about such an important find until she is satisfied it is authentic. There's a huge industry in Asia making excellent copies of antiquities. But if she concludes it's the real deal, she'll report it to the director, and he'll do some more research himself. If he's satisfied, in a few weeks the board will get a report with photographs and authenticating documents, and then there will be a press conference."

"Will the institute get to keep it?"

"Good Lord, no! Something as important as this? No, this is patrimony, part of the nation's history. It will go back to China."

"Could I presume on my rescue of the piece to be allowed to see it all restored before it goes back?"

"They won't restore it here. Think of the repercussions if it's damaged in the process. No, the institute will just pack it as carefully as they can and arrange for the safest and most secure transport possible back to China. Let them make their own mistakes repairing it."

"But what about the law enforcement part? It came into the country illegally, remember. The St. Paul police are conducting a homicide investigation, the St. Peter police and sheriff's department are investigating an assault with a deadly weapon that ended in a death, last night someone shot at Doris Valentine through a window in Wayzata, and I think a suicide in Maple Plain will turn out to be murder."

"But couldn't this be about the Buddha statue?"

"No, Wendy was asking Doris where the Thai silk was."

"Was she? Well, then. What a bloody business! How do you

know all these things? Are you married to a police detective?" he asked.

"No, I'm kind of a civilian detective."

"I thought you owned a needlework store."

"I do. This sleuthing thing is kind of on the side. And I'm not a private eye, either. It's just something I seem to have a talent for."

After a beat, he said, "You are a very amazing person, you know that?"

"If that's a compliment, thank you."

"Yes, indeed it is."

Betsy said, "There are a lot of jurisdictions involved in this, Joe: St. Peter, St. Paul, Excelsior, Wayzata, Maple Plain. I'm surprised the FBI isn't poking around in this already, considering it's a smuggling case."

"Eye See Eee."

"What?"

"Immigration and Customs Enforcement, ICE. As a member of the board of an art museum, I know things like that. They're the ones in charge of smuggling. And I imagine they will be involved in this, if they aren't already. Lord, Lord, what a mess!"

"Is it all right that I told you about the silk?" asked Betsy. "Should I have let Dr. Booker inform you?"

"Oh, it's all right. Consider it payback to Dr. Booker for pretending she had no idea of the importance of that torn and dirty—" He stopped suddenly. "How bad is the damage?" he asked.

"That's another interesting thing," she said. "I don't think it's torn at all." She described how a piece of cloth might be made to appear frayed. "And if I'm right, that means the dirt will come off easily, without leaving a stain."

"Someone was being very clever, it sounds like," he said. "Now, if I might offer to reward you for rescuing this priceless artifact by asking if you would like to increase your pledge, we can both get back to our regular work . . ."

Betsy laughed. "All right, put me down for a five percent increase."

Nineteen

~ · ~

THE door sounded a few minutes later, and Betsy turned to see Sharon Morton coming in. "Is Goddy home from Florida?" Sharon asked.

"Yes, he came back yesterday, but he's not due to start working in the shop until tomorrow. Sharon, I'm so glad you came back."

"Well, when I turned and saw you coming up the sidewalk, I knew you'd put an end to the nonsense going on in the shop."

Betsy smiled. "Is there something I can show you?"

"No, I just wanted to tell Goddy about the chicken quilt he helped me with." Last year, Sharon had decided to make a quilt using the large quantity of chicken-themed fabric she'd been collecting. To make it special, she had done a number of needlepoint, counted cross-stitch, and punch-needle squares for it, too. All selected with Godwin's enthusiastic help.

"Is it finished?" asked Betsy.

"Yes, but I didn't do it." Sharon continued in a rush, "You

know, people will tell you quilting is easy, but it isn't. I couldn't get the cloth cutting right, and when I did, I couldn't figure out how to piece it. Mama finally told me about this woman in town, Karen Kerner, who will make a quilt for people like me who find they've bitten off more than they can chew. Karen came over yesterday to show me the top—and it's *gorgeous*! And her prices are so reasonable! Not that this still isn't going to be the most expensive blanket I've ever owned." She laughed. "I was going to put it on my bed, but now I think I'll hang it on the wall." She paused for a breath, then, eyes apologetic—she was quite a talker, after all—she let it out without saying anything more.

"I'm sure it's beautiful," said Betsy. "And I'm sure Goddy is going to want to see it, no matter how it was finished."

Sharon said, in a much calmer tone, "Anyway, could you tell Godwin? I was ashamed to tell him I sent it out to be done. But it's so beautiful, he'll take one look and know it's not a beginner's work. Meanwhile, I wanted to see the new canvas work Goddy is doing—hey, wow, there it is, all finished!" Canvas work was like counted cross-stitch, except it was worked on even-weave canvas rather than Aida fabric. What Sharon was pointing at was Godwin's recently finished model of Crystal Irises from Nancy's Needle. It featured a single stem of two purple irises surrounded by patterns of lattice, herringbone, smyrna, and other well-known needlepoint stitches. The stitches, though, were not done in the usual wool but instead with finer flosses that allowed the canvas to show through. The effect was of exquisite lace.

"It's even prettier than the picture he showed me! Look how the light changes on the stitches when you walk past it!" The pattern was only twelve dollars, and the eighteen-count canvas wasn't expensive, but Sharon needed the floss, too: five skeins of Caron Watercolors, one of DMC pearl cotton, and five of Rainbow Gallery threads. Betsy was pleased to give Sharon a new project, Sharon was excited at the prospect, and Betsy's bottom line was content. Sharon paid for the project and left smiling.

Betsy was just composing the next line on her ad when the phone rang. "Hello, Crewel World, Betsy speaking, how may I help you?"

"Malloy here. What's up?"

"Hi, Mike. What did you find out about Lena Olson?"

"I don't know why I'm surprised anymore at the things you know or find out."

"It *was* murder!"

"A couple of broken fingernails indicate a struggle, and a heck of a knock on the head probably means she was unconscious when she was put behind the wheel of her car in the garage."

"Oh my. Do the police have any idea who did it?"

"Well, the husband has a solid alibi, and so does the son. So it's person or persons unknown."

Betsy groaned. "Mike, this person must be found!"

"Now, we don't know that Lena's murderer is the same person who killed Oscar Fitzwilliam."

Betsy would have objected to that but hesitated. After all, assigning guilt in advance could lead to serious miscarriages of justice. "Okay, you're right. By the way, I have some new information about that burglary in my apartment building. Remember you said it was a search? I know what she was after."

" 'She'?"

"Yes, the burglar was the woman who was killed at the March Hare in St. Peter. Wendy Applegate."

"You know that for a fact."

"Yes. Well, I'm pretty sure, anyway. And listen, you need to call a Dr. Edyth Booker, the textile curator at the Minneapolis Art Institute. She has the piece of silk that Wendy Applegate was after."

"Where'd Dr. Booker get it from?"

"Me. I brought it to her. Doris brought it back from Thailand wrapped around that statue of the Buddha. She thought it was a rag and threw it away. I rescued it because the embroidery on it looked interesting. But it didn't look like anything I'd seen before, so I didn't want to mess with it until I knew what it was. I finally got a flying appointment with Dr. Booker, but she was—what's that cop word for people behaving suspiciously?"

"You mean 'hinky'?"

"Yes, that's the word. She was astonished when she first saw it, but tried to pretend she wasn't."

"So what the heck is it?"

"One of the oldest surviving pieces of silk embroidery in the world, an important piece of Chinese history."

"Holy cow!" Mike didn't say cow but one of its products.

"Back in the eighties, archaeologists excavated a tomb dating to the second century BC. A woman named Xiu was buried there, covered in layers of silk. Because of the way the tomb was sealed, the silk was almost perfectly preserved."

There was a pause, probably so Mike could write some of this down. "All right, all right, this is too much detail to get over the phone. I want to talk to you about this. Can you come over to the station?"

"No, I'm alone in the shop."

"Then I'll come there—and I may bring some people with me, all right?"

"Yes, of course. Mike, will you do me a favor? Bring me something from Pizza Hut, please. I had to fire my help and I haven't had lunch."

"Who do you think I am, the pizza delivery guy?"

"All right, then, soup and a bread stick from Antiquity Rose."

Mike growled, but when he came by forty-five minutes later, he had a covered foam bowl that gave off wonderful smells and, in a pocket, one of Antiquity Rose's fat, foot-long bread sticks.

With him was a woman, tall and slim, with the most penetrating gray-green eyes Betsy had ever seen. The women nodded politely at Betsy when Mike introduced her as a detective on the St. Paul Police Department. She brought a cardboard box a little bigger than a shoebox to the checkout desk. Inside were layers of Bubble Wrap, and under that the carved stone statue of Buddha. She set it on the desk and stepped back.

"Do you recognize this?" she asked in a quiet voice.

"Why, yes," said Betsy. "It's the statue Doris Valentine brought back from Thailand. Did Mr. Fitzwilliam find it after all?"

"Mr. Fitzwilliam?" she said, and Betsy felt again the detective's eyes on her.

"Eddie Fitzwilliam, the Fitzwilliam's Antiques owner's son. I asked him to call and tell me if he found it." The look was still there and Betsy found herself confessing, "And if he found out anything when he went over the books. And he did, he said there was money coming in that the books didn't account for. So I think that means his father was involved in the illegal import of artifacts."

The detective merely nodded. "You're sure about this statue?" she asked.

"It looks exactly like the one Doris brought from over there."

"Thank you," she said. She wrapped it up again, neither rushing nor lingering in her movements, said good-bye and thank you to Mike, and left.

"Wow," said Betsy, looking at the closed door to her shop after she'd gone through it.

"Yeah," said Mike, blowing a silent, admiring, envious whistle. "She walks into an interrogation room, gives a perp that look, and suddenly he just can't stop talking. She was the only one who wanted to come along, and you can see that's because she had her own agenda."

"Where did she get the statue?"

"It was found in a search of Wendy Applegate's house."

"Why didn't she say that?"

"Why should she? She never gives out information unless she has to, and besides, she doesn't approve of amateur sleuths." He said it as if he himself had never been guilty of this miscalculation.

Betsy sat down at the library table to eat her soup, gesturing at him to join her. "Business is slow this time of day," she said, "so probably we won't be interrupted."

He got out his notebook and clicked out the point on his pen. "What made you decide that piece of silk was important enough that a textile expert at the art institute should have a look at it?" he asked.

"I didn't think it was important. It was a beautiful piece of embroidery, but it was dirty and frayed, and I wanted to know how to clean and repair it. I couldn't find anything like it on the Internet, and with Goddy on vacation I've been too busy to keep looking. So when this man called—his name is Joe Brown and he's a member of the board—about increasing my pledge of support to the institute, I parlayed that into a brief interview with the textile curator there. After the money I gave them last year, I figured they owed me five minutes of their time. All I was hoping for was that someone would give me a time period and a country to focus my research on, and a hint on how to clean it without further damaging it. What's interesting was her reaction."

Mike looked up from his notebook. "You mean her not telling you what she thought it was?"

Betsy stopped sipping soup to say, "*And* talking me into leaving it behind. I think she thought I'd brought it in to get confirmation that it was what it was and that my next goal was to sell it for big bucks." She put on a hard expression. "I wish now I'd asked for it back."

"I thought you said she had a guard outside her office ready to stop you."

Betsy released her scowl with a sigh and resumed her meal. "Yeah, she did."

"So did that article you found tell you how it got from an archaeological excavation in China to a needlework store in Minnesota?"

"It was stolen—twice. First, it was supposed to go to a museum in Hubei, China, but it was stolen en route. It wasn't seen again until last year, when it turned up at an unadvertised auction in Hong Kong. It was stolen again when the buyer shipped it to Bangkok. There's an American doing business in Bangkok, David Corvis—"

Mike lifted his pen, and Betsy paused, while he wrote the name down. She spelled it for him. Then he nodded at her to continue.

"I don't know if he was the thief, but somehow he got hold of it and was trying to sneak it into the United States. He disguised it by making it look like an old rag he was using as packing material. Doris wasn't supposed to open the box it was in, but it never occurred to Corvis that if she did, she'd throw the 'rag' away."

"What do you know about this Corvis fellow?"

"According to Doris, he's an ex-marine who manages a silk factory called Bright Works outside of Bangkok and owns a small export business in the city."

Mike made another note. "This silk, for all that it's rare and historic, does it have much value? I mean if you had managed to get it back, how much could you have sold it for?"

"It was sold in Hong Kong for twenty-five thousand, but the article said that was a low price because it didn't have any provenance—you know, a record of ownership going back to the first owner. God knows what the real value is. That auction wasn't a proper sale; I mean, whoever heard of an auction that isn't advertised? But someone must've heard of it, if it got stolen again on arrival at the airport in Bangkok."

"Unless whoever stole it just picked up a box or two at random," said Mike, the voice of experience.

"Well, yes. I'm sure you know how to check robbery reports, even overseas, right?"

"Yes—and I will, too."

"Good. I wonder who was supposed to buy it here, at this end?"

"Does it have provenance now?"

"I don't know. The description on the Web site that lists stolen art has a photograph of it and says it's one of a kind. I don't think that gives it provenance, though. But I don't think they'd need to know the name of the original thief or of the person who won the auction. Anyway, I'm not the person to answer your question. Would you like a cup of bad coffee? My newly fired employees were supposed to brew a fresh batch but didn't."

"Yes, thanks. Black."

Mike, reviewing his notes, said, "So the art institute won't confirm it's what you say it is, but on the other hand, they won't let us take it for evidence."

Betsy, heading for the back of the shop where the coffee urn waited, said over her shoulder, "I don't doubt that, Mike. It's more than two thousand years old and it will give people new ways to think about the history of silk in China."

"Yeah, well, I'm sure some people will find that useful," he muttered, as one whose job is not the study of Chinese silk but the capture of criminals. Betsy heard him and laughed.

When she came back with a delicate porcelain cup of coffee, she found him shuffling through a thin stack of papers.

"Oh, that's the printout of what I found on the institute's computer." She put his coffee down near his left elbow and pointed to a fuzzy, black-and-white photograph on the top sheet. "That's the silk," she said. "They don't have a color printer for visitors, so it's not very useful. But on the next page is a detail photo that's pretty good. The two pages after that are the article that will tell you about the silk and the tomb and all. Everything beneath that is the rest of the stolen art listing—I didn't know how to prevent the printer from spitting out the entire thing."

Mike said, "May I have these?"

"Sure."

He set them aside and took a sip of coffee, nodding his approval, which told Betsy something about police department coffee. He asked, "Do you think those smugglers knew what they had a hold of?"

"I think so—at least they knew they had something very rare and valuable. Look at all the trouble they took to disguise it when they tried to sneak it into the country."

"There's a difference between 'rare and valuable' and something as wildly rare and historic as the silk you pulled out of the wastepaper basket. I'm wondering who knew what it was. Did Wendy Applegate? Did Oscar Fitzwilliam? Maybe only the person who arranged for it to come over and the ultimate buyer knew, everyone else was satisfied to get a few thousand dollars."

"I don't know about that, Mike. Look how desperate Wendy

was to get it back. Driving to St. Peter in a blizzard, bringing a gun with her—she doesn't seem the type when you look at her background."

"That's true. She must have been fantastically anxious to get hold of it. I wonder who set this up."

"You don't think she did, in conjunction with Mr. Corvis?"

"No, I don't." He sat back and took another sip of his coffee. "Let me tell you something. Smuggling on this level isn't like bringing back some marijuana from Mexico or a little cocaine from the Bahamas. It takes high-level organization and some serious connections. Doris Valentine seems to be innocent, from her behavior since this mess started. I think she was deliberately aimed at this Corvis fellow, possibly by a tour guide or maybe someone at her hotel, and she stupidly agreed to do him a favor. Who set that up, I don't know. But those three ladies who went to Thailand a few years back—that's different. I think it's significant that Wendy Applegate had been to Asia before. And that she had some connections with Asian people in the silk business. I think she's the one who is the link between Corvis and Fitzwilliam's Antiques. Maybe even between Corvis and the ultimate buyer, as you call him. So I don't think we're talking about a nice St. Paul socialite here. Not at all. What we need to know is the rest of the organization. Wendy is dead, so who killed Lena Olson?"

"Could it be the ultimate buyer?"

"Maybe."

"What kind of person would he be?"

"What am I, a profiler?" Nevertheless he thought a few moments and said, "Okay, he'll be someone sane on the outside but crazy on the inside. He's got the same kind of glitch in his brain as those people who are found with two hundred cats in their homes. They call them 'collectors.' But the kind we're talking about will take some dangerous chances to get hold of whatever it is they're obsessed about. They can be secretive about their collection; they'd buy the *Mona Lisa* and hide it in a storage locker or safe deposit box and visit it at night, and never tell anyone they had it. They aren't usually organized enough to run a smuggling operation, so I think our murderer is more likely to be a smuggler than a collector."

"Could they be the same person?"

"Well . . . there are some slick collectors, I guess."

Betsy said, "Okay, who? Who do you think we're talking about?"

"I have no idea," Mike said.

Twenty

༄ ⋆ ༄

BETSY was in the process of closing shop. Sophie was already at the back door, calling in her high-pitched voice for Betsy to hurry. It was time to go upstairs and give the cat her dinner.

The phone rang. Betsy sighed, but answered it cordially, "Crewel World, Betsy speaking, how may I help you?"

"Betsy, it's Carmen Diamond." Her voice was frightened.

"Oh God." Betsy closed her eyes for a second. "Is it Doris? Is she all right?"

"Yes, yes, she's fine, but she's packing up to leave. Phil is going to take her away, and he's making a big secret about where they're going. I tried to talk them out of leaving, but they won't listen."

"May I speak with her?"

"I was hoping you'd say that. Maybe you can talk some sense into her. Hold on."

After about a minute Doris's voice said, "Hello, Betsy." Her tone didn't seem quite as flat as usual.

"How are you? Are you feeling better? You sound better."

"Yes. I look like a combat veteran, but I feel all right."

"What a terrible experience that must have been for you!"

"You know something? I think I'm getting used to it. Getting shot at seems to be my newest sport, and so far I'm not too bad at it."

It was a black jest, but Betsy rejoiced at this evidence of resilience. She forced a little laugh and said, "Doris, you are about the bravest person I know!"

"I don't feel brave, but thank you."

"So where is Phil taking you?"

"I don't know, he won't say."

"Not even to you?"

"He says he doesn't want me to hint where it is to anyone, even accidentally."

"You must know I think this is a very bad idea. Can I talk to him?"

"When he heard it was you calling, he said to say he's sorry, but talking to him won't do any good. He said I could talk all I wanted because this is why he won't tell me where we're going. And you know, since nobody seems to know who's doing this, I think it's not that bad an idea to just disappear."

"Well, if he won't talk to me, I guess I have to lean hard on you. Doris, I think this is a terrible idea. I really, really, really think so. Please, tell Phil you won't go with him!"

"No."

"Oh, but—"

"No."

"Are you sure?"

"Positive."

Betsy sighed. One-word answers meant a mind made up.

"All right, but once this is cleared up, you *will* find a bright new place to move into—at your old address."

"You mean my old apartment?"

"Yes, of course."

"No, I'm not ever coming back there. I'm going to get another apartment."

"Oh please, don't move out on me, Doris!"

"I already have. My rent's paid to the end of the month and I'll give you another month's rent in lieu of thirty days' notice. Betsy, that apartment gives me nightmares."

"But I'm going to hollow it out—both apartments—and make them like totally different places, everything new. I'm calling the contractor tomorrow, and I'll get him started as soon as possible."

There was a silence on the other end of the line.

"Doris?"

She burst out, "Why are you doing this? It costs money to remodel!"

"Well, I can afford it. Plus they're due. Those two apartments haven't been seriously done over since Coolidge was president. You can only push 'retro' so far."

That didn't bring the laugh Betsy was hoping for. Instead, Doris said, "I'm sorry, I can't see how it will make any difference. I'll still know what happened there. And what it led to."

"All right, all right, I can understand that. But will you agree to not sign a lease anywhere else until you see what I've had done here? You've been a great tenant, and I'd hate to lose you."

"I think it's good of you to do this, I really do. And all right, I'll come and look at the result. But I can't promise to stay."

"And I don't want you to make a promise you may find you can't keep. The apartments need remodeling in any case, and you've provided the push I needed to get started. Now, may I ask you some questions before you go?"

Doris breathed a why-should-you-be-any-different sigh. "Sure, ask away."

"Did either Lena or Wendy suggest you go to that silk factory outside of Bangkok?"

"No, how could they? I've never talked to either one of them, all I know about them is what Carmen told me."

"They weren't on your list of people to whom you were sending that daily Bangkok diary?"

"No, I didn't send them my Bangkok e-mails . . . What?" The query was to someone in the room with Doris. "Oh, okay. Carmen says to tell you she was forwarding my Bangkok diary to them."

"So who was it who told you about the factory?"

"The concierge at the hotel. I wanted to see silk being made, but the north part of Thailand, which is where the factories mostly are, seemed so far away, and she said it's kind of primitive up there, no place for a foreign woman to go alone. I asked her if there was one closer to Bangkok, and she told me about Bright Works—that's the name of it."

"Yes, I remember." Betsy had been amused to learn that Thai

businesses often had English names that were only approximately appropriate.

"She even arranged for a driver to come along who could translate Thai into English."

"That was very nice of her."

"Oh, yes. The Thai people are just amazingly kind." A sense of longing came into Doris's voice. "I wish I could have stayed over there."

"I don't blame you one bit. I think those are all the questions I have for now. Thanks, Doris. And may your guardian angel be at the top of his game."

"You're welcome and thank you. Here's Carmen."

"Did she tell you anything helpful?" Carmen asked.

"Yes, I think so. But I wish one of us could have talked her out of going off with Phil. Thank you for calling me, Carmen."

After she hung up, Betsy finished closing up the shop, setting aside the starting-up cash for tomorrow, drawing up a deposit slip for the rest. She would take it to the night deposit drawer at the bank later—in her newly acquired state of alarm, she had a notion that a robber could do worse than lurk outside a business waiting for the owner to come out with a bag of cash in hand.

She flipped the lights off and, with her impatient cat trotting ahead of her, went up the stairs to her apartment.

Supper was a quiet affair, with Betsy deep in thought, trying to figure out where Phil might have gone with Doris. He was a Minnesota native, one of the sort who had always taken most of his vacations within its borders, so he knew the state at a level that immigrant Betsy couldn't even dream of. He was a retired railroad engineer, chummy with fellow railroaders, so he could doubtless have called on one of them to hide Doris—perhaps on a train. He knew people with cabins up in the north woods, many located down some obscure lane deep among the pines. He and Doris could rest secure before a roaring fire in a fieldstone fireplace with no one but the crows, eagles, and foxes as neighbors. It was also possible that he and Doris were flying out of Humphrey or Lindburgh Terminal on their way to Costa Rica or London or Singapore or South Africa. Betsy tossed her napkin down. There was no way to figure out where the two had gone.

Which, come to think of it, might make his plan not such a bad one after all.

Dishes done, Betsy went in to boot up her computer. Doris had put a message onto RCTN about a pattern she was having a problem with. Lillian Banchek had replied privately and Doris's trip to Thailand came up in conversation. Lillian wrote that her ex-brother-in-law had a manufacturing business in Thailand, and she had offered Doris his e-mail address. Betsy and Lillian had exchanged messages both on RCTN and privately for a long time, so Betsy looked to send Lillian an IM. But Lillian wasn't logged on. Betsy sent her a quick e-mail, asking for Ron Zommick's e-mail address and phone number, adding, *This is urgent, so please let me know ASAP.*

She was about to settle down with her bookkeeping program when her phone rang. It was Carmen. "Mike Malloy just left. Does he treat everyone like he thinks they're crooks?" Her tone was crisp, as if she was trying hard not sound as angry as she really was.

"Probably. Until he gets to know them. Was he really rude?"

"No, not rude, exactly. Just . . . Well, he wouldn't take anything I said as true. He'd ask me the same question three different ways."

"Oh, that. That's not suspicion, that's just how the police operate. They want to make sure you understand the question and that they understand the answer."

"Oh? Well, it made me feel uncomfortable."

"On behalf of the City of Excelsior, I apologize."

With a hint of a smile in her voice, Carmen replied, "On behalf of the citizens of Wayzata, I accept your apology."

"Did he get a chance to talk with Doris before she left with Phil?"

"No, and he seemed to think I should have tied her to a chair or something to keep her here until he arrived."

"Mike usually suspects people are out to thwart his investigations. Sometimes he's right, but it's hard trying to remember the policeman is your friend when he's acting like that. Meanwhile, would you care if I asked you some questions, too? While your memory is all warmed up?"

"Among other things," said Carmen with a chuckle. "All right, I want somebody to make sense of this and bring an end to it. Doris says you have a wild card talent for solving crimes. If I can help you do that, I certainly will."

"All right, thank you. When you went to Thailand with Wendy and Lena, whose idea was it to go?"

"Lena's. She's the one who talked to me about it, anyway. It might have been Wendy's idea; she had been to Asia before, not Thailand but Indonesia and Japan and, I think, China."

"How do you know Lena?"

"Through our husbands. They met in college. Richard hunts, and he collects guns. He has some excellent bird guns—shotguns. Lena's husband, Tad, has always had a golden retriever or two. Richard and Tad go out together every fall hunting duck and pheasant, and so Lena and I started getting together with other hunting widows. I didn't get to know Lena well until about five years ago, really. But Wendy and Lena go way back—they were like sisters. Lena introduced me to Wendy. I think they met in high school, actually. I know they both went to Northwestern, both got degrees in fine arts. I'm a U of M grad myself, a master's in education."

"Wendy's husband is a hunter, too?" Betsy asked.

"Oh gosh, no. I don't think Frank knows which end of a gun the bullet comes out of."

"Okay, I think I understand all that. Now, when you three were in Thailand, did you meet a man named David Corvis?"

"Yes. Sergeant Malloy asked me about him, too. But I didn't get to know him or anything, I only met him for about a minute. I saw him with Lena and Wendy in the lobby of our hotel one morning and came over for an introduction. He was planning a trip with them, up north to Chiang Mai, to see silk still being made by women working alone—you know, as individuals. They invited me to go, too, but I'd gotten a tour ticket for Coral Island, in the Sea of Thailand, that was right in the middle of their three-day junket."

"So you didn't go up north with Wendy and Lena."

"No. They came back with some beautiful fabrics and about a hundred pictures. They were all excited."

"Did you see Mr. Corvis again?"

"No, just that one time. They talked about what a great guy he was, but I don't think they saw him again, either."

"What did they say about him?"

"Nothing much, just that he was a soldier who came to Thailand after the Vietnam war and started working in a silk factory. They said he knew just about everything there was to know about silk."

"It was interesting that he ran into Doris, though, wasn't it?"

"Yes. Sergeant Malloy was all interested in that, too. Do you think that's important, that he knew Wendy and Lena and then Doris?"

"Yes, I think it's very important. Carmen, I'm worried about Doris. Did you get Phil to tell you where he was taking her?"

"No. That is scary, isn't it? I know Phil loves Doris and I'm sure he thinks he's protecting her, but I really don't think hiding her himself is a good idea, do you?"

"I've been thinking about that. There are so many places for him to take her, it's impossible to figure out where they've gone. I'm concerned that there's no way to get in touch with them when this is over, but on the other hand, if we don't know where they are, it's not likely the person after her knows, either."

Betsy couldn't think of anything else to ask, so she wished Carmen a good night and hung up.

Her head was too full of conjecture and confusion to focus on recording the day's sales, so she clicked the program closed. Then she saw she was still logged on to the Internet—and that she already had a reply from Lillian. *His name is Ron Zommick, and he's in Bangkok right now, so don't phone him, e-mail him.* She gave Betsy the address, then continued:

What's up? Why do you want to contact him? You're still friends with Doris Valentine, aren't you? You could have contacted her, she has it. She saw Ron in Bangkok, and he showed her around. Do you want him to get you some silk? He may do that for you, if he isn't too busy. I'll e-mail him and tell him you'll be in touch. Don't forget, Thailand is eleven hours ahead of you and on the other side of the international date line, so if you're reading this in the evening, it's tomorrow morning over there.

Betsy thought, *Well then, when it's tomorrow evening there, is it yesterday morning over here?* For a moment she pictured the globe of the earth, one half toward the sun, the globe turning so the leading edge of dawn was always moving west. Somewhere tomorrow had to start; that's what the international date line was for. So no, if it was evening in Bangkok, it was the morning of the same day over here.

Betsy wrote a brief thanks to Lillian, then turned her attention to Mr. Zommick. She tried to think of a way to explain what she wanted without turning it into a very long story. Or scaring him off entirely. Finally she typed:

Hello, Ron Zommick! Lillian gave me your address and said I might ask a favor of you. There is a man in Bangkok named David Corvis. He is an American, an ex-marine, who manages a silk factory called Bright Works near the city and also owns a small export business on Silom Road, name unknown. Can you confirm that he's still at these places and get me his address, at home, the factory, or his export business? Please be discreet about this, he may be a rough customer. I may be able to tell you what this is about later, if you want to know. Thank you.

Betsy Devonshire

She wrote a much longer version, then rewrote it twice, read it over, sighed in dissatisfaction, and before she could change her mind entirely, pressed Send.

Twenty-one

ᏬᎧ ∘ ᎧᏬ

BETSY shut down her computer and sat awhile, trying to make sense of what she knew—but there were gaps. She had too many questions and not enough answers. She thought some more, then decided she needed something to focus her mind. She thought about stitching the sneezing Dalmatian, but it would call for all her concentration. What she was after was something that would leave her free to think and reason and ponder.

She went into her stash of yarn for a ball of mauve wool and some number ten needles. Then she sat down in her most comfortable chair, turned on the standard lamp behind it, and began to cast on stitches. That XOXO scarf she'd been knitting in her imagination at the art institute library had lingered at the back of her mind. It should work up pretty fast—though to make it fun, it should be extra long as well as extra skinny.

Perhaps she should make it as part of next year's Valentine's Day display: Sheepish Love and Kisses? No. Warm Love and Kisses? Better.

Meanwhile, as she had hoped, getting into the rhythm and repetitions of knitting settled her turbulent mind and allowed patterns to emerge.

She thought at first she didn't have enough data on this case to make a guess at its solution. But then she thought perhaps the opposite was true: There was a superabundance of data. Could there be too much? Maybe the problem was that she had collected the data out of order.

She began to list the events as they had come to her, beginning with Doris's return from Bangkok with the stone statue, and then tried sorting them into a chronology. First . . . well, first was the archaeological dig at the Han Dynasty site back in the 1980s that disclosed the embroidered silk. Then the immediate and subsequent thefts of that silk. Then . . . yes, Lena, Wendy, and Carmen's trip to Thailand. Doris's trip to Thailand . . . No, David Corvis's turning up to meet Wendy and Lena, then connecting with Doris. Doris's throwing the silk away and Betsy's retrieving it. Doris's taking the statue to Fitzwilliam in St. Paul. Fitzwilliam's murder. The burglary of Doris's apartment. The trip to St. Peter and the death of Wendy Applegate. Lena's murder. The shooting at Carmen Diamond's house.

As Betsy built a chronology of this complicated case, she looked for a pattern, a set of suspects. To her dismay, there didn't seem to be either.

She knit and thought, but nothing else came to her, and at last she tucked her needles into the ball of yarn and went to bed.

THE next morning Betsy came home from water aerobics, ate a quick breakfast, and as usual, took a few minutes to sit at her computer. She noted on her calendar that she would have double the entries to make on her bookkeeping program that evening. Falling behind on record keeping, the most dreary of small business ownership tasks, was one sure recipe for disaster. She absolutely must make up for her failure of yesterday.

Then she wrote an e-mail to Foster Johns, who had acted as a construction contractor for her before. She asked if he would be available to draw up an estimate for the remodeling of two apartments on the second floor of her building at 200 Lake Street.

When she connected to the Internet to send it, she saw that she had a reply from Ron Zommick in Bangkok:

Got your e-mail. Mysterious! But Lil says I should help you if I can, and I hope you will tell me what this is about as a reward for finding your man. Even though he's dead. Hit and run, outside his Silom Road office. It was in the newspaper, but I didn't remember his name. Happened a few days ago. They found the car that did it, a stolen Mercedes. The story is, some teenagers stole the car and were driving it recklessly. But no one's been arrested. Still want me to find out more about him? Or shall I drop it?

Ron

Betsy just sat staring at the screen. David Corvis, dead. The hair at the nape of her neck stood up.

What kind of murderer could reach halfway around the world? Because she did not for one instant think David Corvis was the victim of a careless teenaged car thief.

She clicked Reply, thanked Ron, and told him not to continue looking into David's business. She would contact him again in a few days, she wrote. She logged off and went to pencil in her eyebrows.

This was far, far too big a case for an amateur like her, she reflected. She should have realized that when she found out what the silk was, and that it had been an object of immense value and rarity sought by international art thieves. Betsy's forte was solving crimes committed by ordinary people, motivated by jealousy or hatred or a desire for revenge. When it was about money, it was the $10,000 left to Bertram by Aunt Kit who was dead under suspicious circumstances—not the sale of a unique piece of ancient embroidered silk. The workings of international smuggling rings were beyond her ken.

She needed to contact Carmen, warn her this was bigger than she'd dreamed, that an armed and dangerous husband might not be enough to protect her. And she needed to tell Doris the same thing. Plus tell Mike Malloy she was backing out of this case. The big problem? Doris was in hiding with Phil. And Betsy had no way of contacting either of them.

She reached for her phone and called Mike's office number. It was before his office hours, so she left a message explaining that she was quitting the case and why. "If you want to talk to me, I'll be in my shop all day."

She went downstairs and opened the shop, then phoned the Diamond house. The phone was answered by Richard. "Yeah?" he growled.

"It's me, Betsy Devonshire. I want to talk to both you and Carmen, if I may."

"She's not here!" Which Betsy was sure was a lie—but she didn't blame him for telling it.

"I just found out that David Corvis is dead. I'm not able to work on a case with international connections, so I'm quitting. Please tell Carmen that someone from Immigration and Customs Enforcement will probably want to talk to her in the near future. This is federal government business now."

"Right." The phone was disconnected by a crash so loud Betsy would not have been surprised to learn Richard had blown it to flinders with his shotgun.

Godwin came in a few minutes late. "It's so dim and gray out, I didn't believe my alarm when it went off," he explained. He looked around the place, decked for Easter in the colors of spring, with here and there the warmer colors of summer starting to show. "At least in here it feels like the sun is shining," he said.

"Well, that's good," Betsy said. "That was the effect we were after, remember? I'm glad it makes it a little less painful for you to come back to work."

"Can I ask you a question?" he said abruptly.

"Of course," said Betsy, taken aback by his tone.

"Why didn't you *call* me about *Doris*? Why didn't you let me *know*?"

"Because you didn't tell me where you were staying, remember? You said you wanted to get completely away from everything up here."

"Oh. Yeah. Well . . ." He shook his head. "I would have come home if I'd known. Have you had any more ideas about who's doing all this?"

"No. In fact, Goddy, I'm quitting. I can't solve this one, it's too big for me."

"Too big? I don't understand."

"This is about international smuggling, possibly run by organized crime. That's not at all the sort of crime I can solve. I'm just in the way. It's too big even for Mike—even for the St. Paul police. This is the kind of crime that Immigration and Customs Enforcement will investigate. Considering that I had never even heard of ICE until yesterday, you can see how out of my depth I am."

"Aw, now—" began Godwin, but he bit the scoffing off before it could begin. "You really think this is some big international crime?"

"I know it is. There was a man in Bangkok who got Doris to bring the stone Buddha back. He had earlier met Wendy and Lena over there, so he's more than likely a part of the smuggling enterprise. And now he's dead. A hit-and-run driver in a stolen car ran him over outside his export business in downtown Bangkok."

Godwin stared at her, his mouth making a small O. "And you think—"

Betsy nodded. "Yes. This particular scam fell apart, the silk came into the wrong hands, and they're covering their steps. Wendy killed the antiques shop owner and then was killed herself, and Lena was killed, and someone shot at Doris—twice, actually."

"What about Carmen?"

"She's been told to go into hiding, but she's staying at home, where her husband, who is a gun collector, is guarding her. I don't know if that's wise or foolish, because the bad people know where she lives. But on the other hand, who could she trust herself to? Who knows how far the reach of these people is?"

Godwin shivered. "Brrrr, no wonder you've decided this is too many for you." Godwin liked old-fashioned expressions, and he had picked this one up from a Mark Twain story.

T HE coffee in its urn had just begun to perk when Jill Cross Larson came in with Emma Beth holding on to one gloved hand. The child was dressed in a cranberry red wool coat with a black collar and cuffs. Heavy leggings knit in khaki wool covered her legs, with matching mittens and hat—the mittens hung loose from the sleeves of her coat by crocheted strings and the hat was in one hand. Emma Beth was radiantly fair, a natural platinum blond, and she turned a very pretty smiling face up at Betsy.

"Going to *Gran'pa's*!" she announced.

"Well, good for you! I hope you have a nice visit," replied Betsy.

Jill was a tall woman, nearly as fair as her daughter. About five months pregnant, her tummy was starting to press against her sky blue winter jacket. She said, "Lars has company. He and his visitors are going to talk *steam* for the next few days, maybe a week, and I thought maybe Emma Beth would get bored or something." She leaned forward, and her light blue eyes took on a special intensity as she said with slow emphasis, "Steam *boilers*, steam *locomotives*, and *Stanley Steamers*, they're going to let off a lot of *steam* over there. And I thought it might be good if Emma Beth and I got out of their way."

Betsy smiled and nodded. "I see." Lars owned a Stanley Steamer, Doris had a boiler license, and Phil once operated a steam locomotive.

A few years ago, Jill would have remained at home with Lars to guard the two refugees from violence. She had been an experienced and highly competent patrol officer. But now she was a stay-at-home mom. And while she could send Emma Beth away, she did not have that option with her unborn son.

"Does Mike Malloy know you're leaving Lars on his own?"

Jill nodded. "He says Lars won't be entirely on his own."

Good. That meant Lars was officially assigned to guard Phil and Doris, and the department would have his back if things got hairy.

After Jill left, Godwin came to say, "Does she think she's being subtle? I mean, *really*!"

"I would rather believe she thinks she's being subtle than the alternative, which is that I'm very dense."

Godwin chuckled. "But at least we know now where they went."

And it's not South Africa, thought Betsy. Or a lonesome cabin in the piney north woods. No, they were right here in town.

"Poor Doris," said Godwin. "Who would have guessed a fun vacation in Thailand would lead to this?"

"Yes," Betsy said thoughtfully, then, "You know, I was surprised when she said she wanted to go to Thailand. But you didn't seem all that amazed. She strikes me as a very quiet person, almost shy. Going to Thailand all by herself isn't the sort of thing I'd expect a shy person to do. What is it you know about her that I don't?"

"Well, first of all, she's not exactly shy. She's . . . she's reinventing herself. She comes from blue-collar people, she worked in a factory. She's always been a little afraid you'll see her trying to act uppity and run her off."

"Why would she think that?" Betsy demanded indignantly. "Because we *never*—"

"No, of course you never," interrupted Godwin. "None of us did. We know how to behave." He sighed. "But we noticed that ridiculous wig, and her overdone makeup, and that her hands were thick and clumsy because she did factory work, didn't we? If she'd really been one of us, someone would have mentioned these things to her, and maybe very gently offered to help her do things better. She saw us noticing. She felt ugly and rough, but none of us said anything, so she wasn't sure how or even if she should ask for advice."

Betsy fell into a half-shamed silence. Then her brain jumped into gear. "So how do you know all this? And why didn't you tell me, at least?"

"Because I didn't know how bad it was for her, not until just before she left. We had this nice, long talk. It wasn't the first one, but the deepest. You know how every so often I swear off dating?"

Betsy nodded. Godwin always fell in love hard and was vastly disappointed when an affair ended. He'd come in to work with his right hand raised, ready to swear—again—that he'd never let love run his life. Which it didn't, until the next time. But she didn't know he took his problems to Doris.

"It's just once in a while, when I can't stand myself for being such a ninny, I go visit Doris, or invite her to visit me. She's a good listener. She lets me pour out my pain and gives me hot cocoa or iced lemonade to drink—or asks me to make some, if it's my place—and tells me what a nice man I am until I feel better."

Betsy felt a squeeze on her heart; she didn't know about Doris's sympathetic nature. She considered Doris a friend, but she didn't know this very basic thing about her. "Apparently you're a good listener yourself."

"My dear, I like to think so. She did tell me something interesting about her trip to Thailand. Did you know the main reason she decided to go was Phil? She wants to look her best, so he can be proud of her."

"Oh, Goddy, that's so sweet!" said Betsy, feeling the squeeze.

"I think she looks amazingly better now that she's thrown that wig away. And that red hair just suits her—so fun!"

"Even her poor hands look better."

"I know. I'm so glad she went. If she thinks she looks nicer, she'll feel more like one of the crowd, and she'll be more comfortable around us, and will feel that we like her."

"Now don't go piling on and on, Goddy. We all like her fine

the way she is, and she's as valuable as anyone in the Monday Bunch. Remember how she joined Shelly and Alice and the others to run the shop so I could go find out who really murdered John Nye? She wasn't a voiceless little mouse in a dark, sad corner."

Godwin drew an indignant breath, then let it out. "You're right, of course. You know how I get carried away when I get an idea. But that doesn't mean what I'm saying about her is a lie. She *did* feel like she was missing out somehow, that she didn't know the right words or get the jokes everyone else was laughing at."

"Oh, then I'm going to have to tell her about something I read in a John D. MacDonald novel once. The hero is feeling depressed and tells a friend he feels the whole world is sitting around a campfire singing songs he doesn't know while he is stuck out in the weeds by his lonesome. And the friend says, 'But don't you know? That's universal! Everyone in the whole world feels like that!' "

Godwin stared at her. "We do?" He frowned and shook his head. "Well, yes, I guess some of us do."

"Most of us, at least some of the time. It's because none of us is truly privy to the ugliness in other peoples' lives. We each think we're the only one struggling, that others have found the secret and we haven't."

"*Sometimes* I think I've found the secret," said Godwin, but more to himself than to Betsy. Then he shook himself and said, "Are you really quitting the case?"

She nodded. "Yes."

"Now that you know where Doris and Phil are, are you going to go over there and talk to them?"

"No. I think it's best if we all just stay away from them, at least for now. Although I'm grateful that Phil did the right thing and got the local police involved in hiding Doris."

Godwin shook his head. "*There's* a really bad case of a person having no idea what's going on in the minds of people around him. He actually thinks no one knows about him and Doris!"

"I don't think that's true. I think all he wants is deniability. He comes from a period when people had private lives and tried to protect that privacy. And good people were ashamed to pry."

"He is kind of old, isn't he? When did that change?"

"Oh, in the seventies," said Betsy with the conviction of an eyewitness. " 'Let it all hang out'—that was the motto." She shook her head. "People thought it was a good idea at the time, but really, some things are not improved by letting in the sunlight."

"Strange ideas old people have," said Godwin. "Do you think you could have found them if Jill hadn't come in and told you?"

"I don't know. Probably not. Finding people who have gone into hiding . . ." She shrugged. "I don't know how to find lost people."

"Makes me wish Mr. Keen were real, and still around."

"Who?"

"*Mr. Keen, Tracer of Lost Persons*—an old radio show."

Betsy smiled. "You and your old radio shows. *Fibber McGee and Molly, Lum and Abner*, now *Mr. Keen*. Who will you be talking about next?"

Godwin could not resist that straight line. He intoned, "The Shadow knows."

Twenty-two

~ ⋅ ~

THE Monday Bunch was in session. It was a subdued meeting because the members were all close friends and Doris and Phil, who were members in good standing, were missing.

Betsy was working on the counted cross-stitch of the Dalmatian. It was a bright but overcast day and the light coming through the front window helped her to see the subtle differences in the shades of white on the puppy's face. Betsy sold all kinds of artificial lighting that advertised itself as "full spectrum" or "just like natural daylight," but while some of the lamps came close, none of them really replicated the real thing. Betsy had no idea why this was the case.

Alice was crocheting another in her endless series of acrylic afghan squares, which she sewed together into blankets sent by her church to African orphans.

Emily was there, knitting a tiny blue sweater, not for the baby she was carrying but for Jill's.

Godwin was nearly at the toe of his white-on-white argyle sock; his fingers moved as if of their own accord while his sympathetic eyes looked around the table.

Bershada was ornamenting the legs of a pair of jeans with dandelions, doing the yellow blooms in turkey work, an embroidery stitch done as a mass of close-set loops. She was currently using a tiny pair of scissors to snip off the tips of the loops forming a flower to give a realistic fuzzy effect.

Nobody was saying much; in fact, nobody had said much during the past half hour.

Finally Godwin sighed, "There, finished!" and pulled the yarn through to finish the toe of his sock.

The others were willing to take that as a signal to wind up, and in a very few minutes, still mostly in silence, they pushed in their chairs, put on their coats, hats, scarves, and mittens, and made for the door.

Their exit was complicated by the entry of Sergeant Mike Malloy. Seeing him made them all pause and try to think of a reason to linger—he looked weighty with news. But Mike was a cop and could command movement with a glance. In a single efficient movement of his head, he caught each woman's eye, and the glint in his own eye made each conclude that her initial decision to go home was correct.

When the Bunch had gone, Mike leaned back, then forward, looking to see if there was a customer in the part of the shop beyond the box shelves. Satisfied that he was there alone with Godwin and Betsy, he allowed an indefinable expression to resolve itself into unhappy excitement. He unbuttoned his heavy wool overcoat and came to the table where the two stood behind their chairs. He touched his top lip with the end of his tongue as he looked for the words to begin.

"May I offer you a cup of coffee, Mike?" offered Betsy.

Thus prodded, he finally spoke, "No, no. I came in to tell you there's been a break in the case you've, ah, been assisting the department with."

Godwin made a tiny sound of interest but quickly stifled it. He did not want to be sent from the room.

"I told you I had withdrawn from the case," Betsy said with quiet reproach.

"It doesn't matter now, because even as we speak the Wayzata police are making an arrest."

"Wayzata?" She frowned at him. "Oh, but Mike, that would mean . . . No!"

"I'm afraid so. They're arresting Carmen Diamond for the murder of Lena Olson."

Godwin groaned softly.

Betsy said, "But that can't be right! Do you mean to say that *Carmen* is a *master criminal*?"

"No, of course she's not," said Mike. "For one thing, none of the murders that we're investigating were done by professionals. A crime boss would have ordered up a professional hit man. A professional wouldn't have bungled the attempt to make Lena's death look like a suicide. And he wouldn't have shot at a reflection in a mirror instead of at Doris."

Betsy stared at him. "But you told me this smuggling operation was run by someone with contacts around the world, someone involved with a whole network of criminals!"

"And I still think that's the case. The overall case, smuggling valuable stolen art into the United States, that is. Something like that is not the work of amateurs or even everyday crooks. But these organizations will hire or involve amateurs or small-time criminals in a particular operation. That's what we think happened here. And when it started to go wrong, when the important artifact they were sending over disappeared, the word went out to the amateurs: find it, bring it back, or something lethal is going to happen to you.

"Oh, I see." Betsy nodded. "That would explain Wendy's journey through a blizzard to St. Peter and her screaming outrage when Doris said she didn't have the silk."

Godwin said, "She must have been terrified. But then, so was Doris."

"And Phil," said Betsy. "And Bershada. And Alice. And Shelly. And the March Hare's manager. That was an altogether terrifying night."

"But she didn't get the silk back," said Mike.

Betsy nodded. "Because Doris didn't have it. I was wondering why Wendy would have thought she did, but when I read the e-mail Doris sent me from St. Peter again, it doesn't mention Bershada, Alice, or Shelly, and it doesn't say they were on their way back here when they had to stop because of the snow. When Wendy opened that e-mail, she must've thought Doris and Phil were leaving town—with the silk."

"Maybe she wasn't actually going to kill Doris but just get the silk back," said Godwin. "And she took the gun to frighten her." Godwin looked inquiringly at Mike.

"I think the decision to kill Doris had been made when Wendy started for St. Peter," said Mike. "Wendy may have felt forced to that decision; maybe it was forced on her by the person who sent her."

Betsy agreed. "They didn't want anyone around to testify that it was Wendy who came down with the gun. Especially after she'd already murdered Oscar Fitzwilliam in his antiques shop."

She looked at Mike, who said, "The revolver Ms. Applegate was carrying that night in St. Peter was the same gun that killed Mr. Fitzwilliam." He raised a forefinger and suddenly realized that he was still wearing his leather gloves. He pulled them off a couple of fingers at a time while he continued to speak. "Here's an odd little detail: She got someone else to load it. His—or her—fingerprints are on the shell casings, not Wendy's."

"Isn't that kind of unusual?" Betsy asked. "If I were going to go kill someone, I wouldn't show someone else my weapon."

Godwin asked, "It isn't hard to load a revolver, is it?"

"No, it isn't," said Mike. "We think the person who loaded it is the person who sold it to her."

"How many shots were fired in the antiques shop?" asked Betsy.

"I'm not sure. Two or three, I think."

"But when she took it with her to St. Peter, the shells weren't replaced?"

Mike squinted at her. "Oh, I see what you're getting at."

"Yes, either she went down there without a fully loaded gun, or she went back to the salesperson and got him to replace the used shells."

"Either of those scenarios is doubtful," said Mike. "So neither is probably what happened. I wonder if the stranger's fingerprints are on all the shell casings." He got out his notebook and wrote something in it. "In any case, I think that's a small detail, easy to clear up," he said. "Her fingerprints are all over the outside of the gun, and no one else's."

"How did he load it without getting his fingerprints on the outside?" asked Betsy.

Mike shrugged that question off without answering it. He was here to deliver a conclusion. "What we think happened is this: These three—Wendy, Lena, and Carmen—went to Bangkok, Thailand, a few years ago and met a man in the export business. Probably the meeting was prearranged by Wendy, who had been buying Asian products for her employer for several years. At first Wendy and Lena started a legitimate import business. But they couldn't make a success of it, so when their contact in Bangkok suggested a way to bypass those pesky customs charges, they made a deal with him. And that was like the camel's nose in the tent. Pretty soon they were accepting stolen goods."

Betsy suggested, "This silk business may have been their first venture into high-end stolen artifacts."

But Mike shook his head. "This is far too high end for them to have trusted it to an untested crew."

"Wait, Carmen wasn't involved in the import business," Betsy pointed out. "Besides, she was out of town when the silk was sent to the United States."

"We don't know what her level of involvement was," said Mike. "And she didn't have to be here to have a role in that silk smuggling deal. Remember, she was supposed to go to Bangkok with Doris."

"All right, but how could she be the one who shot at Doris?"

asked Betsy. "She was in the house with her husband, and the shot came from outside."

"She was in the kitchen by herself," said Mike. "And her husband was in his den by himself. Easiest thing in the world to sneak out the back door, around to the side, and shoot. Then toss the gun into the garbage can to be taken away the next morning, come back around and into the kitchen to tell everyone you had been ducked down beside the refrigerator, too scared to move."

"Did you find it, then?" asked Godwin. "The gun?"

"Yes. In the neighbor's garbage, actually. No fingerprints, of course."

"Not even on the bullets?" asked Godwin.

"But she missed," said Betsy.

"Yes, well, we're talking amateurs here." Mike made a sly grimace at Betsy, because her methods were here shown to be rubbing off on him. "Also, Doris was a friend, a good friend of some years' standing. Perhaps at the last instant she jerked the gun just a little."

Betsy said, "I still don't believe this happened the way you're saying, Mike. I saw the two of them together, and they were very close friends. Carmen would never shoot Doris."

"When your life's on the line—"

Godwin burst out, "Carmen wouldn't shoot Doris for *any* reason! They were like *sisters*!" He turned to Betsy. "You have to *do* something! They're getting it all *wrong*!"

Mike looked at her, too, and seemed about to say something, then didn't.

"Mike?" said Betsy.

"All right, I don't like it, either. I don't know how close those two are, but it doesn't feel right to me, either."

"So what are you going to do about it?"

"It's not my place to second-guess detectives in other jurisdictions. I'm going to go over to the Larson place and tell Lars that an arrest has been made and that his assignment as guardian of Mr. Galvin and Ms. Valentine is ended."

"I don't think you should do that, Mike."

"I'm acting under orders, Betsy." With tired gestures, he pulled on his coat and shoved his hands back into his gloves, and went out.

" 'I am a man subject to authority,' " murmured Betsy, watching him go.

"What?" said Godwin.

"It's from the New Testament. A man was sent to Jesus to ask for a cure for his slave. Jesus started to come to his house, but the man sent others to tell him never mind, he was not worthy to have Jesus come under his roof, because he was 'a man subject to authority,' meaning he had other bosses he had to obey and people he must boss around."

"Poor Mike," said Godwin, looking at the closed door Mike had just gone through. Then he turned to Betsy. "Okay, this puts it back in your arena, girl. It isn't a big, international crime ring doing this but a local amateur. And that means you can figure out who Mike should be arresting instead of Carmen."

Betsy sat down.

"I'll bring you a cup of tea," said Godwin.

Betsy bent sideways and pulled the skinny pink XOXO scarf out of the needlepoint bag on the floor at her feet.

G ODWIN silently set a cup of strong black English tea—with extra sugar for energy—in front of Betsy, then slipped away to sort and stack sales slips at the checkout desk. He kept a covert eye on her.

As he watched, her movements with the knitting needles, at first sharp and jerky, became smooth and regular, and then small and very even. Her lower lip, which had been thrust outward, began to to relax. When that happened, he got out a pair of number six knitting needles and a hank of Berroco Ultra Alpaca Light yarn. It really was very light; a 144-yard hank of it weighed just one and three-quarters ounces.

He had found Berocco's Web site and a set of instructions for tiny sweaters just thirteen or fourteen stitches across. They were actual sweaters, with a front and back and open sleeves, and were meant to be used as Christmas tree ornaments. Godwin wanted to try them out—the instructions said one could be completed in an evening—and if that were true, he wanted to offer a class in knitting them in the fall.

He was doing the striped one, four rows of one color, two of a contrasting color, then four of the first color again. It only took four double rows of the contrast color to reach the arms of the doll-sized garment.

He was casting on an additional six stitches on one side for the sleeve when he heard an exclamation from Betsy.

"What, what is it?" he asked.

"Mashan silk!" she said. "I never said Mashan silk!"

"What's Mashan silk?" asked Godwin.

"Mashan is a place in China, the place where that Han Dynasty silk came from."

"Never heard of it."

"I think only people familiar with archaeological digs in China, or a particular piece of ancient silk, know about Mashan." Betsy picked up the cordless phone from the middle of the table and punched in a number. She listened, punched another number, then said rapidly, "Mike, it's Betsy. Please call me right away." Then she cut the connection and started to make another call. "Goddy, could you go get my coat, please?"

When he came back with the coat, she was saying, "Yes, Jenna told me she thought it was awfully early for that to be starting. Thank you." She put the phone down.

Godwin helped her into the coat. "Where are you going?" he asked.

"Over to the Larson house. I tried calling Mike's cell, but he must have it turned off." She pulled her knit hat on as she hurried to the door. "If Mike calls, ask him to call me right away."

She waved her cell phone at him and was gone.

Twenty-three

❦ ∘ ❧

THE sun had not set, but the temperature had fallen nearly to zero. In just the minute it took Betsy to cross the tiny parking lot out back to her car, the tip of her nose began to sting and the movement of her legs brought icy air up inside her long coat past her knees. She wished she'd worn a pantsuit.

The sky had glowed whitely all day behind a thin, uniform cloud cover which now was darkening as the sun—a mere lighter blur above the clouds—dropped in the southwest.

Betsy started her car and turned the defroster to high as the windows quickly fogged over. It had snowed just an inch last night, not enough to make her summon the man with the little plow on the front of his pickup but enough to freshen up the layers already sagging tiredly over the landscape. Severe cold made the snow whine and groan under her car's tires as she drove out onto the street.

She turned right and went up to where Excelsior Boulevard

came in at an angle to Second Street, and then turned left. Past Maynard's, the nice waterfront restaurant, she turned left again, onto St. Alban's Bay Road.

She drove past the boat sales and service stores, past a pair of identical cottages near where the Stanley Steamer had blown up, past six finer houses behind a row of leafless trees, to Weekend Lane. The little street was only three houses long, ending at Jill and Lars's home on the shore of Lake Minnetonka. The property was over an acre in size, irregular in shape, and set with mature trees. The house had been built as a small cottage, but Lars had built an addition that doubled its size and gave it an attached garage. Lars had also built a big heated shed with a concrete apron in front for his antique Stanley Steamer automobile.

More recently he had surrounded the property with a cyclone fence, for now there was a toddler in residence. Emma Beth could swim, after a fashion, but she was curious, fearless, and inclined to forget instructions when excited—such as not to swim alone. The huge lake at the bottom of the lawn was a glittering attraction to the little girl. And now there was to be another little one with eyes to gleam at the sight.

Not that there was any chance of swimming today; the lake was an immense meadow of snow-covered ice.

The gate that normally blocked the driveway was open, and Betsy drove through. The drive was not plowed, but tire tracks in the snow showed it wasn't very deep. Past a dense set of gray-brown sticks that would bloom with lilacs in a few months, she could see the barnlike shed and off to the right, the cottage. Both were painted a rustic red-brown and had dark brown shingles on their roofs. The driveway split near its end, one part going to the attached garage, the other to the shed.

She looked for, but didn't see, the modest sedan that Mike drove when on official police business. He must have already come and gone. She followed a set of tire prints up onto the apron in front of the shed and stopped. Shutting her engine off, she pulled her cell phone from her purse to make sure it was turned on. It was. So why hadn't he called?

She punched in Mike's number at the police department, but before her phone could begin to ring the car door was yanked open. Betsy looked up to see a man standing there, a gun in one gloved hand. Shocked, she dropped the phone.

He was a tall man, very trim even in a long overcoat of dark gray wool. He wore a stylized dark gray fedora that was almost a cowboy hat, a rakish affectation that made her recognize him at once, though she'd only seen him briefly two or three times before.

"Joe!" she said.

"Hi, Betsy. I'm really sorry about this," he said, and such was the distress on his face that her first impulse was to offer some words of comfort.

But she managed to hold them back—the gun in his hand was pointing at her face, after all—and instead she said, "What do you want?"

"Move over, I'll be driving. We need to go someplace private."

Without moving, Betsy asked, "How did you find me?"

"I followed you from your store. I was hoping you'd stop someplace where I could get to you. I'm glad you did—it makes this so much easier. No, don't get out!"

But Betsy was out of the car before he had finished speaking. "Wh . . . why do you have to take me anywhere?"

"To kill you. Because you know who I am. That is, you know what I am."

Edging very, very slowly down the length of her Buick, Betsy asked in as mild a tone as she could muster, "What are you?" Then she broke and ran down the driveway, veering from side to side, trying not to stumble, desperately hoping it was true that handguns in the hands of amateurs are very inaccurate at more than a few yards.

There was a tiny tug at the sleeve of her coat followed immediately by a loud bang.

She screamed and ran off the driveway in among the tall trees and snow-clogged shrubs. Her feet crunched the snow loudly. Another report sounded, but this time the shot did not seem to come near her. She fled to the largest tree and stopped, heart pounding. She extended her left arm and turned it to look at the back of the sleeve. She saw a small, frayed tear just below the elbow that had not been there when she put the coat on. He'd nearly hit her! She rubbed the hole with her right hand, as if that could erase it.

A troubled silence had settled in. Betsy strained her ears for the sound of footsteps, but could hear nothing. Where was he? There'd been no sound of a car starting up. Was he still on the property? Perhaps he had run away. She began to make her way in the direction of her car, trying unsuccessfully to step quietly.

Here among the trees, the snow had blown into deep drifts. Warmer weather earlier that week had softened the drifts, but now they had frozen up again, just enough to hold her weight briefly. She would step up onto one, and then her boot would crunch through. She had to lift her foot high to get it clear of the crusted snow. Betsy paused very briefly between each step to listen, but still, walking was like working a StairMaster while wearing heavy clothing. In a very few minutes she was gasping for air and prickly with fear-sweat.

Where was Joe? She felt a pressure on the middle of her back, as if someone were aiming a weapon at her, and whirled around to see . . . nothing. She listened intently—was that a footstep? But now there was only silence. The light was failing quickly, she couldn't stay out here in the dark.

Then, all of a sudden, she did hear something. It was like an old-fashioned steam locomotive whistle, except smaller, and not coming from the direction of the one active railroad line near Excelsior.

But she knew what it meant. She was saved.

She turned and ran back toward the driveway just as a large, square-built, flat-fendered, forest green car came rolling smoothly through the gates. So that's why they'd been left open! Lars had gone for a drive with the old car. Betsy stopped before reaching the driveway, looking in both directions. There were a man's footprints besides her own, black on the surface of the drive. She backed up two steps.

Lars hadn't put the top up, and Betsy could see he had two passengers in the backseat.

They were Phil and Doris, laughing as they were pressed to-gether sideways as the antique car bent around the turn into the driveway. Stanleys, having no transmission, generate tremen-dous torque; this model's narrow tires did not lose any of their grip on the snow-covered lane. Lars, behind the wheel, was laughing, too. He reached for controls on the upright dashboard as the old car slowed.

"Lars! Lars!" shouted Betsy, starting to run after it. The trio in the car, startled, looked around at her.

But after her struggles in the snowdrifts, she could run no more than a few strides. Her chest ached, it was impossible to take a deep-enough breath. She stopped and, desperate to warn them with as few words as possible, shouted, "He's got a *gun!*"

Brakes on antique cars are notoriously weak. Lars stopped the Stanley by the simple expedient of throwing it into reverse. The car instantly gave a little hop backward, dumping momentum, at which point Lars closed the throttle and applied the old brakes. Betsy could hear him shout, "Get down, get down!" while gesturing at Doris and Phil, who vanished into the depths of the capacious backseat.

He leaped out of the car, unzipping his fur-edged parka as he ran toward Betsy. He grabbed her by one arm and drew a revolver from a shoulder holster with his other hand, pulling her off the drive and into the shelter of a lilac bush.

"Who has a gun?" he demanded, looking around. He was a very tall man with broad shoulders and big hands. He had blond hair and light gray eyes, and his expression, normally good-humored, was at the moment shockingly grim and preternaturally alert.

"Dr. Joe Brown. He's the murderer, Lars. I was coming here to tell Mike, but I missed him, and Joe followed me."

"Where is Joe now?"

Betsy, with a quaver in her voice, replied, "I don't know.

He shot at me, Lars. I've been running and hiding. If you hadn't come back . . ." She stifled a sob. "He said I knew—and he's right, I do. He killed the antiques store man, and Lena Olson—"

"You can tell me this later," Lars interrupted her brusquely. "Let's get under cover. Come on!"

He hustled her back to the Stanley—he hadn't let go of her arm—and said, through the door, "We have a man with a gun here, and need to get into the house."

"Oh, my God!" muttered Phil from somewhere within the car.

Lars wrenched the door open. "Out, fast!"

Phil came out first, clumsily trying to both hurry and keep his head down. He reached back to assist Doris.

"Drop that gun!" said a voice.

When Phil let go of Doris to spin around, she fell out of the car. She gave a cry of pain as her knees struck the icy driveway.

"Give it up, Joe!" shouted Lars, turning, starting to raise his own gun.

"I'll shoot Betsy first!" countered Joe.

Phil, murmuring words of comfort, helped Doris to her feet, then pulled her close beside him, one arm around her waist. Betsy edged sideways to stand beside Phil.

Then they all faced the man with the gun in watchful, respectful silence.

"I mean it," said Joe. His hand trembled, but his face was clenched with determination.

Lars had not yet brought his gun to bear on Joe. He hesitated, then tossed it aside.

"Who are you, anyway?" Joe demanded.

"I'm Sergeant Lars Larson, Excelsior police," said Lars in an angry voice. "Who are you?"

"Po . . . po . . ." Joe gaped at Lars in clear dismay, then pulled his mouth shut with an effort.

Betsy took this opportunity to identify him. "He's Dr. Joseph Brown," she said. "A member of the board of directors of the Minneapolis Art Institute."

Joe pulled himself together. He grasped his gun more firmly, giving it a little shake and said, "Everybody, just stay where you are!"

"All right," said Lars agreeably, spreading his hands. "Fine. But you're in a lot more trouble now than you were just a few minutes ago."

"Yes, I agree, it's gotten complicated," agreed Joe, "but I think I can manage." He sounded calm now. He turned his attention to Phil. "So who are you?"

"I'm Phil Galvin, retired railroad engineer."

"Who are you?" he asked Doris.

Betsy said quickly, "I'm Betsy Devonshire."

"I know who you are," said Joe. "The source of all my trouble."

"She's not the source, you are!" growled Phil. "Stupid jerk! You're the one killing people over a piece of old silk!" He had wordlessly conspired with Betsy to keep Doris's name out of this.

"You don't understand!" cried Joe, and the gun in his hand wavered. "Nobody was supposed to die! That wasn't the plan at all!"

He began to approach the group, moving at an angle that led him toward the front of the old car, eyes shifting constantly as he kept track of everyone. As he walked, his expression hardened. Betsy was terrified he'd come to a deadly decision.

But: "What kind of a car is this?" he asked, surprising her.

"It's a 1911 Stanley Steamer," said Lars, glancing around at it. Even with its top down, the car was taller than he was. The brass surround of its bolt-upright windshield and large headlights gleamed in the failing light, and its green finish was without flaw. Its big wheels had wooden spokes, painted yellow. A startling touch was a big brass dragon resting on the right front fender, mouth agape. Betsy considered running behind the car—she was sure it was bulletproof. Could doing that get her enough time to pull her cell phone out and dial 911?

Oh, wait. Her cell phone was in her car; she'd dropped it when Joe had opened her car door.

Joe said wistfully, "I wish this weren't happening. I wish we were meeting here as friends. Then I might talk with you about this car. Instead, things are about to get a little tricky."

White-faced Doris took a step backward, trying to put the fender with the dragon on it between herself and Joe, but he took two steps sideways and one step closer so she remained within range of his gun.

"Don't move, sir!" he said to Phil, who had been about to put himself between Doris and Joe. Phil hunched his shoulders and balled his fists but obeyed. "Oh, you haven't been protecting her by your silence, you know," said Joe. "I know she's Doris Valentine. If she had just done what was asked of her, we'd all be just fine." His voice was weighty with anger and unmade threats.

Betsy said quickly, "Joe, I've left phone messages all over the place, saying you're the murderer they're looking for. What good will it do for you to kill us?"

He sneered, "Oh, I'm sure you'd like to convince me of that. But what if you can't?" He pointed the gun at her. "In fact, what if I start off by—"

And suddenly there came an enormous rushing sound. A warm thick fog billowed forward and outward, doubling in sound and size as it did. It clogged the air, engulfing first Joe, then the rest of them. It was warm . . . Oh! Not fog, Betsy realized. Steam. Blinded, she put her hand out and found the smooth side of the car. And that was when she heard a loud, shrill scream, louder than any human throat should produce. She could feel the metal vibrate under the racket.

"Down! Down!" shouted Lars, barely audible over the scream, and Betsy immediately fell on her face. Was the car going to explode?

A shot was fired. The scream was silenced. Had the screamer been human after all?

Then sounds of struggle could be heard: feet scraping, blows being struck, grunts. The steam seemed to roil and Betsy thought she could see figures struggling in it. "Grab his other arm!" Phil shouted. "Ow! Let go!" There was a heavy thud—a body falling?—and more grunting. Then she heard a metallic clatter and slide, and the gun suddenly bumped up against Betsy's side. Joe's gun. Betsy concealed it with an arm.

"Gimme your hand!" That was Lars. "Gimme your *hand*!"

She heard the scraping of feet. The sound of a punch landing, a man's cry of pain. A curse, more grunts and struggling, a sharp, cracking punch, then a panting voice—Joe's: "Stop it! Stop it! All right! All right, I quit!"

A small scraping sound of metal closing on metal—*Handcuffs*, thought Betsy—then Lars calling, "Shut that valve off!"

The rushing noise diminished and finally stopped. The steam rolled upward, thinning as it went. In seconds the air was clear.

"What the hell *was* that?" demanded a rumpled Joe from on his knees, his fine coat pulled crookedly on his body, the effect underlined by his arms pulled behind his back. A bruise was forming on one cheekbone. He was getting up, roughly helped by Lars and Phil. The coats of all three were marred with clean and dirty snow.

"Just letting off a little steam," said Lars, pulling Joe the rest of the way to his feet. "Good work, Phil. And that was well done, Doris!"

Betsy, climbing slowly to her feet, said, "Was that you?"

Doris, speaking for the first time, said modestly, "I just opened the steam relief valves and blew the whistle."

"That's my girl!" said Phil, grinning at her. She looked at him then, and matched his grin with one of her own.

Just then, a very strange sound, a kind of eerie howl, started coming from the car.

Joe staggered backward in alarm, stumbling over the heaps of frozen snow that lined the drive, pulling Lars along with him.

"Get back here, you jerk, it's all right!" said Lars, dragging

Joe forward again. To the others he explained, "The old car sings when she's building a head of steam. Or rebuilding one."

"Shouldn't take long," said Doris. Still standing on the running board, she leaned over the door to look inside. "There's still about three hundred p.s.i. in the boiler."

"That damned old contraption ought to be against the law," grumbled Joe, embarrassed.

"Why, Joe, I thought you just *loved* antiques!" said Lars.

Phil hustled over to help Doris off the running board. He reached out with a gloved hand and caressed the Stanley's flat fender. "Thank God for this old contraption!" he said loudly, in his deaf old man's voice. Then with the same hand, he patted Doris on the shoulder. "And God bless my brilliant, quick-thinking honey!" he added, only a little less loudly.

"Amen," said Betsy to herself, and sat down hard on the running board.

Twenty-four

ꙭ◦ꙭ

A T the police station, Joe was read his Miranda rights. He stared at the uniformed police officer reciting them, eyebrows raised, and when the officer concluded, "Do you understand these rights as I have read them to you?" he nodded. "Do you wish to waive your rights and answer questions at this time?"

A ghost of a smile touched his mouth. "Considering the circumstances of my arrest, I don't think it matters, does it? So yes, of course I'll waive . . . No, hold on. Maybe . . . maybe I'd better not. I think I ought to at least talk to a lawyer."

He was shown to a phone and, since he had no idea whom to call, was permitted to select a name from the phone book. He chose the biggest ad for a criminal defense attorney in the yellow pages, dialed the number, and got an answering service. He was served a lukewarm cup of black coffee while he waited for an attorney to call him back.

Betsy, meanwhile, sat with Doris and Phil in the lobby of the police station under the cool eye of the watch sergeant behind his desk. It had been nearly an hour since they had arrived, and no one had spoken to them other than to ask them to sit down and be patient. Betsy was starting to feel hungry and was thinking of asking the sergeant if they could send out for something when Mike Malloy strode in.

His thin mouth was reduced to a mere line, his eyes were narrow under brows drawn together. He was white with anger, making the freckles strewn across his nose and cheeks look as dark as currents.

She felt a stab of alarm. What was he angry about? Who was he mad at?

She stood and received another shock as his cold blue eyes slammed into her.

"You," he said, pointing at her. "Follow me." He turned and walked away, confident she would obey.

She did, down one corridor, then another. In front of a door in the hall stood Lars, who had somewhere along the way gotten into uniform. When he saw them coming, he straightened into something like attention and reached for the doorknob.

But Mike waved dismissively at him and turned to the other door, which led into his small office. Betsy followed.

She'd been here before, had seen its two metal desks pushed head to head, its twin posture chairs behind them, the identical hard chairs pulled up beside them. Mike pulled off his overcoat and hung it on a wood and brushed-metal coatrack in the far corner. He turned and sat at the neater of the two desks and gestured for Betsy to sit down.

Betsy wanted to know if Carmen had been released. She

wondered if Mike knew that Joe Brown was the real murderer. Had anyone told him of their recent adventure in the Larson front yard?

But there is a time to speak and a time to keep silent. Betsy felt this was the latter. She sat and bit her tongue.

"First of all," said Mike in a thin, hard voice, "I'm sorry I wasn't here when Dr. Brown decided to prove your theory that he was a murderer. I'm very grateful that I'm not standing out at the end of Weekend Lane counting bodies and collecting evidence. It seems you—all of you, Lars, Ms. Valentine, Mr. Galvin, and yourself—behaved with great courage. You did a very *stupid* thing going out there, but the four of you brought down a dangerous man using nothing more lethal than a steam-powered automobile."

Betsy felt her lips begin to tremble and pulled them into a smile. "Thank you, Mike. But I wasn't brave—Doris was the brave one. I couldn't think of anything but running away. I was so . . . so *scared* . . ." To her dismay, she began to cry.

"That's not the way I heard it," Mike said. He leaned sideways to open a bottom drawer and lift out a box of Kleenex, which he handed to her.

She didn't allow the storm to last long; she knew there was a lot of official paperwork to do and didn't want to slow up the process and keep them here all night.

She blew her nose one last time and said, "I'm all right now. What did you want to talk to me about?"

There came a tap on the door, which opened just a few inches. Lars was on the other side. "You goin' to be long?" he asked.

"I hope not. Is someone talking to Ms. Valentine and Mr. Galvin?"

"Yeah, Sergeant Windemere just got here." Windemere was Mike's partner, the occupant of the other desk.

"Fine," said Mike, nodding. He was pulling a yellow legal pad from the center drawer and apparently didn't notice that Lars had carelessly pulled the door to without checking to see that it latched.

He wrote something at the top of the blank page and said to Betsy, "Tell me about Joe Brown."

"He's a murderer, Mike," said Betsy. "He killed Lena Olson and he tried to kill Carmen, and I wouldn't be surprised if *he's* the one who murdered poor Oscar Fitzwilliam, instead of Wendy. You check those fingerprints on the shells in the revolver—I'll bet they're his."

"How did you come to this conclusion?"

"I started by thinking he might be the collector."

"What made you think that?"

"Someone told me he was an expert in Asian art, that he already has a collection of very old and fine artifacts. Nobody else I know who was involved in this mess has those credentials. Plus, Wendy and Lena were amateurs, and probably Mr. Fitzwilliam was an amateur, too, so this was likely a local operation. That meant the buyer—the collector—was local. And he kept turning up, calling me every couple of days about raising my pledge to the art institute."

Mike stopped writing. "So?"

"Well, it's not time for the pledge drive to start. I didn't realize that at first, it wasn't until today that I called and found out the drive isn't scheduled for another ten days. What he was really af-ter was to know if I knew anything about Doris and the silk." She smiled. "Funny thing, I actually told him about this old silk rag I found the second or third time he called. I started to describe it to him but got interrupted. And since I didn't know what it was, my partial description was so far off he didn't recognize it."

She stopped her narrative to ask, "Have you seen it, Mike?"

He shook his head. "No. I've seen that photograph of it you obtained. I don't think it's particularly Chinese-looking, but I'm certainly no expert. Funny-looking animals, especially the bird. If you had described it so he recognized it, and he said he wanted it, what would you have done?"

Betsy had to think about that. "I'd have said no. But he couldn't have tried to buy it from me, not without hinting that it was something special. He had no claim to it otherwise."

"So the only way to have gotten it from you would have been to steal it. And you'd have ended up dead like Fitzwilliam, be-cause he'd've had to kill you to keep you from telling anyone he was asking about it."

Betsy felt her mouth go dry. She swallowed hard and said, "That's a very ugly thought."

Mike sighed, made another note, and asked, "Now, you say you didn't ask about the fund drive until today. What made you suspect him earlier?"

"I called him to ask him to get an appointment for me with an expert in textiles at the art institute, which he very kindly did. So, naturally, after I saw Dr. Booker, I told him next time he called that the silk I found wasn't a variant on a contempo-rary design but an important silk artifact from the Han Dynasty.

And he was terrifically impressed, of course. He asked me if I knew what a privilege it was to hold a piece of Mashan silk in my hands. But I never specified Mashan to him, so how did he know?"

Mike wrote that down. "Nice catch," he murmured.

"Thank you. Mike, why did you turn off your cell phone?"

"You mean earlier today? Because I was helping handle an arrest. Why didn't you phone the police station in Wayzata?"

"I did. But I didn't know the names of the investigators over there, so I think the person I talked to only pretended to write down my message that they were arresting the wrong person."

"You were a little excited by then, probably?"

Betsy felt herself blush. "Yes, probably. I may have shouted at her—the person who took the call."

"Uh-huh. Next time, don't shout. So let's get into the events of this afternoon. Why did you go over to the Larson place?"

"I wanted to talk to you, I was hoping you were still there. But when I got arrived, no one was there at all." Betsy described what happened next in as calm a voice as she could manage.

When she finished, Mike said, "And you think you behaved badly? I agree Doris Valentine is the heroine here—she deserves a medal—but you were in there swinging, and never lost your head."

"If you could have seen me running up the drive, screaming my head off—"

"That was exactly the right thing to do at that point. Yes, he shot at you—and missed, which is what happens ninety percent of the time. Don't believe what you see in movies or on TV;

even cops are lousy shots at anything more than four or five yards. If someone pulls a handgun on you, run. And scream. Maybe someone will hear you and call the police."

Betsy nodded. "Jill told me that once. And not to go with someone who gets into your car. Get out and run. Good thing I remembered that."

"Yes, because if you'd gone off with him, you'd've been a long time gone."

There came that gentle tapping on the door again. Betsy turned. The door swung halfway open and Lars stuck his grinning face in.

"There's someone wants to talk to you," he said.

"Who?" asked Mike.

"Dr. Joseph Brown. He's in the room across the hall. It seems I accidentally left your door open and then I accidentally left his open, too." He nodded sideways. "He's right across the hall. I guess he overheard you two in here and realizes he's cooked."

"Hasn't he lawyered up?" asked Mike.

"He called one," said Lars, "but he asked if he could call back and cancel."

"Did you let him?"

"Not yet."

"Well, don't. Let the lawyer get here so Doctor Joe can tell him in person. And call me when he arrives, I want at least three witnesses."

M IKE asked Betsy to sit tight and went out to speak to the attorney when he arrived. The man wore a face famous from television ads. He was calm, sincere, deep-voiced, and, after several minutes talking with Joe in front of witnesses and several more alone, convinced. He shrugged, bestowed business cards on anyone who'd take one, and went home.

But Joe was convinced, too. Given the Miranda warning yet again, he waved it off saying, "I could hardly be more busted than I already am, right? So never mind, never mind. Ask me anything you want."

"Who shot Oscar Fitzwilliam?" asked Mike at once. They had gone into the police station's tiny interrogation room, a bare, spare place with a small wooden table and two hard wooden chairs, all bolted to the floor.

"I did. It was an accident, really. Wendy went to get the silk and he said he didn't get it from the courier, Doris. Wendy believed him, but I didn't. She brought the carved stone Buddha away with her as proof that Doris had come in. This was the fifth or sixth item Oscar had handled for us, but far and away the most costly, and I thought he was getting greedy. I went down to put the fear of God in him, and while I was waving the gun under his nose, it went off. I didn't mean to kill him. I searched the place but couldn't find the silk. And now I know he wasn't trying to steal it from me, I'm . . . sorry it happened."

His confession was being watched by several people, investigators from Wayzata and St. Paul—and Betsy, too. They were in Mike's office, gathered around his desk, looking at a television monitor. A tiny, discreet camera in an upper corner of the interrogation room broadcast a picture of Joe sitting upright in his chair, a pose somewhat at odds with his relaxed tone of voice. The picture was in poor-quality black-and-white, and the microphone hidden with it could have been replaced by two tin cans connected with string and gained somewhat in fidelity.

Joe burst out, "Nobody was supposed to get hurt! What we were doing was illegal, of course, but not dangerous or even, to my mind, wrong. Museums routinely acquire more things than they can display. Most of their beautiful artifacts are hidden away, did you know that? Only a fraction is on display at any given time, so people who might appreciate them never get to see them. My way, at least one person, a person who could care for them as well as any museum, who would lay loving hands on them, admire them. And it wasn't like I was depriving the world of them forever. I had a codicil added to my will that these things I had to keep hidden were to be brought out and given—*given*—to the art institute."

"I'm sure the art institute will be very grateful to learn its gifts from you came over the dead bodies of citizens of the greater Twin Cities area," said Mike dryly.

Joe bowed his head.

Mike asked, "How did you learn there was a very valuable piece of embroidered Chinese silk for sale, anyhow?"

"From a man named David Corvis. I'm not sure how he got hold of it—he always played his cards close to his vest, which of course was intelligent of him. Though it didn't save his life, did it? He's the one who got me my first illicit artifact, a five-thousand-year-old bronze bowl taken from a tomb in the Halil Rud valley in Kerman Province in Iran. I think it came through England—I know there was a court case about a large group of objects taken from that tomb. Then there was a temple bell from Burma—Myanmar, I beg your pardon. My favorite was a broken pot half filled with Roman coins found in a field in Normandy, broken by a farmer's plow. That didn't come from David, but from another source, currently watching the years slip by from inside a French prison. That was the queen of my collection, that pot of coins, though the silk would have dethroned it. Some of the coins in it are brilliant uncirculated— from the reign of *Caesar Augustus*, isn't that amazing?"

"Amazing," said Mike. "But then came the chance to acquire this piece of embroidered silk, and you wanted it."

"More than anything." Again there was pain and regret in Joe's voice. "More than anything. I almost had it. But I didn't even get to see it, much less hold it in my own hands!" He lifted them as if to demonstrate. "I wish I could make you understand how envious I am of Betsy Devonshire!"

"I can appreciate that."

Betsy got up and walked out of the office.

"Acquisition fit," she muttered to herself, as she walked toward the lobby. She had experienced them—and she catered to a clientele frequently afflicted with them. "Gotta have it"—that was their motto. They'd see a spectacular canvas or the silk lamé braid from Rainbow Gallery—sixteen colors!—and just have to have it, all of it. Betsy knew it wasn't the nicest trait to have, but she had appreciated it in her customers. She hadn't really understood how ugly it could be until Joe Brown. So a few people had to die so he could run his fingers over a really old piece of embroidery, that was fine with him. He wanted it, to gloat over, to *possess*. In his mind, any price was worth paying to satisfy that desire.

But he didn't possess these things. They possessed him. There was a man in town, an infamous miser also named Joe: Joe Mickels. The two were alike in their need to possess things—although Mickels did not, would not, murder to amass more money. Brown would—he had murdered—to acquire an addition to his store of ancient, valuable, and unique things.

The root of all evil was not money, but the love of money. The love of *things*, putting that love above all else, had led to a series of horrific crimes. Betsy pushed her fingers through her hair. She had *liked* Joe. He was charming and amusing, intelligent and successful. But there was a big hole somewhere in his soul. A hole he tried to stuff full of things.

Was it something that could have been fixed when he was younger? Or was it an innate lack?

Betsy came into the lobby and saw Phil and Doris sitting side by side on a wooden bench under a window. They saw her come in and smiled at her, so she went over to say hello.

"This is taking a long time, isn't it?" she said. "Are they making you wait?"

"Yes," said Phil. "Mike's partner, Sergeant Windemere, is having our statements typed up. Once we sign them, we can go home."

"This is so awful, I'm sorry it had to happen."

Doris said, "It's all right, really. We're fine. And it's *over*, we don't have to stay in hiding anymore."

Betsy looked at Doris and realized that in fact she was all right. That flat, distant look she had carried about these past two weeks was almost gone. Betsy smiled, "You do look much better. I would have thought you'd be ready for a hospital room by now, after all that's happened."

"It was the steam," said Doris. "He was coming toward us, I knew he was going to shoot us—starting with you—and I just had had enough. I wasn't going to allow that. Lars had shown us the starting up process, naming the valves and gauges, explaining how everything worked. Well, of course it wasn't exactly like the boilers I've tended, but on the other hand, it was *steam*, and I *know* steam. I've seen what happens when you open a valve at a hundred and fifty pounds of pressure. There was over five hundred pounds of pressure in that Stanley boiler, and I thought it might be at least a distraction if I released it." She laughed softly. "Well, I should say! The result was even better than I had hoped." Smiling she added, "And then I pulled the wire that blows the whistle—just to mix things up a little bit more."

Phil laughed, too. "Clear the track! The four forty express, comin' through!" He put his arm around her. "I'm the locomotive engineer, and I'm standing there like a pillar of salt. She's running the show! I'm going to give her my engineer's cap! It was my most prized possession—until I met her! Doris Valentine, the finest steam driver in the state of Minnesota!"

"Well, I should say!" echoed Betsy, rejoicing with the two of them. "Blessings on you, Doris! Blessings on us all!"

Author's Note

There really is a piece of Han Dynasty silk over 2,000 years old. Embroidered with a pattern of birds and other animals, it was found in the well-sealed tomb of a woman whose name was Xiu. (The pattern of a Phoenix at the back of this novel is an excellent representation of the bird.) But the silk made its way to a Chinese museum in Hubei where, as far as I know, it rests to this day. (On the other hand, the theft of priceless artifacts is a real and serious problem around the world.)

Han Phoenix

The **Han Phoenix** is stitched
on gleaming white 28-count Jubilee fabric,
in full- and half-cross-stitches, over two rows,
using two full strands of silk ("2 over 2").

*A photocopy enlargement
of the pattern and key
will make the stitch symbols easier to read.*

Stitches

left half-cross-stitch
right half-cross-stitch
full-cross-stitch
backstitch

**Outline eye in backstitch
using Gloriana #011.**

Key:
(Half-size symbols indicate left and right half-cross-stitches.)

Gloriana # 011

Kreinik Silk Bella #7086

Kreinik Silk Bella #2016

Kreinik Silk Bella #7082 (or raw Thai silk)

Stitch four full-cross-stitches, one on top of another.
This makes a four layer full-cross-stitch that is thick and big, resembling a knot.

Belle Soie "Rouge"

Gloriana #019

Gloriana #124

Gloriana #124A

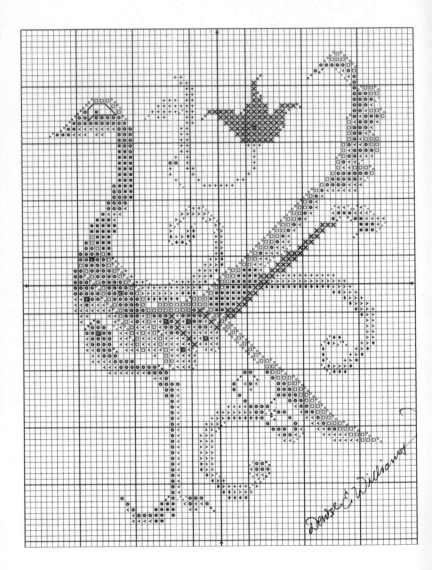